GW00630886

...ical College, where he edited a student magazine, and has worked in public and academic libraries.

Since 1981 he has published over twenty books, mostly in the field of historical biography. His miscellaneous writing includes contributions to *The Oxford Dictionary of National Biography* and *Guinness Rockopedia*, articles and reviews for various national and local journals and websites, and booklet notes for compact discs. He was a consultant for the BBC documentary *The King, the Kaiser and the Tsar*, first shown in 2003.

He lives in Devon with his wife Kim. *The Man on the Moor* is his first novel.

BY THE SAME AUTHOR

History and biography

Frederick III, German Emperor 1888 (1981)
Queen Victoria's Family: a Select Bibliography (1982)
Dearest Affie [with Bee Jordaan] (1984)
Queen Victoria's Children (1986)
Windsor and Habsburg (1987)
Edward VII's Children (1989)
Princess Victoria Melita, Grand Duchess Cyril of Russia (1991)
George V's Children (1991)
George III's Children (1992)
Crowns in a Changing World (1993)
Kings of the Hellenes (1994)
Childhood at Court 1819-1914 (1995)
Northern Crowns (1996)
King George II and Queen Caroline (1997)
The Romanovs 1818-1959 (1998)
Kaiser Wilhelm II (1999)
The Georgian Princesses (2000)
Gilbert & Sullivan's Christmas (2000)
Dearest Vicky, Darling Fritz (2001)
Royal Visits to Devon and Cornwall (2002)
Once a Grand Duchess [with Coryne Hall] (2002)
William and Mary (2003)

Music

Roxeventies (1982)
The Roy Wood Story (1986)
Singles File (1987)
Beyond the Summertime [with Derek Wadeson] (1990)

John Van der Kiste

The Man on the Moor

Troubador Publishing Ltd
9 De Montfort Mews
Leicester LE1 7FW, UK
Tel: (+44) 116 255 9311
Email: books@troubador.co.uk
Web: www.troubador.co.uk

ISBN 1 904744 23 0

Cover from a painting by Kate Van der Kiste

Typeset in 11pt Plantin Light by Troubador Publishing Ltd, Leicester, UK
Printed by The Cromwell Press Ltd, Trowbridge, Wilts

t² is an imprint of Troubador Publishing

Author's Note

This is a work of fiction. While the historical figures and major national events referred to in these pages did exist, all the characters in this novel are entirely imaginary.

As a historical biographer whose previous works have included a life of Kaiser Wilhelm II, I cannot emphasise too strongly that any theories about him and an illegitimate son in England have no foundation in fact, and do not exist outside the following pages.

My particular thanks for general advice, encouragement, and reading through the manuscript at various stages go to my wife Kim; my mother Kate; and my friends Ilana Miller; Marcia Willett; Sue Woolmans; Paul Rendell; and Miles Tredinnick.

Chapter 1

George Stephens heaved a sigh of relief as he tidied a bulging folder on his desk and replaced the gold-nibbed fountain pen in his drawer. Glancing at the clock on the wall, he saw that there were only a few minutes to go before he would be walking out of the front door of Smith & Hanbury Insurance at Bayswater for another weekend, and boarding the 1.40 from Paddington for Ashburton. Beyond the latter destination lay the rolling expanse of unspoilt Devon terrain, not to say beckoning wilderness, that was Dartmoor. Just a few hours out of the world's largest and busiest city, and without having to seek foreign shores he would be setting foot in an entirely different world.

Dartmoor – what soothing visions the very name conjured up to the deskbound working man of London, driven by the necessity of earning a monthly salary. The labyrinth of twisted, gnarled trees of Wistman's Wood; the triumphant peaks of Haytor, Greator, Brentor and others; the striking rock structures of Combestone Tor, Bonehill Rocks, and Bowerman's Nose; the clapper bridge over the East Dart at Postbridge, a scene that had launched a thousand postcards; the gently winding Avon...

He sat up with a start as the door opened.

'Wake up, George. You're still in London, you know.'

Not for much longer, he said to himself as Charles Shepherd tapped him playfully on the shoulder.

'Don't tell me, old man. You're off to Devon again for the weekend?' George nodded. 'Well, have fun. I'm sure you will. Don't forget those of us who are stuck in Bayswater.' Charles glanced out of the window. 'If the weather is as good down there as it is here at the moment, you'll be all right. In fact, I may go and stretch my legs out on Hampstead Heath. The metropolis has its compensations.'

George smiled at his colleague.

'Hampstead's pleasant enough. Not as good as Devon. But then, what is?'

1

'You and your west country!' Charles laughed. 'I've never been west of Hampshire myself. And I'm proud of it.'

There was a gentle knock on the door and in walked Paul Jenkins, a newspaper tucked under his arm.

'Going out for lunch, gentlemen? And if so, would you care to join me?'

'I'd be delighted to,' Charles replied. 'As for Mr Dartmoor, he's heading for the great wide open spaces out west again.'

'How long are you staying this time?' Paul asked.

'I should be back on Wednesday,' George told him.

'You'd better. This office can't function without you. Or indeed without any of us. In the meantime, the rest of us will be keeping an eye on this historic city of ours.' He opened his newspaper. 'Come on, George. Just think what you're missing up here. You've never tried going to the theatre, have you? One of these evenings you really ought to come with us and see a good play or two. Or even a bit of opera?'

George shook his head. 'Not for me, thank you. The great outdoors gives me all the theatre I want.'

'Very poetic of you. Ah well, have it your own way.'

Charles shot a sidelong glance at the paper under Paul's arm. 'Anything in the news we ought to know about?'

'Not much. Except our friend the Kaiser making himself ridiculous again.'

An expression of acute discomfort flickered across George's face and he looked away, hoping the others would not notice. At a furtive frown from Charles, Paul tried to cover his tracks by swiftly changing the subject. 'Oh, some more suffragette antics. Mrs Pankhurst's petticoat infantry are now going round armed to the teeth with parasols, smashing shop windows in Piccadilly. And everyone thinks the weather is going to become much hotter in the next few days.'

There was an awkward silence, then Charles spoke, anxious to dispel any lingering feelings of embarrassment.

'Well, the two of us had better be on our way. Enjoy your weekend, George, and give our regards to the moors. Oh – and don't forget to send us a postcard!'

'I know I made a bit of a gaffe there just now,' Paul said ruefully as he and Charles walked along the street in pursuit of a suitable place for lunch. 'But why oh why is our George so damned touchy on the subject of Germany?'

'I'd love to know just as much as you. One of the big secrets of our time. But do you remember old David?' Charles nodded at this reference to a recently retired colleague. 'He always warned me not to bring up anything in conversation to do with Germany when George is around if I could help it. And particularly nothing to do with the Kaiser.'

'And did David ever explain why?'

'I asked him, but he didn't know. Something to do with his family background, he thought. But he wouldn't be drawn, whatever his knowledge, or lack of it. But then what family has George got? He's unmarried, and as far as I know there never has been a wife, unless he was widowed or divorced early. He could have been, for all I know. And in four years of working with him, not once have I heard him mention a word about brothers or sisters. Let alone any reference to his parents.'

'That makes two of us.'

'In fact, I've never known anybody give quite so little away about himself, apart from his obsession with Devon.' He smiled. 'Perhaps he has a lovely young woman down there whom we don't know about, or even a couple of children he doesn't want to admit to.'

'Maybe. There's a devil of a lot to him that we know nothing about.' Charles looked pensive. 'Remember a couple of months ago when the papers were full of that business about the Kaiser's daughter getting married in Berlin? King George, Queen Mary, the Tsar and almost the whole of the *Almanach de Gotha* were there. And George was unusually quiet that week. A bit on edge, even. Not that he's ever been that talkative at the best of times. But I thought even one or two of the regular clients seemed to notice the difference in him.'

'I can quite understand people not wanting to talk about that pompous ass. The Kaiser, I mean, not George. But it's almost as if he has some sort of skeleton in his cupboard about the man.' Paul stopped dead in his tracks as a sudden thought struck him and he looked at Charles. 'Good heavens, you don't think they're related? Bastard brothers, or something?'

Charles smiled. 'A member of our staff related to that strutting great fool? Surely not!'

3

'But now you mention it, can't you see a bit of a likeness? That sort of look in the eyes?'

'If we tried hard enough, we could probably see little resemblances in all our friends to somebody famous. Take your glasses and moustache, for instance. Has anybody ever told you that you look like the late Dr Crippen?'

Meanwhile, as the train pulled out of Paddington heading west, George felt at one with the world. Much as he enjoyed living and working in London, the place he knew better than anywhere else, he had grown to love and appreciate the tranquillity of the west country, Dartmoor in particular.

Although he normally came only during the summertime, he wondered what it was like during late autumn, or even winter. Many a time he had been told of the area's sometimes inhospitable nature. Bitter winds, heavy rain, and thick snow were all to be expected, with stories of hardy souls venturing into the more remote regions of the moor and never returning. Winter in such an atmosphere was not such an appealing prospect, maybe, but autumn might be a different proposition. Watching the leaves changing colour had always fascinated him, and he tried to imagine what his favourite Devonshire views would look like, with oak and beech shedding their golden foliage for another year, leaving the evergreen Scots pine as undisputed kings of the skyline.

And Stead Farm, the address of Roger and Mary Strong at Holne, was virtually open house for the asking where he was concerned. They were now in their late fifties, or maybe even their early sixties. Devonians simply stopped ageing once they reached the age of forty, or so it appeared. He had stayed with them on every visit to Devon for the last four or five years, and they had become just like uncle and aunt. They never asked him for any payment for their bed and board. Instead of cash there had always been a tacit understanding that he would provide them with a couple of bottles of wine and sherry, perhaps some good steaks as well for supper one night. Their children had long since flown the nest, and they shared the farmhouse with their tomcat Mole, so named because of his rich velvet-like coat, the terror of the local mouse and rat population, and their golden retriever Rex, a placid beast who made up in looks and temperament what he lacked in the guard dog department.

Only a few hundred yards from their front door was the thirteenth-century Church of St Mary, with its striking tower and beam roof. While George was not a regular churchgoer and could hardly call himself a particularly religious person, he always experienced an indefinable sense of inner peace every time he visited the church. He had attended morning service on Sundays during his last two visits, and was very flattered when the Reverend Michael Noble shook him warmly by the hand on leaving as if he was one of the regular parishioners.

On his last visit they had invited Maud as a supper guest one evening. Maud Watts was a lively, uncomplicated girl of about twenty-five, who lived a few miles away at Buckfastleigh and sometimes came over to give Roger a hand with odd jobs around the farm. Her mother Emily had acted as a virtual housekeeper a few years earlier when Mary was laid up with a broken ankle and spent months in plaster, grumbling endlessly that if she couldn't get back to her pots and pans, her sweepin' and dustin' soon, she would go mad. Not half as mad as her poor husband and friends who took the brunt of her frustration until she was better. At the time George had wondered whether there was an element of match-making on their part. They coy way in which Roger and Mary had been casting sidelong glances at both of them had unsettled him a little, and for a brief moment it had crossed his mind to ask them about it afterwards. But on reflection he realised it was probably just a little private joke, and he had no desire to spoil a very pleasant few days by causing them any embarrassment.

Thinking it over on the way back to London afterwards, he had to admit that Maud seemed rather a good sort. Could he afford to give in his notice at Smith & Hanbury, invest some of his savings in setting up house and home at Dartmoor, and take a farming job locally? Alternatively, he had sometimes considered setting up his own business in the area, or looking round for a partnership with somebody who might be counting down the months to retirement. Dealing in local paintings, or antiquarian and secondhand books, appealed to him on the surface. As yet he had only a passing acquaintance with Devon artists, and a knowledge of literature and books which could best be described as comprehensive rather than scholarly.

5

Nevertheless with a little research, reading up, talking to the right people, and a knowledge of business gained from several years at his desk in London, it would surely not be beyond him to make a career in buying and selling in the fine arts. Life on the farm would be more physically demanding, and he wasn't sure it was the answer for him. Maybe the more gentlemanly occupation of selling books or paintings was a better idea.

Then again, maybe it was not the right time to consider a change of career. He had never been an impulsive man, and the last thing he would do was to make a snap decision. It was impossible to envisage Maud marrying him and coming to live in London. Perhaps she didn't regard him as anything more than a good friend. But if Roger and Mary were inviting her over again while he was staying this weekend...well, let fate take its course.

It was impossible for him to deny that for thirty years – almost his entire life – he had had this love affair with the area. Though they lived at Brighton, his mother had some remote family connections with Devon. Although she had hardly ever talked to him about her own family, he had vague recollections of her telling him about a cousin – or was it an uncle and aunt – who had lived there and often invited her to stay when she was a child. When he was four she had taken him to stay in a cottage near Princetown and gone exploring with him nearby, and immediately he had felt an affinity with the rugged, ever-changing landscape. Even when he was small he had loved to lie on his back and watch the different cloud formations drifting across a bright blue midsummer sky, or sit on a rock on the high ground gazing at the patchwork, as he put it, of fields, pastures, meadows, open landscape, bounded by stone hedges and wood-lands dotted around, as far as the eye could see.

One of his earliest memories was the sunny August morning walking across the stepping stones of the East Dart and then going to pick whortleberries on Laughter Tor, finally getting a lift back with Tom Crocker the local carrier. He and his mother must have spent half the day out, collecting enough to fill two generously-sized cans, getting their hands and fingers cheerfully stained purple in the process – but the pie she cooked that night was delicious. Nearly thirty years later, he could still recall the taste.

When his sister came along, there were less holidays in Devon. With two extra mouths to feed instead of one, they tended to go and stay on the Sussex coast more often than not, and that usually meant playing on the beach instead. Charlotte used to love swimming or wandering along the shore, collecting shells and examining rock pools and fishing with a tiny net, although she never caught anything exciting. Their mother appeared to be equally content with the moor and the beach. But he found the seaside boring, and although there was something to be said for old historic Brighton, with its regency associations and old narrow streets, he preferred getting back to the moors. Of course, little sister usually got her way as the baby of the family.

Thankfully that was a long time ago. She was now married and living in Gravesend – well, that had been her first married home, though they had lost touch soon afterwards. He had not seen her since the wedding, and he wondered if she ruled her husband with the same rod of iron. Or had she finally met somebody who had the good sense not to treat her like the spoiled brat she was in those days? He hadn't been at all impressed with her husband, a self-important solicitor who was in the running for selection as a parliamentary candidate for some seat in the home counties. But if he could keep her in order, all well and good. After the wedding he felt that they richly deserved each other.

With or without Maud, he could look forward to leaving Smith & Hanbury, wave goodbye to his lodgings in Bayswater for good, and move to Devon altogether. Of course he would miss the good-humoured bustle of London, its trams, its winter fogs, and its Cockney paper vendors. There would be no more walks around Westminster or Chelsea Embankment looking at the Thames, no more regular visits to the National Portrait Gallery or the British Museum, no more strolls across Trafalgar Square under the reassuringly familiar presence of Nelson's Column and Landseer's lions. Despite the grime, the noise, and the breathless pace of London, city life had its compensations. Anybody with proper respect for the history, traditions and heritage of Britain, he thought, must take pride in living and working in the city that was the hub of the universe. Still, he would get used to it. In any case, the situation might not arise for another twenty years or so. Until then, Dartmoor would be his home from home.

For a few minutes he was lost in thought, looking at the view outside. The panoramic view of London's suburbs gave way gradually to woodlands, green fields and meadows, and the gentle yet insistent rhythm of the train had a soothing effect. A harassed-looking woman sitting opposite him, with two small and initially restless noisy infants, managed to stop them from trying to fight each other after terse looks from a middle-aged, smartly-dressed gentleman in the corner. George smiled benignly to himself. Those children might have been Charlotte and himself once upon a time.

As they drew towards Reading, his eyelids were becoming heavy. Just before they reached Exeter he woke, sat up with a start, and blinked at his watch in disbelief. Where had the afternoon gone? He *couldn't* have been asleep all that time.

Chapter 2

At Stead Farm, on the edge of the village of Holne, Roger was finishing off a cup of tea in his kitchen. Mary had just come downstairs after changing sheets and putting a freshly-laundered quilt on the bed in the little spareroom, and was humming to herself as she tidied plates back into a cupboard.

"E's chosen a good weekend this time, 'as our George,' she said brightly as she joined him at table, helping herself to a biscuit as she cast an appreciative glance at the sunshine through the windows.

'Aye,' Roger grunted. Rex walked through the door wagging his tail and came to lay his head on his master's knee. 'Remember that last weekend, it poured an' poured. Thought it were never goin' to stop. 'E were so disappointed, like. Quite spoilt 'is plans to go for a walk and birdwatchin".

"E likes 'is walks on the moor, does our George. 'E don't get none of that in the city.'

'Young lad like 'im ought to be comin' to live down 'ere for good. That there London no place for a lad like 'im. I'd soon get 'im workin' in the fields. Put a bit o' colour in 'is face an' some muscle on those skinny arms of 'is.'

Mary playfully flicked her duster at him. 'Now, you know George's got 'is job in London. 'Tis all very well for us farmin' folk to talk like that, see, but 'e's in a different world, like. 'Sides, 'e enjoys 'imself much more down 'ere if 'e don't see it all the time.'

Roger nodded in mock resignation. 'Always knows best, me dear. An' I s'pose 'ee'd be a-motherin' 'im all the time. Weren't born yesterday, were I?'

'But 'e's got no parents of 'is own, as 'e?' She looked at her husband thoughtfully. "As 'e ever said one world to you about his mother an' father?'

Roger shook his head. 'Can't say 'e 'as. Must 'ave died when 'e was young, like. Or maybe 'e's adopted. S'pose 'e might be an

9

orphan, a Barnardo boy or somethin' like that. 'Ear about 'em in all walks of life, you do. But ain't none of our business really, though, is it? As me ol' Pa used to be sayin' to us, it don't matter where you come from, it's what sorter person you're like that really counts. Now when's 'e comin'?'

'Oh, sometime this evenin', I'll be bound. Before dusk, even. Usually gets off 'is train over to Ashburton, an' then 'e takes a wagonette on from there, but if it stays fine, I expect 'e'll 'ave a good walk first. Stretch 'is legs, like.'

'Aye. But not all the way from Ashburton?'

'Why not? 'T'ain't that far.'

'Maybe not. But s'pose 'e'd give 'imself a good appetite into the bargain if 'e did. An' 'e'd be eatin' us out of 'ouse an' 'ome.' George chuckled as he moved back to dodge another flick of the duster.

'Tribute to me cookin', I'd 'ave yer know, Roger Strong. Mary's farm'ouse fare is best in Devon. Best in the world. You always said so y'self!'

George with his suitcases alighted from the train at Ashburton with a spring in his step. Though he was conscious of not having had anything to eat since lunch, he did not feel at all hungry. If anything, these long train journeys only seemed to diminish his appetite. He could either take the four-seater horse-drawn wagonette straight to the Strongs' front door, or take a stroll around the town first and then have a pint of bitter in the Rose and Crown. What better way could there be to celebrate his arrival in the fair county of Devon?

Nearly an hour and a drink later, he climbed aboard Geoff Coombe's vehicle as the only passenger. Good old Geoff always seemed to have a kind of sixth sense and know somehow when he was coming. Ashburton station wouldn't be the same without his trusty conveyance, his horse, and above all his cheery smile.

'Good day, Mr Lloyds,' was Geoff's customary greeting. Never George Stephens, but always Mr Lloyds. He had used the nickname by way of a joke ever since finding out George's line of business, and it had stuck. 'And how is the world of insurance treating you?'

'Oh, the same as usual, thank you, Mr Coombe. I enjoy my work, and the company of my colleagues in the office, and I like to keep busy. But it's always good to come back here.'

'And so I should think, young sir. I wouldn't live in London for all the horses in England. Country born and bred I am, and ever shall be. By the way, would you mind if I didn't take you all the way down to Stead Farm this time? I've got a couple of packages that have got to be delivered to Mitchelcombe, which is a bit out of the way, and the missus will have something to say to me if I'm not back for my tea. So if I can drop you off in the village, that would help. The weather looks set fair, so you don't mind the extra walk, do you?'

'Not at all. The village it shall be.'

It made no difference to George. That would mean a stroll of barely a mile, and on a sunny evening in July what could be more pleasant, even with a case in each hand? Moreover it would save Geoff and his horse from having to negotiate the steep hill, to say nothing of saving him from an encounter with a rolling-pin wielding wife. He presented Geoff with a pocketful of change, they shook hands cordially and he got off near the pub.

To set foot once more on that welcoming terrain of bracken and gorse, and in high summer, was to enter a different world entirely. This domain which was home to skylarks, stonechats, wheatears and above all majestic buzzards on the wing, dotted with rivers, streams and tors, made him feel ten years younger. He walked a few hundred yards along the track, feeling with a sense of barely-contained excitement the soft ground beneath his feet, looking to where the sweeping beds of light mauve ling and rich magenta bell heather would come into flower in a few weeks, punctuated by bright sprigs of yellow-gold gorse which often seemed to last all the year round. Tiny yellow tormentil twinkled on the ground, campion positively sparkled like little pink jewellery in the hedges. Standing proudly on their own, or pushing their way up through the emerald green bracken, were tall, sturdy foxgloves which had just come out and were threatening to dwarf everything else. Twisted hawthorn trees and the occasional rowan, with berries about to turn orange and then scarlet, dotted the horizon.

Beside one lay the skull and part of the ribcage of a sheep. Poor creature, he thought, but it was probably old and had had a full life. And after all this wasn't such a bad place to go.

He sat down on a rock to pause and take it all in. Once he

could smell the place again, he knew he was back where he belonged. How would he describe it to a stranger, he wondered. It was difficult to define – a combination, he supposed, of bracken, moss and soil, not to mention the bright enamel flowers of gorse with their subtle aroma of almonds, especially in sunlight. There was always the scent of wild honeysuckle in the evening as well. As his eye swept across the horizon, he felt that there was nothing to compare with a Dartmoor sunset. The sun was enveloping the skyline in a rich warm glow and playing on the running brook. Suddenly the bewildered bleating of a half-grown lamb, temporarily separated from its mother until she caught up with it, distracted him momentarily from his reverie. In the distance he thought he could hear the familiar plaintive mew of a buzzard, perhaps a pair. Another moment and maybe they would come into view, circling gracefully overhead.

In a little while he would be back at the farm and have his feet under the kitchen table with Roger and Mary. Of course they would want to know all about what he was up in London, or would they? Did they only ask him every time out of politeness, or out of genuine curiosity over how the other half lived? They had probably never been out of Devon, or even away from Dartmoor, themselves.

He yawned expansively. It had been a long day, and in spite of that nap on the train he now realised he was more tired than he had thought. A few minutes' rest wouldn't hurt, as he lay down on a soft dry piece of ground and closed his eyes.

As afternoon rolled into evening and there was still no sign of George, Roger and Mary decided he must have missed the train.

'It's not like 'im not to let us know if 'e's changed 'is plans,' Mary commented a little peevishly as she gave the kitchen table a final wipe. 'Always so reliable, like. All that there train's fault, if you ask me.'

'Jes' as well Maud couldn't come to supper tonight, then. But I aked 'er an' she'll be round givin' me some 'elp tomorrow, so she'll see 'im then.'

Mary stared out of the window, thinking deeply. 'D'you think 'is 'eart fluttered for Maud last time?'

''Ard to say, like. Shy, that's 'is problem. I think she liked George, but 'oo's to say if she just thought of 'im as a friend.

It's not as if they were courtin', is it?'

'Well, 'e's' a different class from 'er. They say it matters, but if two people are fond of each other an' that, doesn't really matter that much, does it? Maybe we'll see what 'appens if she comes to supper tomorrow night.' She shrugged and looked down at Rex. He wagged his tail eagerly, and she bent down to pat him. 'An' we thought George was goin' to take Rex for 'is walk tonight, di'n't we?'

'Oh, 'e'll turn up, don't 'ee worry,' Roger reassured her. 'If there's trains tomorrow, 'e'll be along then. Jes' stop frettin', woman, an' let's get upstairs. I'd best be gettin' up bright an' early tomorrow mornin' to sort them tools out in the barn. Needs me beauty sleep, like.'

Cycling back from Ashburton to his home near Hexworthy on Monday evening, Tom Dobson had scarcely a care in the world. That weekend, after what had seemed a very long wait, he and Katie Braithwaite would be going to tie the knot in town.

It would be the second wedding for her, poor girl. Married just two years previously, she was scarcely back from honeymoon before her Arthur suddenly collapsed. Nobody ever knew for certain, but from what they could gather, he was suffering from some kind of tumour. For weeks she had nursed him faithfully while he lay in bed, going downhill, eventually into a coma and then death. Poor, poor woman – a widow at nineteen. At first she had shut herself away from the world as soon as the funeral was over, hardly wanting to see anybody outside her immediate family. But Tom, an odd jobbing gardener who could work wonders with any kind of edible fruit which grew in England, lived in the next street but one, and helped her parents out in their garden whenever he had an hour or so to spare. They found him a pleasant, cheerful young man, just the kind of person they needed to come and take their unhappy daughter out of her miseries. One thing led to another, and at the last new year's eve dance in the village hall he had popped the question. On Saturday he would take her to St Andrew's Church, place the finest ring on her finger that his humble savings from a gardener's wages had been able to buy in Exeter, and she would become Mrs Dobson.

He whistled a few jaunty bars of Mendelssohn's *Wedding*

March to himself as he rode past the moor gate and downhill to Holne. His old schoolfriend Ronald Smith was going to play the organ for them, and there were still one or two details to be sorted out over the music. Were they going to have a piece from Katie's favourite composer Handel, and if so, was it to be the *Largo* or that other one of which he could never remember the title? Would *Lead Us, Heavenly Father, Lead Us* be the right opening hymn, or should it be *Love Divine, All Loves Excelling* instead? Lost in blissful contemplation of the service and everything which would follow it, he barely took in that apparently sleeping form by the roadside until he was halfway down the hill.

At that point it dawned on him that perhaps he ought to stop, go back and check. Something about the position of that body did not look quite right. He cycled to a halt, dismounted and pushed the bike uphill again until he reached the level, and approached the spot with a growing sense of horror. Kneeling beside the body he took a deep breath, lifted the right wrist, and felt for a pulse.

At once his worst fears were confirmed.

Unable to believe that anything so dreadful could have spoilt the serenity of this summer evening which had begun so gloriously, he climbed back upon the saddle and made straight for the police station.

Chapter 3

'It *can't* be George, can it?' Paul looked at Charles in amazement across his desk in the back office.

'I wish to heaven it wasn't,' Charles answered sadly. 'But it must be him.' He pointed to a small paragraph on the morning paper, informing them that the body of George Edward Stephens, an insurance clerk at Bayswater in his early thirties, had been found beside a track near the Dartmoor village of Holne. The cause of death was unknown.

'But how could he have died?' Paul said, after the cold reality of it had sunk in. 'I mean, he was always in pretty good health. It's not as if he had a weak heart, or anything like that. And he could hardly have died of exposure or hypothermia on a warm night in July – let alone during the day.'

A cold fear gripped his heart. 'I can't see why, but do you think he might have had any reason to take his own life, do you think?'

Charles frowned. He could hardly visualise the man with whom they had shared an office for the last few years behaving in such a way, but George had always played his cards so close to his chest. There could have been dark secrets below that apparently tranquil surface.

'None I can think of. What would have driven him to do so?'

'With someone as secretive as that, we'd never know. For all we known, he might have had money worries, or –' Paul shrugged. 'He kept his own counsel so much. We could guess all day and we'd never be any the wiser.'

They both sat, lost in thought, bewildered at the sudden tragedy of a colleague who had been there with them in such good spirits only the previous week. He should have been walking through the door with or just before them every morning, as he had almost every weekday morning for months on end. '*Good weekend, George?*' '*Yes, thank you, splendid weather, lots of walking, plenty of birdwatching, everything as usual. Can't*

15

wait to go back again.' Now there was a sudden emptiness, a void where there had been flesh and blood.

Their contemplative mood was interrupted by an abrupt knock at the door and a man walked in without waiting for them to call him in. He was dressed neatly with a small case in his hand, and though he looked outwardly calm, they detected a sense of brisk efficiency, even urgency about him.

'Gerard Cross, reporter for the *Western Morning News* at Plymouth,' he introduced himself as he produced a business card to confirm the fact. 'I must apologise to you gentlemen for arriving unannounced like this, but pressing business brings me here.' They all shook hands and introduced themselves as they invited him to take a seat.

'Now, gentlemen, I take it you have seen the sad news of George Stephens' demise?' They nodded. 'And I understand you knew him well?'

'Oh yes,' Charles said without thinking, as Paul nodded.

'Maybe,' Paul added slowly, choosing his words with care, 'maybe we should qualify that. Between us we have worked with him for about three years. We always liked him and respected him as a colleague, but – I can't say we really knew him well as a person.'

'Something of a man of mystery,' Charles volunteered.

Mr Cross nodded as he scribbled away at his pad. 'Go on, please.'

The others looked pensive, then Paul carried on. 'Mr Stephens never spoke of any family. Well, of course there must have been relations, but – in all the time we worked with him, he never once alluded to his parents, or any brothers or sisters.' He looked from the reporter to Charles, who nodded in affirmation. 'No wife, or lady friend either. Bit of a loner. He liked going round museums and things like that on his own. I don't think he really mixed with anybody.'

'So I take it he never socialised much?'

'Very little. Once or twice he would come and have supper with us and our wives, but we got the feeling he was never very comfortable about doing so. Rather ill at ease when it came to making small talk. The last time he came round to my house, Joan – that's my wife – was so embarrassed by it that I decided I couldn't really invite him again. And we've tried to interest him

16

in the occasional night out at the theatre or that sort of thing, but he never showed any enthusiasm.'

'Did he live on his own?'

'Oh yes. In lodgings locally, not that I've ever seen them.'

'I see. Was he a Londoner born and bred, do you know?'

They shrugged.

'I suppose you could say he had a kind of Middle England accent,' said Charles after a moment.

'In other words, no accent at all,' Paul proffered. 'He could have come from anywhere.'

'Anything else? Did he have any particular interests outside his work or, if I may dare to use the word,' here he hesitated, before lowering his voice, 'what you might call obsessions?'

Charles and Paul looked at each other.

'He was mad about Dartmoor,' Charles remarked. 'It was as if he could hardly wait to get out of London sometimes and on the train for Devon. And he told us once that if he wasn't working here, he'd like to work down there instead. Maybe running a bookshop or an art gallery. How seriously he meant it, I don't know, but he was obviously very much in love with the area, so it wouldn't surprise us if he did make a tentative move in that direction.'

'That fits in with the general picture we have already. Was there anything else that you can think of?'

Paul took a deep breath. 'Well, I suppose –' He hesitated for a moment, but the reporter's prompting eye made him realise that anything was relevant, no matter how trivial it might seem. 'Germany.'

'Anything specific about Germany?'

'The Kaiser.' Paul and Charles came out with the words simultaneously. If it had not been such a solemn occasion, they might have almost laughed.

'Now we're getting somewhere.' There was the hint of a gleam in Mr Cross's eyes as he looked from his pad to their faces. 'Would you venture to suggest that he was a passionate admirer or otherwise of the esteemed Wilhelm?'

'Hard to say,' Charles told him. 'I suppose you could say that perhaps he was obsessed, or something very like it. There was a senior clerk in this office who warned us when we started work, to keep off the subject of the Kaiser within Mr Stephens' hearing. He didn't tell us why, though. In fact, I'm not sure whether he knew himself. But he would never let himself be drawn on the matter.'

'Do you think I might speak to this clerk?'

'No, he retired some time ago, I'm afraid. I think he moved to Ireland. We've long since lost touch with him anyway.'

'Perhaps some of the other staff would be able to enlighten us?'

'Little hope of that, I'm afraid,' Paul advised. 'If anybody knew Mr Stephens at all, it was us. As we said, he kept very much to himself. Everybody else found him even more remote. They all liked him – in fact, I don't think any of them ever said a word against him. But they all found him a bit – well, strange. Not exactly strange, so much as withdrawn.'

'Two final questions. Do you know if he was fluent in the German language, either written or spoken?'

They shook their heads.

'Not as far as we know,' Charles volunteered.

'He could have been,' Paul chipped in. 'We never knew about it, but – well, as you can see, there was very little we knew about him or what he did in his spare time. Even if I could speak or write half a dozen different European languages, which I can't, there's no good reason why anybody else in the firm should know. Except perhaps for professional reasons, of course, like interpreting any foreign correspondence which we receive in the office.'

'Exactly. Now, during the time that you worked with him, do you know if he ever went to Germany? Or travelled anywhere abroad at all?'

'I don't think so,' Paul replied.

'If he ever left London, it was always to Devon,' Charles added. 'Unless – I suppose he could have, but – well, he never seemed to be away long enough. He could have slipped across the North Sea during the summer, but he never mentioned it.'

There was a pause, then Paul asked, 'What was the cause of death?'

'There was no appearance of foul play, but police investigations are continuing.'

After making a few more notes Mr Cross opened his case, and was about to announce his departure, when Charles stalled

18

him. 'Does all this come as a surprise to you?'

'I suppose a reporter should never be surprised.'

Charles felt slightly irritated with the man and his reluctance to impart any further information, but he was careful to conceal his impatience. Even so, he felt there was nothing to be lost by broaching the question. 'Mr Cross, do you know anything we don't about Mr Stephens?'

'It would surely be wrong of me to prejudice my position or my integrity by speaking out of turn, gentlemen. However, since you have been kind enough to give me a few minutes of your time, I can tell you something.' He lowered his voice a little. 'But I would ask you to respect my confidence in this matter. I have your word?'

They nodded.

'Very well. When the police examined the contents of his pockets and luggage, they found a few pages of documents in German, and some maps. I am not at liberty to say what those maps were of.'

'Not Dartmoor?' Paul asked.

'Not Dartmoor, I can assure you. Please don't question me further. My lips, regretfully, are sealed on the matter. But I will tell you one more thing. They found a pair of photographs in a small folding ornamental frame. One was of a woman who looked rather like him, but about twenty or thirty years older. They think it was probably of his mother.'

'And who was the other picture of?' asked Charles, who was fairly sure he had suddenly guessed.

'Not the German Emperor?' Paul broke in, astonished.

Mr Cross looked him in the eye and nodded grimly. 'And with that, gentlemen, I really must go. Time and tide wait for no man.' Rising to his feet, he held his hand out again to both in turn. 'Once again, thank you for your time.'

Meanwhile, at Holne, Tom Dobson's discovery and the subsequent police investigation dominated all local conversation. Sergeant Donald at Ashburton knew Roger and Mary Strong well, and had met George briefly a couple of times on previous visits although they had done no more than exchange the odd 'good morning'. He had taken it upon himself to call round at their cottage and break the news, as well as take a brief statement from them in which they confirmed George's regular visits as well as his intention to stay with them again that weekend. As to his background, they agreed that they would help if they could. There was so little to tell about George, apart from what a pleasant young lad he had always been. But they could not throw any light on his family background or circumstances.

When Donald mentioned the possibility of a German connection Mary was speechless, while Roger muttered that he 'seemed too much of a nice young English gentleman to go gettin' 'imself mixed up with that there bunch o' Berlin monkeys.'

'But 'ow did 'e die? We mean, was 'e killed, or 'eart attack?'

'The coroner will let us know in due course.'

'Were there any sign of a struggle, like?' Roger asked.

Donald shook his head emphatically.

'Sorry, Mr Strong. I'm not at liberty to say yet. But when we know more, I will see to it that you are kept informed.'

Holding a newspaper under her arm, Ethel Stephens closed the front door of her lodgings in Brock Road, Peckham, with one hand and clutched a battered wooden walking stick in the other. She stopped for a moment to check in the pocket of her threadbare coat to satisfy herself that she had brought the key. There it was, beside the small bottle of gin she carried around with her. For sustenance, as she put it, as well as her one true friend in a cruel uncomprehending world which never seemed to understand her. Husbands, lovers, children, dogs, who needed them, she often thought to herself. She'd tried them all during her fifty-six years, but none of them could compare with a nip of gin, or perhaps a drop of Scotch when she could afford it. As long as the money didn't give out on her in such little time as she felt she had left on earth, that was all that mattered.

A little unsteadily on her feet despite the stick for support, she made her way towards the police station in the next street, stumbled up the steps and through the door to the reception desk. Banging the counter with a clenched fist to draw attention to herself, she caused Constable Turner to sigh as he recognised her. Somebody had to draw the short straw, he said to himself as he walked towards her. What a pity it had to be him again.

'Good morning, Mrs Stephens. And what can we do for you?'

'Don't you good morning me, officer,' she retorted, her voice slightly slurred. Years of perfecting what she took to be an upper class accent had only partially concealed her cockney roots. She spread the paper in front of her at the page containing the report of George's death, stabbing at it fiercely with the finger of her right hand. 'Why wasn't I told? Why do they never tell me anything? My own son, and they let me find out from the newspaper. Or leastways, from my neighbour, who had the kindness to show me this.'

He looked at her with sympathy, somewhat startled that she appeared more indignant than upset. 'May I offer my con–'

'You may, young man. Why wasn't I told?'

'I'm sure the authorities meant to notify you as –'

'Authorities!' She clutched at the desk to steady herself. 'It's all authorities, isn't it? You're all the same, each and every one of you. Do you know something?'

He looked at her anxiously, realising that he would not have much choice in the matter.

'My son's names are not George Edward, I'd have you know. Were not. He was called Frederick William Victor Albert, after his father.'

'Do I take it your husband is no longer alive?'

'Don't ask me!' She almost spat the words at him. 'Had three husbands I have, and they all left me in the end. How do you expect me to know where they are? I'm talking about William's father.'

Turner rolled his eyes. Not again, he thought.

'Everybody knows who his father is. What does he care about it, or any of us?'

I know, he thought grimly. I've heard it all before. Just then she lost her balance, clutched at the desk for support and fell on the floor. He moved out quickly to help her to her feet. She had hit her head on the side of the desk and seemed mildly dazed but otherwise unhurt.

'Come and sit down and have a cup of tea, Mrs Stephens,' he said reassuringly as he helped her towards a chair. He resisted the temptation to add that a little more tea and a lot less alcohol would solve a good many of her problems.

By the following Tuesday the report of the post-mortem had

21

reached the papers. The cause of George's death, it was established, was a severe blow to the head, leading to brain haemorrhage. As his colleagues at work had said, he had previously been in excellent health, and there was no indication of a weak heart or anything which might have indicated a fit or seizure. The most likely explanation was that it was an accident. He had probably fallen and hit his head on the road, but something about the position in which the body was found made the coroner suspect foul play, and an open verdict was recorded.

Mr Cross had evidently done his work well. In the *Western Morning News*, there was increasing speculation on George's German connections. While it would be rash to suggest that the carrying of a photograph of His Imperial Majesty Emperor William indicated paternity or a close relationship, people could readily be excused for thinking thus. Nobody recognized the face of the woman in the other picture, and there was no inscription on the back, but its age, and the likeness, made it more than likely that she was his mother. The documents and maps were being examined by police, and as to their contents, an excited community could but guess.

Roger and Mary pondered with amazement on what looked disturbingly like the Jekyll and Hyde nature of their late guest.

'They're sayin' 'e were up to spyin' for Berlin or somethin' like that,' Mary commented incredulously to her husband one morning as she was scouring out a saucepan in the kitchen.

'That's nothin' to what they were sayin' at the bar in the Red Lion last night,' Roger countered, washing his hands at the sink. 'They think 'e's related to German royalty. Son of that there Kaiser Bill, if 'ee can believe it.'

'Never! Surely not our George? Sorter thing us only reads about in them magazines, stuffin' people's 'eads with such nonsense, like. But George always seemed so quiet.'

'Aye. They say the quietest ones are the dark horses. If 'e were that quiet, what did 'e 'ave to 'ide? Must 'ave known we wouldn't 'ave liked puttin' up someone mixed up with mischief like that. Or the son of this country's enemy.'

''E's not 'xactly this country's enemy, yet. Though 'e's certainly not our friend, the way 'e cavorts around the place. But do 'ee think George's death really was an accident, Roger? Could someone 'ave gone an' murdered 'im?'

'If 'e was involved in monkey business, someone probably 'ad their reasons for wantin' to get rid of 'im. I don't know nothin' much about this German business, like, but if they wants war with us, they must be makin' plans. Why they buildin' all these warships, if they ain't goin' to use 'em. Cost a pretty penny, or mark or whatever. Our own navy buildin' dreadnoughts to keep up, when they could be spendin' money lookin' after the old an' the sick an' givin' our nippers a proper education.'

'Changed your tune, eh? You always used to tell us you didn't 'old with education. Said all young men oughter grow up to be good farmers or gamekeepers, lookin' after the land an' the animals, an' the women good wives an' mothers.'

'I did think that once, maybe.' Roger scratched his head philosophically. 'But times are changin' and you gotta go wi' the flow. I look at it like this. We need brains in this country now. England an' Germany both want to be top dog, an' where's it goin' to end? As for this business of Germans gettin' people over 'ere to do their dirty work for 'em, and watchin' people all the time, you never know, do you? An' if George were caught up in it all...'

'I can't believe it, Roger. Good quiet country folk like us, an' a prince in our bedroom? Or a spy?'

Roger scowled as he shook the water off his hands and reached for a towel. 'If what's you be a-sayin' is right, then whose side would 'e be fightin' on if push came to shove? Would it be King an' country, or Bill an' 'is mob in their fancy spiked 'elmets an' uniforms? If 'e were still alive, 'e might 'ave been our enemy. Or might be soon!'

'Oh, Roger, what a thought!' She shrugged helplessly, and picked up a large basket of washing to sort out and hang over the stove. 'We don't know for sure. Mustn't gossip, eh? The dead can't defend their selves, an' we best not let our tongues run away with us, like?' She paused to look closely at a couple of garments, feeling how damp they still were. 'Now 'ow about givin' me an 'and with these clothes, an' if you can put 'em into that basket I'll 'ang 'em out to dry. Then I'll sort us out a nice bit o' bread an' cheese for lunch.'

23

Chapter 4

At the premises of Smith & Hanbury, the staff's minds were likewise concentrated more than they ought on the astonishing circumstances of their late colleague. Mr Pargeter, the office supervisor, had been asked by head office to instruct his employees not to speak to any representatives of the press on office premises, but direct them straight to him if necessary, and to be extremely circumspect in any dealings they might have with reporters in their own time – as if they needed telling. As Charles and Paul were the only ones who had really known George, they realised that the order was directed mainly at them. They agreed to impose a rule on themselves not to discuss the matter at work.

Conversation at lunchtime was a different matter. At first they were regretting not having been able to attend the funeral, being as they were, probably the only people in London who really knew George well. Now they were beginning to reconcile themselves with the extraordinary knowledge that rumours of his parentage were perhaps true.

'Now they keep telling us the German Emperor is his father,' Paul said one day as they went in search of refreshment, 'I'm starting to see a resemblance. Something about that look in his eyes, for example.'

'You're right. I'm not sure I want to believe it, but – if it is the truth...'

'But what about his mother? Is she really this woman in Peckham or Deptford, and if so, do you think we ought to go and see her?'

Charles shook his head. 'Best left alone for the time being, I'd say. If it really is her, then my heart goes out to the poor soul. But it might make a difficult situation worse. And if the police do know her, then there's always the chance that she might contact us. Or they might bring her in on some enquiry if there is a further investigation. Goodness knows what that would lead to.'

'The Palace might be involved.'

'The Palace? Oh yes, I see what you mean. The King being his cousin, and all that. But it's not the first time there have been royal pretenders. Mostly madmen, trying to make a nuisance of themselves or with some letters that they think will help them in a swift bit of blackmail. What makes them think they'll succeed where others have failed so spectacularly, I wonder.'

They made their way along a crowded pavement and resumed their conversation over a cup of coffee some minutes later.

'It looks increasingly like someone wanted George out of the way,' Charles mused, taking a sip and holding the cup in both hands. 'This knock on the head sounds pretty suspicious, to say the least. I've never been one to believe in spying theories. It all sounds too far-fetched for me. But this theory about his parentage, which still sounds rather extraordinary. Do you really think it's possible?'

Paul nodded, a little reluctantly.

'Like you, I've never been one to jump to conclusions. But it all points to somebody wanting him dead. And if it was at imperial court level, this makes it all the more likely.' He sipped his coffee contemplatively. 'They might not have meant to – well, eliminate him. It could have been a bungled kidnap attempt.'

'And he put up a struggle, you mean? Possible, I suppose.'

'It would explain his extreme sensitivity to any mention of Germany. Do you know anything about these people in Devon he used to go and stay with? A farmer or somebody running a guest house, I think.'

'He did let slip some mention of it once.' Charles stopped and looked at him open-mouthed. 'Now you're not going to suggest he was at the centre of a spy network on Dartmoor!'

They finished their coffees in silence. Although both were worldly-wise men in their early thirties who were reluctant to make wild assumptions, it was apparent that a drama was unfolding beyond their eyes of which they would be spectators, if not unwilling participants. They viewed the prospect with not a little apprehension.

Ralph Hillman stepped out of his cab at Stafford Terrace, Kensington, and walked up the steps to the front door of No. 14. Now in his late sixties, retired from his appointment as Clerk to the Justices in Exeter, he had moved to Holne shortly after his wife's death. His days were now occupied mainly with a little birdwatching, reading, and with acting as joint churchwarden and sidesman at St Mary's. Two or three times every year he travelled by train to London to stay with his younger brother and sister-in-law.

Alfred Hillman had earned himself a comfortable living as a merchant banker, to say nothing of a series of shrewdly-timed investments. Their grandparents had been Devonians, and he owned a small house near Honiton where he generally spent part of every summer. He had assured Ralph that, when he retired from his life of commerce in London, he and his wife Louise intended to look for a more spacious dwelling in Devon and make their main home there. Perhaps he would keep a *pied à terre* in Kensington from which he could make occasional forays to the capital.

With this case of the man on the moor, as everyone had begun referring to it, engaging almost everyone's attention, Ralph was more than pleased that he had chosen this particular week to be with his brother. A straightforward man who believed in minding his own business, he had little time for those who had nothing better to do than gossip about other peoples' private lives, and he was finding the atmosphere at Holne increasingly tiresome. It was unfortunate enough, he maintained, for this young man to be found dead in strange circumstances, without all this distasteful speculation as to what those circumstances might have entailed, or ill-founded theories on connections with foreign powers. Until the police had pronounced definitively on the matter, it was nothing to do with anybody else. The modern world, it was his belief, would be a far better place if people did not pass judgment on others until they were in possession of the full facts.

Five minutes later he and his brother were comfortably ensconced in armchairs in his drawing room, under the watchful eye of a large oil painting of their grandfather – a genuine John Everett Millais, Alfred said, although nobody was quite sure. A newly-opened bottle of malt whisky had pride of place on a salver at his elbow. Normally it would not have come out until after dinner, but his brother felt the need for a little additional refreshment after his journey.

'You always knew a good Scotch,' Ralph complimented him. 'Thanks to Grandpa Francis, yes.' Alfred glanced at the portrait. 'Taught me all I knew about whisky. And they always said that nobody had a more discerning palate for the best.'

'Not that he was bad when it came to vintage wines, either.'

'True. But whisky was always his speciality.' Alfred paused, puffing on his Havana. 'Now, tell me a little more about this business out at Holne.'

Ralph gave an involuntary frown. Much as he might have disliked the idea of talking about it, he knew that his brother would be longing to know directly from him, instead of from the national papers.

'The investigations are still continuing,' he said, exhaling a cloud of smoke from his own cigar. 'I can't add much to what has been in the press. Young man from London, found dead, might have been an accident, possibly murder. German spy, or even a by-blow of the Kaiser, if you believe half the ridiculous stories going around the village. Which I don't,' he added as an afterthought.

'Any son of that conceited ass would probably be happier in the next world than the present one,' Alfred observed. 'If we're not careful he'll have all Europe by the ears. What a pity good old Teddy isn't still at the Palace. The Kaiser was scared stiff of him. But now he thinks he's the number one when it comes to the pecking order of Europe's sovereigns.'

Ralph nodded. 'Of course, there's always Franz Josef in Vienna.'

'Oh, that poor old man. I daresay the Emperor of Austria is probably a nice enough old soul in his way. And he's had his share of family troubles, with his wife getting stabbed, and that misguided son of theirs doing away with himself and his mistress. Not to mention that ridiculous business in Mexico, with his brother falling foul of the natives and getting himself shot. But he's too old to have any sort of impact on affairs. Do you know, I always think of him as a kind of elderly headmaster sitting in his study, working away solemnly until they carry him out in a box. No, I believe the future of Europe belongs to strutting Wilhelm and his toadies in Berlin. For better or worse.'

'For worse, I'd say', Ralph murmured. 'And I'd much rather we weren't part of that Europe.'

27

'Absolutely. The mainland of the continent may have to meet its day of reckoning, although I have no doubt the French would prove to be tougher adversaries than they were last time. For all we know, Wilhelm could turn out to be quite a reasonable sort of fellow under that ridiculous mask and those uniforms, and he would be more so if only he could stop his tongue from running away with him. But none of this alters the fact that if half of what they say is true, it was a bastard son of his who was found dead not so far from you.'

'Mere conjecture.' Ralph shook his head. 'Unless or until somebody can prove otherwise.' Though he was fond of his younger brother, he had frequently been mildly irritated by the way in which Alfred had often deliberately taken the opposite point of view from him in family discussions. He had always put it down to a youthful desire to show off, but if so, at the age of fifty-six it was high time he grew out of it.

'And you don't feel at all excited by the thought that your community might have been harbouring a spy for the Huns?' Alfred eyed his brother, a faint gleam of mischief in his eye.

'You know me better than that, younger brother. The stuff of cheap tawdry adventure stories.' He paused for a moment. 'The latest rumour going around is that a couple of men with German accents, possibly officers in the army, have been seen in the Holne area, and that they were the murderers. Not that I believe a word of it.'

'You are too sceptical, Ralph. Always were.' Alfred reached for the whisky bottle and topped up their glasses. Although he knew that at his time of life he should be taking the issue more seriously, he could not resist this opportunity to tease his over-serious brother a little. 'Sometimes they say that these things have to be the truth only because they are too impossible for fiction.'

Have it your own way, Ralph longed to reply, but he restrained himself with a lame 'Who knows?' Having spent much of the day travelling, he was tired and not really in the mood for argument. A good meal, perhaps a short brisk constitutional afterwards, and a nightcap before retiring to bed for the night would suffice.

'We think we might know the young man's mother, though. Or know somebody who knows her.' Realising that Ralph might

28

become a little testy if the topic of conversation was prolonged too much, Alfred hesitated, but at the look of mild curiosity on his brother's face, he was encouraged to go on. 'Canon Richardson, who lives a couple of streets away. Do you remember when he came to dinner last time you stayed?'

Ralph nodded. 'Chap who told us he had been out working with the missionaries in Central Africa, and then became a minister in the East End?'

'That's him. Now there's an Ethel Stephens who lives in Peckham, his old stamping ground. Louise was talking to him the other day, and she found out that he knew her. Unless there's somebody else of the same name, the chances are that she's the mother of this young man.' He puffed on his cigar again, evidently thinking hard. 'From what I hear, this woman has had a pretty hard time. As they say, her life is probably not one that would be accepted at any insurance office, and this business won't have made things any easier for her. Apparently she went to the police after it all happened, though what came of it if anything I don't know. If there's something we can do to help her...'

'What do you suggest?' Much as Ralph's head told him to let well alone in such a situation, his heart – not to mention his role as churchwarden – told him that any assistance or even the merest shred of moral support he could offer was not to be dismissed without a thought. 'I met this George Stephens once, last year, was it? No, it must have been two years ago, because it was the same summer as the King's coronation, and I was chairman of a committee in charge of organising a street party for the children. I had to go in to the church at Holne to collect something, and I found Stephens inside wandering around. He seemed to be taking quite an interest in the brass plaques on the wall, and especially in the inscription of a 17th century slate marble tomb on the floor. Dated 1647, it was, and I think he was intrigued by the fact that it dated from the civil war. Commemorating some family that was distantly related to the Courtenays of Devon. That stuck in my memory.'

'So you spoke to him?'

'Oh yes, I made myself known, and we passed the time of day. We chatted for a bit, and it was plain that he was keen on history. Seemed a nice enough fellow, I suppose, but apart from that, he didn't have much to say for himself. I asked him where he was staying, and what brought him to Dartmoor, but he wasn't giving much away. I put it down to shyness, but afterwards I thought there was an air of mystery about him. More than met the eye.' He knocked back the rest of his whisky. 'Not that it makes any difference with regard to doing anything for his mother, of course. Let's see what Louise has to say on the subject.'

'I'm sure I could speak to Canon Richardson,' Louise assured them brightly at dinner, as they made short work of their pheasant and vegetables, not to mention two generous bottles of Burgundy. 'I was going to go and see him on Thursday to make arrangements for the next Bible reading group, but I can contact him tomorrow morning, as long as he's at home.'

Organising meetings and people, and not necessarily in that order, was one of the great passions of Louise's life. If friends sometimes found her a little domineering, and suspected that she ruled her happy-go-lucky husband more than he was prepared to acknowledge, they never minded. At worst she might be a busybody, but her goodness of heart was always self-evident. If any of them ever needed cheering up after a bout of illness, a friendly word when they were feeling down, or any kind of moral support, she would be around with her hand on the doorbell almost before they knew it.

'You never knew this Ethel Stephens, did you, dear?' Alfred asked.

'Never heard of her before all this.' A look of intense sadness came into her large blue eyes, which until then had twinkled so brightly that they almost seemed to be laughing. 'She must be brokenhearted. After all, it's bad enough to lose a son in the prime of life, without having all these undercurrents attached.'

'So what can we do?'

'About Mrs Stephens? Well, I always say a little bit of sympathy never came amiss. If we find out where she's living, I can take her flowers. Do we know if her son's funeral has taken place yet?'

'There was a private ceremony nearby at Leusdon, a few miles away,' Ralph informed them. 'The vicar at Holne was ill and his locum is pretty young and inexperienced, so we contacted the rector of Leusdon and he agreed to arrange matters. Though it was a modest little service, it was the least we could do for the poor man, to let him rest in peace. I read a lesson from the First Book of Corinthians. And the rector gave a very good address, seeing we barely knew anything about him at all.'

'Poor man! George Stephens, I mean. Going to your final resting place on earth without any of your family there. It doesn't seem right, does it?' She looked at them resolutely, almost defiantly. 'In that case, his mother needs another woman's sympathy more than ever. I know, Alfred – perhaps we could invite her round here for dinner one evening.'

Alfred almost choked on his potatoes.

'Steady on, my dear! Not that I mean to be cold-hearted, but – well, you don't know anything about her.'

Louise looked at him in surprise. 'What else do we need to know about her?'

'I think we should at least find out something about what sort of person she is, before we start writing the invitation, what?'

For all her desire to spread sweetness and light throughout the world, Louise knew when her impetuosity sometimes ran ahead of commonsense.

'Oh yes, Alfred, you are right. I'm sorry. But promise me you will think about it? Remember, it's simply to cheer up some poor woman whom nobody else wants to know...'

'We'll see, my dear. You have my word.'

Ralph watched their expressions carefully. He was torn between two conflicting desires. One was a wish to play what part he could in ameliorating Mrs Stephens' lot, as befitted a churchwarden, not to say a man of comfortable means who was evidently in a position to help the less fortunate. The other was a sense of caution, a resolve not to find himself in a position which none of them could control. There was always the possibility that this Ethel Stephens might be some kind of compulsive liar, even an imposter. His sister-in-law was the kindest person in the world, and nothing would hurt him and his brother more than to see her made a fool of by a convincing actress.

Chapter 5

Towards the end of the week the police called on the premises of Smith & Hanbury to interview Mr Pargeter, who had testified unstintingly as to George's good character. Beyond telling them what a conscientious and cheerful if rather shy and introspective young man the late Mr Stephens had been, and that he would have had no hesitation as regards recommending him for promotion if the matter had arisen, he could say almost nothing. After that the police had spoken briefly to most members of the staff in turn, but only Paul and Charles were in a position to tell them anything of importance.

No personal items had been left in his desk at work apart from a couple of pens, but by the first week of August, George's lodgings had been cleared out by his landlord. Francis Worth had been a London policeman himself, until a leg injury sustained while pursuing a burglar had made early retirement necessary. He was happy to cooperate with the officers who called round to the house in Bath Street to take a statement, and make arrangements to search his rooms for any papers or possessions which might add in some way to the tantalisingly little they knew about him.

Neither Charles, Paul nor their wives had ever seen the premises where their reclusive colleague had lived. When they went to the police station after the search, they did not know what to expect. The 'personal effects', all carefully listed and brought along, included a much-folded, very creased passport with his photograph, and a set of diaries. To their disappointment they could find no sign of a birth certificate. How they would have liked to find one and see what entry there was if any as to his paternity. However there was a small collection of books including a Holy Bible and Book of Common Prayer, a few recent espionage novels, among them William Le Queux's *The Invasion of 1910* and Erskine Childers' *The Riddle of the Sands*, some volumes of nineteenth-century English verse, a well-worn field guide to

British birds, and a handful of books about contemporary Germany and the Kaiser, some with sentences and passages of text heavily underlined in blue or red pencil.

When Charles and Paul glanced at the covers of the diaries the policeman, reading their thoughts, picked one up and flicked swiftly through the pages. It was a small standard pocket diary with a full week to each double-page spread. Most of the pages were blank, and the few exceptions merely had brief names and times of day, presumably appointments. They were all like that, he said. Nothing there for any prospective biographer of the man.

'There's something a bit odd about this passport, though. It's pretty battered, but look at all the handwriting and those date stamps on it. I know I don't see many passports, but I'd guess that someone's tampered with it. As if they've tried to use it to prove a point, or make it seem something that it's not.'

'I've never seen a passport before,' said Charles. 'I thought it was something they did away with in the last century.'

'Some people have them, if they travel abroad regularly. It could make things easier for anyone if they have an accident. Or if they're involved in official business. But if this young man had one, what did he need it for?'

'To make it look like he was in the habit of going abroad, you mean?' Paul asked.

The policeman nodded. 'I think it's genuine. They're not easy to forge. But I still think it could have been, shall we say, clandestinely altered.' He cleared his throat. 'This conversation doesn't go beyond these four walls, of course.'

Next they turned their attention to a rather tattered dark blue postcard album, full of cards showing various scenes from Berlin, carefully mounted in small black adhesive corners on dull brown leaves. A couple of worn light blue envelopes contained a handful of photographs, mostly in misty hues of sepia, showing a small boy – evidently George – with an even smaller girl, doubtless a younger sister, and their mother.

'So what do you think this tells us about the deceased?' the policeman asked, regretting that he had to deal in such a matter-of-fact way with this mournful business.

'It fits in with this German side,' Paul remarked, studying a hand-tinted view of the Brandenburg Gate. 'Look at those novels, for instance. Aren't they the lurid adventure tales that someone in government was complaining about, because they thought the authors were trying to whip up ill-feeling between us and the Germans? I read one of them myself to see what all the fuss was about, and it seemed rather sensationalised. The Emperor and his military staff sending their soldiers to infiltrate our civilian population and try to capture Oxford Street, and that sort of thing.'

Charles murmured in agreement. 'What George thought of them, I'd love to know. Ever since we knew him, we had been mystified by his reaction to any mention of Germany. He always seemed very sensitive about it, but – now I've seen this, it's all beginning to fall into place.'

The policeman looked at him thoughtfully. 'And what do you make of this theory of Mr Stephens being the son of the Kaiser?'

Paul looked at him gravely. 'A couple of days ago, I'd have had no hesitation in saying it was absolute nonsense. But after being confronted with this lot, now I'm not so sure.' He scrutinised a badly-creased photo of the woman and her children, the boy aged five or six at a guess and the girl little more than a babe in her mother's arms. The boy, he was convinced, must be George. On the back was scribbled, 'Brighton, 1886?', in handwriting which he recognised as being that of George. 'Either that, or a pretty pronounced case of hero-worship.'

'Increasingly a case of still waters run deep, I'd say,' Paul added. 'I'd always assumed he was just rather shy. But now it looks like he certainly had a lot to hide. Almost as if he was leading some kind of double life. It's a strange thing to say about one of your friends who has suddenly died. But – well, there's no other word for it.'

'What about the things that were supposed to have been found on him after he died?' Charles asked.

'There wasn't much,' said the policeman. 'Least, when I say not much, it could have been quite significant. A few handwritten papers in his case which looked like they were in German, but they were in such a state that nobody could make out what they said. All torn and screwed up, looking like they had got wet at some stage and later been dried out. And a plan of some harbour –' Charles and Paul held their breath as he searched his memory for the place. Not Chatham, Portsmouth, Devonport, or some similar place in Britain of strategic defence importance?

'It wasn't in England, I remember that. Began with K, it did. Kiel, that's it.' They breathed an inward sigh of relief. If he had been spying, then presumably it was for the right side as far as they were concerned. Though it must have been rather foolish of him, they thought, to be carrying a map of Kiel Harbour on him at such a volatile time.

True to her word, Louise Hillman had made it her mission to go and speak to Canon Richardson on the morning after Ralph's arrival. From first thing that morning she had chattered of nothing else but 'poor Mrs Stephens' with a single-mindedness that her husband and brother-in-law found rather wearisome, and they could not conceal their relief when she left the house to hail a cab for his vicarage in Deptford.

'I have not seen Mrs Stephens for some time, not for almost a year,' he told her as they made themselves comfortable in adjacent armchairs over a pot of tea in his drawing room. 'But after reading the papers, I do indeed intend to call on her to convey my sympathies as regards this most distressing news about her son.'

'I should like to come too, if I may,' Louise said. 'If you don't think it would be an impertinence. She does not know me, but – well, with my brother-in-law having known Mr Stephens, albeit slightly, I think it would not be out of place. And if there is anything I can do, just by offering to help or giving comfort.'

'Most commendable, Mrs Hillman. You always were a kindly soul.' He leaned across and patted her hand, resting on the arm of her chair, and coughed gently. 'Mrs Stephens has never been in what we may call fortunate circumstances. I believe she has very little money to live on, and as is often the way with ladies in such a position, I regret that she spends rather more on spirits than is wise.'

'Has she ever talked to you about her family?'

'She has mentioned her son and daughter from time to time. I understood that the son worked in some kind of office in London in a clerical capacity, and that the daughter was married and living somewhere in the south-east. But she never referred to them by name, I must add, which always struck me as rather odd.'

'As if she was subconsciously distancing herself from them, wouldn't you say. Does she strike you as one of these people who seems to want to bring down a curtain on their past?'

'I think you have a point there.'

'What about a husband?'

He shook his head resolutely. 'I do not recall any mention of a husband. And neither any reference to His Imperial Majesty.'

Louise was not sure whether this was the answer she had expected, but she nodded. 'How old would you say she is?'

'In her late fifties, I should imagine. Possibly more. It may of course be that a hard life has aged her somewhat before her years.' He shook his head a little sorrowfully. 'When I think of what has become of such people, I think we must feel truly thankful that we have not been the same way. There but for the grace of God indeed.'

Louise looked around the room, her eyes scanning rows of books on the shelves, wall-mounted glass cases of stuffed tropical birds, ornaments – antique pottery jugs and what looked like a pewter tankard – on the mantelpiece, lost in thought. She was overwhelmed with a desire to meet Mrs Stephens, but she knew that if she did so she would find it very difficult not to ask her questions. Any probing for information, no matter how kindly meant, could give an impression of rudeness. Even being thought as some kind of detective, or even heaven forbid a police informer.

Nevertheless it was a risk that must be taken. She was not the kind of person who would let such a possibility deflect her from a chance to do good.

'Mrs Richardson and I have a sick parishioner whom we have promised to visit this afternoon,' he said after a few moments' contemplation. 'Recovering from a fever at home. We will be taking her some good nourishing soup and perhaps a book or two. But if you like, perhaps we might go in search of our Mrs Stephens tomorrow morning. I wonder – there is always the possibility that she might not be at home. Maybe I should call first to see whether she would be willing to receive us?'

Louise shook her head. 'Let us take the chance, Canon. I had not arranged to do anything in the morning, apart from writing letters, but they can wait.'

'Very well, Mrs Hillman. In that case I will call for you in my cab at, shall we say, around ten-o'clock?'

As she took her leave of the Canon, her heart trembled a little at the prospect of this meeting with a stranger who had been through so much. Yet it was outweighed by the realisation that here was somebody who desperately needed comfort and help in a hostile world which, from what she had just heard, had not treated her all that well.

Canon Richardson was as good as his word, and the clock tower of Kensington had barely finished striking ten the next morning before he rang the bell of the Hillmans' house at Stafford Terrace. Moments later Louise issued forth in her best hat and coat. She had wondered whether it might not be tactless to dress too smartly for such a visit, but she had always been brought up to believe that a lady must be seen to advantage when in public, and anyway Mrs Stephens might feel she was being patronising if she did make an effort to dress down. The Canon was wearing his best frock coat and top hat, which immediately reassured her.

Some fifteen minutes later they reached Brock Road. Louise looked around the run-down street sadly, not with the air of superiority which might have befitted somebody in her finery, but out of pity for the people who lived there. She suddenly felt a little uncomfortable in her smart outfit. In Stafford Terrace it had seemed all right, but *here* – well, it was not quite another world, but she sensed such a difference as she looked at the grimy houses with their peeling paint, broken or boarded-up-windows, and rubbish on the pavements. Still, it was too late to do anything about it now. She could hardly go back and change. She looked at the Canon with mild envy. He could wear the same thing anywhere he went and never feel remotely self-conscious about it.

She stood behind him as he knocked on a dilapidated door which had evidently been painted grey some years before. There was the sound of shuffling footsteps and it opened slightly, then slowly a little wider, as a surprised face looked out.

'Mrs Stephens!' The Canon doffed his hat and beamed. Louise noticed he did not offer her his hand to shake, interpreting it as a desire not to seem patronising to someone from a lower class who may have been unused to such niceties.

Ethel peered into his face with dull, tired eyes.

37

'Why, it's Canon Richardson,' she said at last, her voice and expression revealing no emotion. 'Haven't seen you for a long time. When was the last? My memory isn't what it was.' She looked at Louise with curiosity, mingled with contempt. 'And who is this?'

'I don't think you know Mrs Hillman.' Ethel appeared immune to the jollity of his tone, murmuring, 'Pleased to meet you, I suppose,' under her breath as Louise smiled nervously, increasingly ill at ease and, though she would never have admitted it to anyone else, slightly afraid.

'You'd better come in,' she said coldly, looking vaguely at the Canon. Louise was beginning to wonder if she was included in the invitation, but he gave her a kindly look as if to reassure her that their hostess's bark was worse than her bite. They followed Ethel in though the passage to a dirty, untidy kitchen around which hung a pungent smell, predominantly of stale vegetables and damp clothes.

'Can't offer you anything,' she muttered. 'I'd let you share some of my medicine, but this has got to last me until tomorrow.' She pointed at a half-full bottle of gin. The Canon nodded to himself, while Louise felt that this probably said more about the woman's circumstances than anything else. Especially at this time of the day.

'Now what brings you here, Canon?' Ethel asked with her back to him, poking around on a shelf as if looking for something.

He cleared his throat. 'We came to express our deepest condolences.'

'On Frederick William, you mean?'

Louise looked bewildered and opened her mouth to speak, but the Canon silenced her with a let-me-do-the-talking look.

'Your son.'

'As I said, Frederick William.' She turned round to face him. 'Can you spare us a cigarette, if you've got one.'

Without a word he felt in his pocket for a case, passed her one and lit it. She took a couple of puffs, coughed, cleared her throat, and ushered them into an adjacent living room. There was a small wooden table, three assorted and rather rickety-looking chairs, and no other furniture to speak of but a small and rather badly scratched chest of drawers. They sat down, the

38

Canon offered Louise a cigarette which she declined, and took one himself.

'You're wondering why I call him Frederick William, when everyone else calls him George, aren't you?' she said, her voice becoming hoarse and croaky. 'I named him that after his father. The Kaiser in Germany, you know.'

She looked at them with a hint of pride, and they nodded politely. However fantastic this might sound, it would not do to provoke an adverse reaction in which anything might happen.

'We met when he was in England before he got married. You see, I lived at Windsor in those days, in a place in a street not far from the castle, and one of the times he came to stay here, he used to go out rowing with one of his servants on the Thames. One day I was walking by the river, and he invited me in the boat with him. I didn't believe him when he told me who he was, but he insisted he was Prince William of Prussia, and he had the right accent for it. We went and stayed in a small inn that night, and I think he must have given his military governor the slip. Good job his grandmama at the top of the hill didn't know what he was up to, otherwise they might have put me in the tower. It was only after we had said goodbye the next morning that I remembered what had happened during the night.'

For the first time since their meeting, her features broke into the ghost of a smile. 'You being a man of the cloth and a lady, I won't make you blush by saying any more about that. But he gave me some lovely trinkets, a brooch and necklace, earrings, just the sort of thing you'd expect a prince to give his ladies. I've still got them, after all these years. I never wear them now, but sometimes I take them out just to have a look at them.' Her voice gave way to a fit of coughing. 'And then a few weeks later I found I was with child. It had to be his. So that's why I called him Frederick William. You know those were the prince's names?'

Taking refuge in acquiescence, the Canon and Louise continued to nod with expressions of keen attentiveness.

'But then he went back to Germany, and married his princess from wherever it was called. Schleswig Holstein and all those other places.' She shrugged her shoulders with a look of resignation, and drew on the cigarette again. 'Always the way, isn't it? They can't marry the likes of us, because they're not allowed to. Got to have their princesses to keep the blood pure, and all that.' With a sarcastic laugh, she added, 'It will be different when the revolution comes, won't it? Do you believe in revolution, Canon?'

He cleared his throat politely.

'Our Lord did expel the money-changers from the temple, after all.'

'You won't be drawn, will you?' she said, a little aggressively. 'Have you ever read Karl Marx? I haven't, but there are people who told me about him. I know he's dead, but he's left his books behind him, hasn't he. For others to read, and turn the tables on those who have everything and shouldn't have.' She waved a finger at Louise who sat impassively, beginning to wish she had not come after all. 'What do you think, Mrs Hill?'

Louise wondered whether to correct her, but decided it would only risk provoking confrontation.

'I don't know,' she answered with forced brightness. 'We never know what's around the corner, do we?'

Mrs Stephens rolled her eyes in despair.

'You're all the same, the lot of you. No opinions of your own, or if you have, you're afraid to say so. Well, I don't regret anything that's happened. I had my son, he went away, I moved here, and now he's gone. But I suppose I lost him when he left me, didn't I? Whatever you have, you lose it in the end. Who wants people or possessions? You go out of this world with what you came in, don't you? And I don't expect I'll be around for much longer.' She coughed again.

Surely not, Louise was tempted to say, but she bit her lip.

'You mustn't say that,' the Canon said reassuringly.

'No, it's true. My lungs will do for me soon. I've had my life, and I won't grumble. Haven't got a lot left, have I?' The slight slurring of her words and the smell of gin on her breath added to the matter-of-fact manner, the lack of self-pity which Louise and the Canon found slightly bewildering.

'If there's anything we can do –' the Canon ventured, but she interrupted him.

'No, Canon. You are a good man, but I've got all I need for as long as I need it.' She looked around her. In any other circumstances it might have been mildly comic to hear somebody who obviously had so little in life to speak thus. 'And you, Mrs Hill. I don't expect you're used to seeing somewhere like this, are you?' If there was a sneer to her words, Louise rode above it as she smiled reassuringly, resisting the temptation to correct Mrs Stephens as to her surname. 'But I respect you for coming. There's not many of your class that would come to a house like mine,' adding rather ungraciously as an afterthought, 'all dressed up to the nines like that. I expect I could feed myself for a week on what you paid for that gown. A month, even.'

As they stood on the pavement waiting for their cab, the Canon reflected with a touch of sadness on what they had just seen. He had been prepared for it, although it did not make it any easier to bear. Yet nearly forty years in the church had taught him that there were many people who were in similar straits, and with the best will in the world there was only a very small amount he could do to alleviate their burdens. He could talk, offer comfort, provide a sympathetic ear, and promise to pray for them, but little more.

While she would not have cared to admit it, Louise was considerably shaken. It made her shudder to think that if the Canon had not been there with her – or rather, had she not been there behind him, letting him take the lead – then that woman would have gone for the jugular. She did not feel any dislike for the bereaved mother; on the contrary, she was full of pity, yet she could not but feel a twinge of revulsion. Whether it was for the bitterness she harboured against herself, for coming to such a poor house in her best clothes and being treated with such thinly-veiled dislike, or for a system which allowed such poverty and squalor to co-exist only a few minutes away from the City of London, its wealth and grandeur, she could not say.

How right, she thought, her husband had been the other evening to curb her impetuosity when she had been on the point of issuing Mrs Stephens an invitation to dinner with them. She was no snob, but the woman would as likely as not have made plain her ingratitude for any such kindness. With her defiant pride in her poverty, she would certainly have resented the Hillmans for being patronising.

'Well, she didn't eat us alive after all,' the Canon observed, adding with a puckish grin, 'Mrs Hill.'

'No. Poor woman! But what I can't get over was the cold-blooded way she dismissed the memory of her son in that casual manner. Like easy come, easy go. When he was probably the only family she ever had – apart from this daughter, about whom we are none the wiser.'

'I will make enquiries about her. Somebody of my acquaintance must have some knowledge of her, and a meeting would be in order.'

Their cab drew up and they climbed inside the vehicle, saying farewell to Brock Street without regret.

Chapter 6

In his sitting-room at Cumberland Drive, Paul was taking a well-earned quiet few minutes in the evening with the newspaper and a restorative glass of brandy. Joan had retired to bed early. She was still convalescent from a severe attack of influenza during the late spring, and found staying up late beyond her for the present. Paul would follow her a little later, but needed time on his own first to catch up with the news.

Life at Smith & Hanbury was at last resuming its regular rhythm after the unwelcome excitement of recent days. While he and Charles would always remember George Stephens with sadness and regret, he hoped they could draw a line through the situation and get on with their lives as before. In any case, he and Joan had a suspicion that, after four years of marriage, at last they might soon have another little life clamouring for their attention. He was particularly looking forward to becoming a father, though he had sometimes thought that Joan might not be too keen on the idea of motherhood. Never mind, he thought, she would come round to the idea. After all, she would have to.

Running his eye down through the headlines for the main stories, he was relieved that this time there was no mention of the Stephens case. Nevertheless there was not much comfort to be gleaned elsewhere. Industrial unrest in the mines; more suffragette protests; escalating arguments about Home Rule for Ireland; and a particularly unpleasant domestic murder case in Shoreditch. A neighbour had summoned the police, who had had to break into a house and find a woman and five children, one a babe aged less than a year, all with their throats cut, and there was no sign of the husband...

A ring at the doorbell startled him. Folding the newspaper and placing it on the table, he got up and went to answer it. He came face to face with a coachman, and a smartly-dressed woman looking at him with a sense of some urgency. Beneath the flustered exterior there was an apologetic look in her eyes.

'You are Mr Jenkins, of Smith & Hanbury?' He nodded. 'Charlotte Waters. I believe you used to work with my brother, George Stephens?'

He blinked in surprise.

'Do come in, Mrs Waters.' The servant took her coat and waited in the hall, while Paul showed her into the sitting room, and she eagerly accepted a glass of brandy.

'I'm so sorry to disturb you at this time of night,' she said a little breathlessly. 'I should have written to you first really. But ever since the police told me who my brother's friends at work were, I felt I had to come and see one of you. I couldn't find Mr Shepherd's address, so I felt I had to turn to you.'

Looking at her as she spoke, he now saw something in her face of a resemblance to George.

'It's rather odd, but he never mentioned having any sisters,' he said. 'Or brothers.'

'That doesn't surprise me.' She gave a mirthless laugh. 'I'm afraid that George and I were total opposites, just like night and day. We never really got on with each other as children, you see. When we were small I think he resented the fact that there was a younger sister to get his mother's attention. It's only natural, I suppose. Happens all the time in families, doesn't it? Looking back on it, I don't think our mother really spoilt me that outrageously. No, it was the sort of sibling rivalry that elder brothers generally grow out of. But George never did.' She sipped her brandy. 'Oh, that's another thing. His real names were Frederick William – I *think*.'

There was another hollow laugh. 'Fine state of affairs, isn't it? I hardly knew my brother as an adult, and now his mysterious death makes news headlines. And what's more, I realise that I'm not sure what his real names were. It's like something out of a novel, isn't it?'

'We always knew him as George at work.'

'He might have changed it officially by deed poll. You see, he always had this wish to be known as George Edward. When he was small he was forever with his nose in a book, and it was usually something to do with English history. We lived in Brighton, and he was fascinated by the Pavilion, probably because of its associations with the Prince Regent and all that. I was quite fond of walking on the beach and the Pier, because I

44

always liked collecting seashells and things. But apart from that I didn't care for the town much, it seemed awfully dull. Anyway, I'm getting off the point. He got this idea that George Edward were the most English-sounding names there were, so he decided that was what he was going to be. I suppose it must have been after George IV, and the last Prince of Wales – King Edward, that is. Whenever I wanted to tease him, I used to call him Georgie. He didn't like that, he must have found it rather undignified. Mother called him Frederick William because she and –' here she hesitated, her face clouding as if recalling some hateful ghost from the past – 'father were so keen on anything to do with Germany.'

Paul's eyes lit up at the mention of her father, but he knew the question would have to be broached with care. 'His father –'

She rolled her eyes with the transparent boredom of one who has been asked the same tiresome question too many times. 'All right, I know exactly what you're going to say. That his – our father was the German Kaiser?' With her free hand she gripped the arm of her chair tightly, and Paul could sense her cursing inwardly. 'Let me make it quite clear, Mr Jenkins. Our father's name was Anthony Stephens, and he was a railway engineer. He was born in Streatham, and his parents were local people.' She swallowed nervously before continuing her tale. 'He walked out on us when I was a few months old. Whether it was because he and mother didn't get on and were always arguing, or whether there was another woman involved, I just wouldn't know. But our mother obliterated every trace of him from our lives that she possibly could, and I would never have known the first thing about him if it hadn't been for a cousin who had the common decency to tell us the truth.'

She took another sip of brandy. 'What happened to my father, nobody seems to know. He'd be about sixty, so he could still be alive.'

At the increasing tone of distress in her voice, Paul looked at her with apprehension, as if she was about to cry. He waited for her to carry on in her own time.

'All this business about the Kaiser is complete fabrication, I can assure you. Thank goodness! Unless somebody knows something that I don't, which I grant you is possible. It's not easy trying to piece your family history together when the only

45

person you can rely on is a cousin who may not know all the facts himself. It if hadn't been for Claude, I'd have been completely at the mercy of my mother's fevered imagination.'

She shook her head sadly. 'When father disappeared and simply vanished into oblivion, my mother took to drinking too much. And she got it into her head somehow that she had had a fling with the Kaiser when he was still Prince Wilhelm, on one of his visits to England before he was married. Whether it was to cover the shame of father walking out on us, I don't know. That might have been something to do with it, but I think it was just a mixture of her stupid imagination and this love of everything German. She used to go on about Wagner and Beethoven, and it wasn't until I was almost grown up that I even found out who they were. She spent a lot of time in a sanatorium, and we were brought up by a couple of aunts. They used to tell us that she couldn't look after us properly because she wasn't very well, and we saw her at such irregular intervals that she was more like a distant aunt to us than a parent. And she used to go about telling people she had had several more husbands, all of whom left her. Unless the rest of the family were trying to protect us from something unpleasant, I'm fairly sure there was only one.'

Her voice faltered, and she dabbed at her eyes with a hand-kerchief. 'I'm sorry. You mustn't think I'm reproaching her in any way, because I don't see what else she could have done. She had a hard life – in fact, we all did. It wasn't an easy childhood for us, but we made of it what we could.'

'Do you still see her?'

'I wish I did, but I haven't seen her for a long time. I've tried to find out where she lives, but all I know is that it's somewhere in central London. Somebody told me that it was in the Peckham or Southwark district, but I've tried to trace her without success. She came to our wedding, but she was plainly out of sorts that day. As if she hadn't really wanted to come at all.'

'Did George share this love of Germany, or do you think he was rebelling against it?'

'I think she rather put him off the country. He seemed to be mildly interested in it for a while, but I got the feeling that it was just to please her. She had this great idea of trying to send him to university at Berlin or Bonn, but of course there wasn't any money. And I don't think he ever went there. Or anywhere abroad at all, in fact.'

Paul wondered whether he ought to mention the matter of the suspect passport he had seen, but decided that this was not the time to tell her that he had seen her brother's possessions of which she probably knew nothing.

'And what about your husband?'

'Oh yes, I should have told you about that. James and I have been married for five years. He has represented North Buckinghamshire since the second election of 1910, and in the spring he was promoted to under-secretary at the War Office. We have two small sons, David and Thomas, and he keeps saying they must grow up to be interested in politics, so they can follow him into Westminster one day. He wants to found his own little dynasty!' She tried to say this with a laugh in order to lighten the atmosphere, but rather unconvincingly.

'And how did your husband and brother get on together?' Paul asked, cursing himself as soon as the words had left his lips. He could have been rather more tactful.

'Not at all, I'm afraid. Again, I had the feeling that George didn't really want to come to our wedding, but was only there out of a sense of family duty. James spoke to him once or twice during the reception, but he told me afterwards that he wasn't exactly impressed with him.'

She lowered her voice and continued rather hesitantly. 'It was one evening when we had been married a few months. I said something about George, some casual remark, nothing important. But James was tired, and he'd been drinking. He doesn't drink often, I must add. And he told me he'd never met such a damned idiot in his life.'

Paul blinked, evidently startled.

'I know I shouldn't be telling a complete stranger all about this, but...' She put her empty glass down and clasped her hands together tightly. 'I felt I needed to tell somebody. It hasn't always been easy.' He saw at once that a world of loneliness lay behind those five words. 'And what I'm really afraid of is that my mother is going to go and make an exhibition of herself about it, especially if reporters should catch up with her. Or if she went to the papers herself, it could be even worse. Matters are precarious enough already between us – England as a nation, I mean – and Germany. And I can't let anything jeopardise James's career at the war office. His constituency officers think he could be in the cabinet one day, but if anything ghastly was to happen...' She held her hands out in a gesture of appeal.

'Did you still see your brother regularly?' asked Paul.

'No, I'm afraid not, that's almost the worst part of it. I knew where he lived, and I did write to him asking if we could arrange a meeting – several times, in fact. We sent him a Christmas card every year, and we always put our addresses on everything we sent – James's house in town, and the country house in his constituency. But he never answered once. After a while I gave up writing. What else can you do if your brother seems to want to shut you out of his life?' The look of desperate sorrow in her eyes made him feel utterly helpless.

'If there's anything I can do,' he said lamely, knowing it was a hollow rhetorical response rather than a suggestion of anything positive.

'Thank you, Mr Jenkins.' She rose to her feet and shook his hand warmly. 'You've listened to me, and you don't know what a help that's been. I promise I won't make a nuisance of myself, but do you mind if I contact you again if – if – well, there is anything?'

'Not at all. It will be my pleasure.' He smiled, feeling that his courtly manners masked only helplessness. Still, a shoulder for her to lean on was better than nothing, especially if his first none-too-pleasant impressions of her husband were accurate. Until that evening he had barely heard of James Waters, and what he had learned from the Right Honourable Member's wife did not encourage him to probe too deeply.

'And I must have kept Mr Crompton waiting outside longer than I meant to. Our coachman, I should have explained. I've never resorted before to bringing him out with me on an errand like this, and I don't mean to make a habit of it. But it really has been rather an exceptional case. Anyway, we must return to my house in Pimlico.

As they took their farewells, he saw her and the man out and locked the front door behind him, his mind raced back over their conversation. He believed that everything she had said carried the ring of truth, but until he knew a little more about her and her husband he was reluctant to commit himself. Meanwhile, it was getting late and he needed his sleep.

48

Underneath a cloudless summer sky, Sergeant Donald and Constable Fox cycled along the track from Holne to Poundsgate. It was rumoured that two Germans, possibly army officers, had taken over Little Tor Farm Cottage.

'Weapons an' all,' one young farm hand had come to the police station at Ashburton to tell them. 'They must 'ave 'ad some 'and in the death of that city gent, eh?' While Donald was reluctant to commit himself in the absence of greater knowledge, he knew that duty called for some kind of reconnaissance. And young Constable Fox needed to accompany him for moral support, more for his brawn than his brain. Six foot three and broad-shouldered with it, Francis Fox was of a peaceable disposition except when aroused, and as a youth his peers had soon learnt that he was not someone with whom one would willingly argue. Should Donald encounter any violence on his mission, Fox's presence would be invaluable.

The gateway and entrance to Little Tor Farm, the Cottage and its garden lay almost at the top of a hill, and both were quite out of breath by the time they propped their cycles against the hedge and unlatched the gate. Sitting on the lawn in a deckchair, taking advantage of the August midday sunshine, was a thickset man dressed in a suit and high collar, smoking a cigar and studying *The Times* intently. At the approach of the policemen he lowered his paper and glanced at them superciliously over the top, before continuing to read. Fox was relieved that he had not sprung to his feet, clicked his heels and saluted them, for with the mild irreverence of his twenty-five years he knew he would have been unable to stop himself from laughing.

'Good afternoon, sir.' Donald smiled brightly, under no illusions as to what was unlikely to prove a friendly encounter. 'And might I have the honour of knowing your name?'

The man lowered his paper again and stared at Donald with an air of superiority.

'I cannot see why you should wish to know, but for your information, my name is Count Otto von Andrewitz, and I am a Lieutenant of the First Potsdam Grenadiers.' Detecting their surprise at how little trace there was of a German accent in his voice, he continued, a little less icily. 'I sometimes think that I am more English than the English. You see, my mother had the good fortune to be born in London, Greenwich to be exact. Her father was a Major in the Wiltshire Yeomanry, and she used to accompany him and her mother sometimes to attend the army manoeuvres at Berlin. Which is how she met my father.' He laughed heartily. 'So you see I have one thing in common with His Imperial Majesty. I too have an English mother.' As an afterthought, he added, 'But her name is Marianne – not Victoria! And my wife is called Marianne as well.'

'And you still come to England regularly?' asked Donald, careful not to appear too eager in his pursuit of information.

'I come every summer. And sometimes in the winter, when I bring my wife and we stay in London. But in the summer, the countryside is sweeter, do you not think?'

'I agree with you there, sir. Lived on Dartmoor all my life, I have, and I'm sure there's nowhere just like it.' He checked himself for a moment, then decided to continue the questioning albeit delicately. 'So what brings you to such an out-of-the-way place?'

The Count looked him carefully in the eye before answering. 'There are few places better for watching birds than here. Do you watch birds?'

'Yes. When I get the chance.' Donald was not fully convinced of the man's ornithological interest, but he let it pass. He glanced casually at the garden. 'Quite a nice little spot to rent on your own, isn't it?'

'Ah, but I am not alone. I have a colleague staying with me, a senior officer who has served the Fatherland faithfully for nearly fifty years.'

'And he enjoys birdwatching too?'

The Count frowned. 'Why do you wish to know?'

Donald shrugged. 'Oh, idle curiosity. Nothing more.'

Constable Fox was faintly aware of a gimlet-like expression in the Count's eyes and shuffled uncomfortably, feeling that anything he said out of turn might cause unpleasantness. Suddenly fate intervened, in the form of a couple of butterflies flitting over a small spray of deep purple buddleia only a few feet away. He walked over with measured tread and crouched down to catch a closer view before they darted away.

'Red admirals,' he said as he returned and the other men looked at him. 'You will understand my being distracted by them when I tell you that's the first time I've seen a pair together all season.'

The Count roared with laughter.

'The red admiral. His Imperial Majesty's favourite butterfly! And no doubt it is the favourite of His Majesty King George V?'

Donald and Fox joined in the laughter good-naturedly.

'Of course,' Donald added. 'But the admiral, naturally, rather than the red!'

There was a pause, then he turned to Fox. 'Time we were getting back, I suppose.' There was time for one last effort at subterfuge before they left. Trying to sound as casual as possible, he remarked, 'We've got an appointment to see some friends of this chap who was found dead a short while back.'

The Count looked at him, opened his mouth as if to speak, then evidently thought better of it. Donald wrestled with his thoughts but decided to take the chance.

'You wouldn't have heard anything about it, would you, sir?'

'We know nobody in this area! How do you think we would have heard?'

Donald shrugged, doing his best to sound casual. 'Don't know, really. At the shops?' He glanced at the newspaper, and assumed that it would have been collected in person, rather than delivered. 'Perhaps when you went out to buy that paper? Or any food or groceries, maybe? The whole village has been talking of nothing else for days.'

The Count pursed his lips and emitted a noise expressive of ignorance and contempt. 'Village gossip! And you are expecting me, a complete stranger, to know about it?'

'I don't expect you to, sir. But if you did happen to hear anything...'

'I will say this, my good man.' The Count had adopted a patronising tone, not unlike that of a headmaster addressing a particularly stupid pupil. 'This young chap has evidently been very foolish. Maybe he has been involved in certain matters which should not concern him. But that is all I am prepared to say.'

Donald involuntarily raised an eyebrow. 'You knew of this man? Saw something about it in your newspaper, maybe?'

The Count hesitated for a moment. 'I did read something, as it happens. And as I told you, maybe he has behaved very stupidly. I repeat, that is all I am prepared to say on the subject. If you are police officers, perhaps you should arrest me myself. And Count

51

Linevitch, who is indoors.' A cynical smile played around his mouth. 'But what could you arrest us for? Unless you have a very good reason, then we will see to it that you will bitterly regret your action, if you live long enough!'

Donald looked at him impassively, his years of police service having taught him the virtues of hiding his feelings under a mask of outward imperturbability. Fox felt himself starting to redden with anger, but he bit his lip and said nothing.

'Very well, sir,' Donald said calmly. 'I don't think we need take up any more of your time. Good day to you.'

As they mounted their bikes for the ride back to Ashburton, Donald and Fox realised that their new acquaintance evidently knew a good deal more than he was prepared to reveal.

'How do two German officers come to be staying somewhere as remote as this, anyway?' Fox asked. 'I mean, who owns the cottage?'

'Chap called Priestley, unless I'm mistaken. He hasn't been seen around here much lately, though. In fact, he may have sold the place to somebody else for all I know.'

A few minutes of pedalling back, and Donald knew where he had the best chance of finding out.

Chapter 7

Within a couple of days both the Counts had gone. The discovery had been made by Michael Hobbs, the milkman who delivered each morning and discovered the cottage completely deserted. Within twenty-four hours their sudden disappearance was all over Holne and the surrounding area, and nobody could talk of anything else. At the Red Lion, some patrons were convinced that they had been arrested. Although nothing had appeared in the papers, people were ready to suggest that they had not merely rented the place, they had commandeered it and had the unfortunate family who lived there taken away under armed escort. That they had been taken into custody for questioning in connection with the suspicious death of George Stephens seemed beyond question.

Sitting in the lounge bar, Tom and Katie took the news in carefully. A resilient young man, he had been badly shocked by discovering the body in the first place, but he was determined not to let it spoil their special day. They had celebrated their wedding in style on a gloriously sunny Saturday, with the church packed out for their ceremony. It was as if nearly the whole of Holne had come to wish them well. After a week's honeymoon enjoying equally fine weather in a cottage close to the Welsh border, they had returned to make their home in Ashburton. On finding out that Roger and Mary Strong had been expecting George that weekend, Tom went to make his number with them after they came back, and both couples had become firm friends.

It was only right, Tom decided that evening, that the Strongs should hear about these rumours directly from him the following morning if possible. He had planned to go up and see them anyway, mainly as it had been a particularly good summer for strawberries and he had promised them some of their surplus. There were far more than he, Katie and their parents could eat their way through in the next few days.

Anyway, Roger and Mary seldom saw a newspaper, and in a

small community gossip was bound to become so distorted that there was no knowing what lurid form it would take by the time they heard anything more definite. All it needed was for some joker to sink one pint of beer too many and start mouthing off in a German accent about an imminent declaration of martial law in the village.

'So you think they've gone an' got the Germans an' that they might 'ave killed 'im?' Mary asked as she bustled around the stove, making Tom and herself a pot of tea the next morning. Katie had gone to see her mother who was unwell, and Roger was working on the farm.

'We don't know for certain that he was killed,' Tom said carefully. 'People still think it might have been an accident.'

''Ere, come on, Tom, we none of us were born yesterday, like. It were no accident.' She waved the kettle fiercely as if to give added emphasis to her words. 'Someone killed 'im, and if what the papers is sayin' is true, them Germans 'ad a right good reason for doin' away with 'im. Why else would the police 'ave arrested 'em, then, if it weren't for murder?'

'We don't know yet. Somebody said that a cache of arms was discovered at the cottage they had rented. And if that's the case, they might have been taken for questioning about that rather than the death of George. It's not official, but I'm sure we will know before long.'

'Official my foot. 'Ave it yer own way. 'Spose they might be innocent after all, but it sounds mighty fishy to me. Did you ever 'ear such goin's on down 'ere, of all places?' She poured the boiling water into the pot and slammed the empty kettle down so fiercely that Tom almost jumped. 'Young man found dead by the roadside, an' Germans pokin' around all over the place. They mus' be up to no good, I'll be bound.'

She turned round to beam at him, and put two steaming mugs of tea on the table in front of them. 'But 'tis good o'you to come and tell me. 'Ow would I be kept informed if it weren't for the kindness o' folk like you, Thomas Dobson.'

She pulled up a chair and sat down facing him. 'Now 'ow's Katie? You must bring 'er with you next time. She's a fine girl, your wife, but I think she needs a bit more weight around 'er middle, if you don't mind me talkin' personal. Let me know when you're bringin' 'er, an' I'll do you both a cake. Nothin' like one o' my cakes for ruinin' your figure, but all in a good cause.' She chuckled. 'You ask my Roger when 'e comes in. Skinny young fellow when I married 'im. Yet when we celebrated our first anniversary, 'e could 'ardly get into 'is weddin' trousers.'

'Rum business eh, them Germans up at Little Tor?' Alf Cuthbert remarked, briskly mopping the bar in front of him at the Red Lion.

Sergeant Donald took an eager gulp from his pint of bitter. 'Rum business indeed. We can't prove anything, mind, but something about that Count Andrewitz made me think he was putting on an act. I think he knew a lot more than he was prepared to let on.' He looked at Cuthbert. 'You don't know anything else, do you?'

Alf shook his head. 'Not me, officer. Never done nothin', I can assure you.' He held up his hands with an expression of feigned horror. 'All my customers know, or at least they think they do. Give 'em an unexplained death and every Tom, Dick and Harry round these parts know everything, or they think they do.' He suddenly looked thoughtful. 'I used to know the fellow who owns the farm and cottage. Dick something – Bishop – Priest – Priestley, that's it. He was a widower, and he was always coming in for a drink or two and a chat in the evenings, but he ain't been seen round this way for some years.'

'I remember Dick, but not that well. Only met him once. Does he still own the cottage? Sold up, moved, or whatever?'

'Might 'ave done. Just a moment, I'll ask the wife. There's nothin' goes on within ten miles of Holne that escapes the missus.'

With that he disappeared for a minute, to come back with a jolly-faced buxom woman behind him.

'Evening, Sergeant Donald. Don't think we've met, have we? I'm Isobel Cuthbert.' They shook hands. 'You were asking about Dick Priestley's place, Alf tells me.'

Donald nodded. 'That's right. Particularly whether he still owns it or not. You know about our, ahem, friends from Germany?'

Isobel roared with laughter. 'You're talking to the town crier, Sergeant. Why buy a newspaper when I can tell you all the interesting goings-on for the price of a drink, eh?' She walked round to the other side of the bar and beckoned him over to a table in the corner of the bar where they sat down and made themselves comfortable.

'I know I can trust you, being an officer of the law and all that,' she went on, lowering her voice slightly. 'But obviously you'll be choosy in who hears all this. For one reason, some of this stuff I only know from hearsay and I wouldn't swear it's all true. Most of it is, I'm pretty sure, but I'm not one to go blabbing to all and sundry unless I'm certain. And besides, I don't want it all laid at my door for that same reason.' She grinned. 'Everyone calls me a gossip, and I don't mind. Friendly gossip, like. But if it's going to cause mischief, I keep my great mouth shut.' She looked at him for assent and he nodded sagely.

'Now, as far as I know, Dick Priestley still owns the farm. Lives in Cornwall now, unless I'm mistaken. He must be pushing sixty or seventy if he's a day, and he's too old to do the hard graft himself, but he left the whole cottage and farm on the hill just above it, and everything else to his daughter and son-in-law. Eleanor and Edward, their names are. I think they still do a bit of sheep farming, but they don't spend much of the year there. Edward has got some business in Southampton, or that area, and lives there. Maybe he'll give that up and come back to the farm full-time when Dick pops his clogs, maybe he'll sell up. But that's not really to the point. What you need to know is this. Now, Constable, you've lived here some time, haven't you?'

Donald scratched his head. 'Let me see – twenty years odd. In fact, it'll be twenty-one years come December.'

'I thought so. Do you remember that fire on the farm some time ago?'

'Now you come to mention it, yes. That hot summer of 1906, wasn't it?' He made a quick mental calculation. 'Seven years ago, that's it. Wasn't there something a bit peculiar about it?'

'You never spoke a truer word.' He voice sank to little more than a whisper, as she looked around to confirm that nobody else was in earshot.

'Dick Priestley is a man who's always liked the good life. He used to spend most of his profits on the gee-gees, so they say. You're not to quote me on this, but the word was that he got his fingers burnt about then. It may have been something to do with a run of bad luck at the race track. Although somebody did tell me that it wasn't that at all, and he'd purchased some bonds or made investments that crashed pretty heavily and he ended up considerably the poorer. I don't pretend to know a lot about these things, and whether it was a combination of the two, I can't judge on that either. But it would certainly fit in with what we know about him. Anyway, that fire destroyed most of his out-buildings and quite a lot of his tools and machinery. You could see the smoke for miles around here.' She hesitated before continuing. 'And they think it was deliberate. You get the picture?'

'Started by him, you mean?'

She nodded. 'It's not for me to point the finger. But the insurance company did some investigating, and they didn't like what they found. They never managed to prove anything as far as I heard, and I don't think anybody was charged with arson. But while they didn't actually accuse him of fraud, I think they found some get-out clause in his policy to suggest that he'd been careless, or something. Not that I know the p's and q's of the legal side, but that's how the situation went as I understood it.'

'So they didn't pay up in the end?'

'There you've got me, Sergeant. I suppose they must have had some good reason for not doing so, or at least withholding payment until or unless they were satisfied that he wasn't to blame. Which is where we get these German types coming in. I think you met them, didn't you?'

'Constable Fox and I met one of them the other day. What was his name – I've got it, Count Andrewitz. He said his mother and wife were English.'

'Did he tell you what his wife's name was?'

He thought for a moment. 'Marianne, that's it.'

'Marianne Bennett. I don't know her, but what I can tell you is that she's a distant relation of Dick Priestley.'

While Donald had mastered the art of containing surprise in public, in this case he failed as he whistled in amazement. Only a few customers were in the bar, chatting to themselves, but from the bar Alf looked across at them and grinned broadly.

'If my wife is tellin' you bawdy stories, officer, I'll see to it that it don't 'appen again.'

They laughed as Isobel pulled a face at him.

'That bar is going to be spotless tonight, Alf Cuthbert. Spotless and gleaming like a moonlight lake, so I can see my face in it. Either that or you sleep downstairs for a week.'

Once the merriment had subsided and the remaining patrons had added a few good-natured remarks directed at Isobel on her conjugal duties, she continued talking to Sergeant Donald in the same half-whisper as before.

'As I was saying, Marianne Bennett is some relation to Dick. Third cousin, or something like that. And it seems she got her husband to bail him out and finance him. Or at least pay to make good the fire damage, replace everything he had lost, and so on.'

'Paid for it, or lent him the money?'

'Again, I don't exactly know. But what I did hear was that Dick allowed the Count and Countess to come and stay in the cottage whenever they wanted. Or for the Count to bring his friends to stay. I suppose the usual plan is that he brings one or two down as guests from Germany every summer while she goes to see her family in England, as it's the only chance she gets. They live in the Birmingham area, I think. Now we come to mention it, I don't think she's ever actually been down herself. Maybe she doesn't like the area, or perhaps she and her husband are separated, or happier living apart. Alf and I have never met either of them.'

'They don't come in here, then?'

Isobel roared with laughter. 'A German Count and his good lady wife in here? No, they're much too grand for us, and it's just as well. I can just imagine him walking in here, clicking his heels and standing to attention as he orders a flagon of beer in a German accent. He'd probably give me a salute when I've poured them. Then I'd be rolling around the floor until I do my insides an injury.' She patted his hand playfully. 'Just think of the papers, Sergeant. I can see it now. Devon publican's wife court-martialled for making fun of a German officer!'

He joined in her laughter genially. 'As long as they don't ask me to arrest you. And do they have exclusive use of the cottage at Little Tor Farm when Priestley's daughter and son-in-law aren't there?'

'I suppose they might. They run it as a sort of guest house for part of the year, just to keep some extra pennies coming in instead of it staying empty. Or they did for a while – I know they have had English people there before. But the Count has been back at least once every year, and he keeps to himself pretty well all the time. There might be a more sinister purpose to it than that, there might now. I don't know.'

'After this, everyone is bound to think so.'

'And who can blame them?' She looked up at Alf. 'Back with you in a moment,' she called to him and rose to her feet.

Sergeant Donald got up and thanked her as they shook hands again.

'And if I hear anything else, Sergeant, you'll be the first to know.'

Chapter 8

Paul had slept none too well after Charlotte Waters' visit. He felt more deeply involved than ever, though powerless to do anything. And though he had always felt that George was a man of mystery, now he decided he was even more of an enigma than before. For a moment he had a sneaking suspicion that she might have made some of her story up, and almost at once he was ashamed with himself for having allowed such uncharitable notions to cross his mind. Her sincerity seemed beyond reproach, her words had the ring of truth, and if that was the case then she deserved every sympathy. First that difficult childhood, an absent father and an unstable mother, and now a husband of whom, he suspected, she was rather afraid. Fate had evidently not dealt her a good hand of cards.

He was relieved when Charles turned up early at Smith & Hanbury the next morning, so they could have a chance to talk over the matter without interruptions.

'I know James Waters,' Charles remarked when Paul had finished his account of the previous evening. 'Or rather, I know of him. A friend of Alice used to work for him when he was in banking, and said he was an arrogant little fellow, if I recall his words correctly. Very much your self-made man, who was born with hardly a penny to his name, and by solid hard work and a lucky investment or two has got a handsome fortune tucked away somewhere. As for Charlotte, she's in her late twenties, I think, and he must be a good twelve years or so older. Fiercely ambitious, not the type likely to let anything or anyone stand in his way once his mind's made up about anything. And as you say, he seems to have set his sights on high office. Whether he sees himself as a future Prime Minister or not it's hard to say, but if he has his eye on a seat in the cabinet, it wouldn't surprise me.'

'And the last thing he wants is the likelihood of any scandal attached to his name. Or any kind of family embarrassment.'

'Exactly. If you're working for the War Office, you obviously wouldn't want it to be known that you had such a close connection with Kaiser Wilhelm. Particularly now we've got all this talk of naval and military estimates in the Reichstag, and our own cabinet getting increasingly restive about increasing the fleet just to keep abreast. It's getting harder than ever to find anyone in government circles who thinks we can get through the next couple of years without war in Europe – in other words, with Germany on one side and ourselves on the other. If as much as a whisper of this business about her parentage or her brother's supposed origin was to get out, Waters must realise he could well find himself returning to the back benches by Christmas.'

'And if his wife should be the unwitting cause of his downfall, he won't be inclined to make it comfortable for her.' He thought back to the veiled expressions of fear in her attitude last night. 'Whether he bullies her or not I don't know, but I get the impression she's afraid of him. The last thing she would want to do is prejudice his career up the political ladder.'

'In her position, I'd say the same. I've just thought – what about those things we saw of George's at his lodgings? We really ought to give them back to her.'

'I was going to ask your advice about that. I didn't say anything about them to her last night, but until or unless we know where their mother is, she must be his next of kin.'

'You didn't tell her where he lived, I take it?'

Paul looked at him pensively. 'No, I did wonder whether I ought to, but it placed me in a difficult position. If I had given her his address, it would have been hard for me not to tell her about us being shown his books and all that other stuff. She's the one who ought to have seen them first, and if she knew that we'd been there before her, it would have looked rather intrusive of me.'

'I see your point. If someone else had stumbled across my long-lost sibling's possessions, I'd be pretty sensitive about it. Particularly in circumstances such as these.'

Only then did Paul remember that he still had no idea of Charlotte's address. He made a mental note to call at the police station later and inform someone that at least the dead man had a sister and brother-in-law who could easily be traced.

James Waters let himself in through his front door with two things on his mind. One was a glass of good brandy, and the other was a word with his wife. Marsh the butler took his coat and hung it up in the hall as he went into the drawing room, seated himself in an armchair, and waited for the inevitable glass and his paper to be brought to him. Marsh's reward for his devotion to duty, apart from a handsome wage, was acknowledged as ever with a curt nod.

Ten minutes later, having emptied his glass and scanned through the paper, he called for Crompton.

'Mrs Waters, if you please.'

'Beg your pardon, sir. Mrs Waters is not well and has gone to lie down.'

'One of those damned headaches of hers, I suppose. It's her usual excuse when she knows she's done something I don't approve of. Send her to me!'

'Very good, sir.'

He stared out of the window, tapping his fingers with increasing impatience on the arm of his chair. After some moments Charlotte appeared, looking pale and haggard.

'Sit down!' he rapped without glancing at her. 'Now, what's this I hear about your going about paying visits in town without telling me – on your own?'

She sighed. Trust James to make such a fuss, she said to herself. 'I went to see a man who worked with my brother.'

He turned to face her as she sat down in a chair opposite him. 'His name?'

'Jenkins. Paul Jenkins. From Smith & Hanbury in Bayswater.'

'I do know where that confounded brother of yours used to work!' His voice took on a thinly-veiled hint of sarcasm. 'What I did not know was that you had asked my permission.'

'I was going to. But you were out on committee business, and –'

'And you couldn't wait until it was over!'

'I'm sorry, James. But I was perfectly safe. Nothing –'

'Never mind that!' He looked angrily at her, the obvious suffering in her face only irritating him even more. 'Have you any idea what could have become of you? Or what would happen to my reputation in the House, if it comes to that? What do you think they'd say if they heard that I was letting my wife go gadding about, walking unescorted on the streets of London after dark!'

'I told you, James. I was perfectly safe. And I was not alone

62

and unescorted. Do you really think I would be as foolish as that? Crompton was with me all the time, and we took a cab.'

'So I suppose that makes it all right, does it? Very well, what did you want with this Mr Jenkins?'

''I wanted to see if he could tell me anything about my brother. Or my mother.'

'And could he?'

'Not very much. But at least he could tell me about what sort of person George was. After all, I hadn't seen him for years. And if I need anything else, I think he is prepared to help.'

James stood up and put his hands behind his back with the pompous air which she disliked even more than his sudden anger.

'The best way he can help, Charlotte, is by keeping his nose out of your private life. Our private life. Have I not told you time and time again that if any of this foolish business gets out, it could finish off my career? You scarcely need to be reminded that I have just been appointed to my first post in His Majesty's Government. If the press is to get wind of any nonsense, even if it is a pack of lies from start to finish, where do you think that will leave me? Or my sons?' They're my sons as well, she said to herself, but she did not feel up to making an issue of it. 'And what do you imagine this man can do anyway?'

'I don't know. But, remember I hardly knew my brother.' James snorted and tried to interrupt, but she ignored him as she continued. 'His colleagues must have known him better as a person than anybody else, and they may be able to shed light on something about the circumstances in which he died. You must admit it's the least I can do. He was part of my family, after all. And I hadn't seen him since our marriage.'

'Whose fault was that? He was the one who never bothered to maintain any semblance of contact once we were married. If I remember, you did make the effort yourself, and where did it get you?'

Any more of this, Charlotte thought to herself, and she would either burst into tears or strike him. 'I know, James. But he was part of my family.'

'Well, you have another family now. Your husband and sons. And you owe it to us not to do anything which might sully our reputation. Particularly mine.'

She had heard it all before, but her headache was particularly trying. Even if she had been feeling stronger, she knew that it was pointless to argue. As for him, he vowed silently that if he had been living a hundred years earlier, he would have marched round to the offices of Smith & Hanbury, summoned his brother-in-law's colleagues, and horsewhipped them on the spot, or even challenged them to a duel on Hampstead Heath. It was lucky for them that they all lived in gentler times.

'Very well,' he growled after a moment. 'Back to bed with you, if you must. And it will not happen again. As my wife, you should never forget that you have certain obligations to follow and you will do as I say. I do not want to have to lock you inside the house, like some husbands do to their wives, so don't force my hand. Do I make myself clear?'

As she tried to make herself comfortable in bed once again, despite the hammer-like throb in her head, she cursed herself. This, she knew instinctively, was not the way to deal with James. How many times had she put up with being treated like a disobedient child, just for the sake of a quiet life? He always seemed so apologetic afterwards, or at least showed an element of contrition in his behaviour for the next day or so. No straightforward admission that he was sorry if he hurt her – he had his pride, of course – but he evidently didn't mean to be so hurtful.

If only she stood up to him for once, what would his reaction be? His love for her would surely see it in the right spirit – a little call to order, nothing more. Yes, he only had eyes for her and their children – *our* sons, James, not *your* sons. It was her calling in life to support and cherish him as a good wife, to indulge him as she should, to cherish, honour and obey, but -

Next time, she told herself. She would choose her moment. Just as long as she didn't have a miserable headache like this to deal with as well...

Since she had accompanied Canon Richardson to Brock Street and been glad to come home in one piece, Louise had tried to put the business out of her head like a bad dream. Though it had crossed Alfred's mind that morning to try and dissuade her from going, he knew from experience that she was not easy to talk out of something once her mind was made up. If she discovered that she had bitten off more than she could chew, it might prove a salutary lesson for the future. Her reluctance to initiate any discussion about it afterwards seemed to suggest the latter, and neither her husband nor her brother-in-law felt like bringing the subject up themselves.

As for Ralph, he did not particularly want to be reminded about George's fate, sad though it was. He was relieved when their conversation turned to more wholesome matters, like plans for spending an afternoon in St James's Park or Kensington Gardens, followed by an evening at the music hall.

Yet any hope that he may have escaped from further echoes of the case for the rest of his stay in London were dispelled when Alfred came across a couple of paragraphs in the paper one morning at the breakfast table.

'Well I never! I see they've sent a couple of Germans packing in Devon,' he remarked, picking up his coffee. Louise had just left the room but Ralph looked up attentively, leaning across as his brother indicated the relevant section. Under the heading, GERMAN OFFICERS ASKED TO LEAVE ENGLAND, it announced in a few lines that two army officers from Potsdam, Count Otto von Andrewitz and Count Max von Linevitch, had been requested to return to Germany after having been questioned by police at Ashburton, in connection with the discovery of a quantity of rifles and ammunition at a house in Poundsgate in Dartmoor, Devon.

'Anything to do with this Stephens case, do you think?' Alfred glanced at his brother.

'Hard to tell. It could be mere coincidence. But unless they've got some pretty good reason to suspect them of foul play or murder, I suppose the press could hardly make any reference to it. It wouldn't do to jump to conclusions.'

'You must admit it seems a bit ironic, though.' Alfred smiled grimly. 'Two Huns in uniform come across to a remote corner of Devon where they think they won't be noticed, bump the fellow off, and then get told to make themselves scarce, maybe for something completely different. Strange are the ways of the world.'

With a grunt he turned to the racing pages.

Charlotte sighed as she looked around the seventy or eighty people who had come to participate in another of James's garden parties in the grounds of Lower Brook Manor, their country house near Aylesbury in his constituency. With her natural shyness she had initially dreaded these occasions, having to meet and make small talk with all these strangers. She would far rather have spent the time reading to the children, or by herself with her sewing and knitting. Somehow she had steeled herself to take them all in her stride, although she still could not wait for them to finish. The usual crowd were here – the great, the good, the self-satisfied and the boring.

Thankfully at least one person who did not fall into the latter two categories was there, she said to herself as the Right Honourable Sir Gregory Hall-Adamson, Bart, came ambling slowly towards her. A touch of gout made it necessary for him to walk with a stick in his left hand. With his stovepipe hat, mutton-chop whiskers and a well-worn suit which placed him firmly in the middle of the last century, he looked like someone out of a story by Dickens, she thought mischievously. As James' predecessor, he had sat as member for North Buckinghamshire for almost forty years, a period of distinguished public service which included a spell as parliamentary under-secretary in Gladstone's last government, and had retired at the last election a few weeks after celebrating his seventieth birthday.

'Good day, Mrs Waters, ma'am.' He raised his hat with a flourish, then lowered his voice respectfully. 'Please accept my deepest condolences on the death of your brother.'

'Thank you, Sir Gregory.'

He waved his hand aside. 'Oh, call me Gregory, or Sir G if you want, like everybody else does. Is everything else well with you these days?'

She nodded half-heartedly as he looked at her searchingly. It was impossible to conceal anything from the wise old bird.

'Well, my brother George –' She proceeded to tell him about the rumours of his parentage as he listened with growing amazement. 'And the worst of it,' she ended, 'is that James is angry lest it should get out, and that it will spoil things for him.'

'His climb up what old Beaconsfield used to call the slippery pole? Or a senior post in the cabinet, eh?' He shook his head decisively. 'I can't see that it will. He's imagining things. By Gad, if I had heard this from anyone else, I wouldn't have believed it. But I'm not going to go acting like the town crier, believe you me.'

'No, thank you, Gregory. I knew I could rely on you.'

He cleared his throat before continuing, a little hesitantly as if weighing his words first. 'You'll forgive me asking, my dear, but James isn't, in a manner of speaking, taking it out on you in any way, is he?'

It was her turn to look astonished. 'Oh no, nothing like that. But he does seem worried and irritable. About what it will do to his chances of promotion, or that the ministers might use it as an excuse for passing him over.'

He looked around them to make sure nobody else was listening. 'Balderdash!' he grunted. 'I'm sorry, but the idea is preposterous. I know what you're thinking. It's the old knife in the back situation, isn't it? Waters has got a family skeleton in the cupboard, some blighter says, so let's suggest he's not right for the job. Maybe someone with their eye on the main chance. Am I right?'

'More or less.'

'Let's get this clear. Your husband is a first-class member of Parliament. Since we elected him, he's proved he's a good speaker, has a splendid grasp of detail, sticks to the facts when making speeches in the House and in committee. Doesn't waffle on to hide his ignorance. Most important, he hasn't made any enemies in the ranks, as far as I can see. The opposition have plenty of respect him as well, and you can't say that of all of 'em. Do you remember that first debate he spoke in, on the employment welfare provisions, when he made an absolute meal of that damn fool spokesman for the other side who hadn't bothered to find out his facts properly before he opened his mouth? Everyone else does, and afterwards he had them eating out of his hand. You mark my words, he will go a long way. If he has a fault, and who of us haven't, he's a trifle sensitive to these things. Worries too much about his image. Now when I sat in the House, I always told them that they could say what they liked about me. The worst thing for us chaps at Westminster is when they *don't* talk about us. It means we're not important. We're so vain, and my, how we hate it when nobody takes any notice of us.'

He laughed, and such were his infectious good spirits that Charlotte could not help laughing either despite her anxiety.

'If you don't believe me, perhaps you'd better ask our friend over there.' Coming towards them with a ready smile was Philip

Hemsworth, assistant treasurer of the constituency association. They exchanged the customary greetings, and Sir Gregory tackled him gently. Hemsworth was well aware of the rumours, and only needed the most cursory of explanations.

'I can't see that it would threaten your husband's position, Mrs Waters,' he told her without a moment's hesitation. 'One or two of the chaps hate the Germans like poison and they might try and make an issue out of it, but they wouldn't get far. The rest of them are far too sensible to let their judgment be knocked off course for such a petty reason.'

'There you are,' Sir Gregory remarked triumphantly. 'If it would set your mind at rest, I can have a word in his ear on the subject. Tell him he's not to lose any sleep over it, what?'

'Oh thank you, Gregory. But you won't tell him I put you up to it, or anything like that?'

'You can rely on me to cover my tracks.' He winked conspiratorially. 'I can always tell him there's been a bit of gossip in the committee rooms. Or even Lady H-A and I chewing the fat over it at dinner? You know what a gossip my good wife is!'

'Oh yes, I meant to ask. How is Lady Hall-Adamson?'

'She's all right. Had a touch of the old fever this week, so she hasn't come here today, but she's well on the mend. We'll have you and James to dinner to celebrate when she's back on form, what?'

Catching sight of another friend, he waved his hand in recognition.

'Now you'll have to excuse me, my dear. I simply must go and talk to that chap. Bit of a bore between you and me, though he means well. But I will see you and James before I go this afternoon.'

Good old Sir Gregory, she reflected as he and Hemsworth moved away. He had always been one of the few genuine friends she had in the constituency. She always felt the better for speaking to him, but her mood of mild euphoria did not last long. Walking determinedly towards her was Sophie Clark, whose husband Oswald represented the adjoining seat of Buckinghamshire South-West.

Oh yes, Sophie assured her lightheartedly in that affected voice of hers, when Parliament was sitting she hardly saw Oswald from one day to the next, but wasn't it *marvellous* now that

Members could command a proper salary, which they couldn't until two or three years ago, and how he was making all these *wonderful* investments in stocks and gilts, and how he only had a majority of just over three hundred last time in Buckinghamshire South-West, but it *really* didn't matter if he lost his seat at the next election as they had their eye on a absolutely priceless little property near Paris which he had been planning to buy from friends anyway, and Paris had so much more *style* and *atmosphere* than staid old London these days, and with its place in the fashion and art world it *really* was the place to be, wasn't it? Of course, politics wasn't Oswald's entire life, and it simply wasn't a woman's business to follow all those *tedious* debates in the House. But she *really* couldn't agree more, and what did she want to take an interest in politics for, as she found it so much more rewarding when she helped out in those soup kitchens in Stepney and Bethnal Green, and oh my *dear*, don't those poor people think it simply *marvellous* that somebody like her should have time to come and do all these *divine* things for them.

Charlotte listened resignedly, knowing it was useless to try and get a word in edgeways once Sophie was talking at full spate. Years of patience had helped her to put up silently with such insufferable types, though sometimes she wondered what on earth she had done to deserve such a woman taking up her time. She had only met Oswald briefly on social occasions a couple of times, and found him a pleasant, unassuming fellow. He was indeed fortunate if he hardly saw his wife and had to put up with her self-congratulatory prattle from one day to the next. With relief she noticed another of the members' wives walking up to them, gave her an ingratiating smile and proceeded to take Sophie off her hands. Thank goodness for small mercies, she thought as a maid approached her with a platter of savouries in each hand.

'Excellent woman, Mrs Clark, don't you think,' James remarked to her that evening after everyone had gone and they stood on the garden verandah, taking advantage of the fine evening and watching a golden sunset. 'If they ever give the vote to women – God forbid – then she might not make a bad MP herself.' He laughed cynically. 'But she'd have more sense than to get ideas above her station. You know, dear, you ought to see about getting on to one of her committees for charitable work in the East End. How would you like that?'

'I do help to organize the bazaars here every month. And there is the clothing collection for the hospitals, which I am involved in sorting out.' She groaned inwardly. The last thing she wanted was to be one of Sophie Clark's underlings, particularly if any of the rumours about her private life and affairs were true. Either Oswald was a fool or a saint to put up with her.

'Yes, yes. But I thought you'd like a new challenge. Get to meet a few more people.' He looked at her coldly. 'You've always got an answer, haven't you? The moment I suggest something, it's so often a case of I've got this, I've got that. I don't know what's the matter with you.'

'All right, James. Just let me think about it.' She had heard all this before, but it was useless to argue. The less verbal resistance she put up, the more likely he would be to lose interest. If she was lucky, maybe this was the last she would hear of it.

Tom and Katie came to supper with Roger and Mary, having given their word to be lured by the promise of one of Mary's cakes. She had also prepared a mouth-watering salad with cold meats, bought some cream to go with the strawberries Tom had given her, and to round it off Roger uncorked two bottles of homemade wine.

'So what's this 'bout lettin' them Germans off the 'ook, then?' Roger asked.

'The vicar was telling me about it when I went to help dig his raspberry beds,' Tom informed him. 'All seems like a lot of fuss about nothing much. There were a couple of rifles at Little Tor Farm Cottage in Poundsgate, but no vast armoury or anything. So the press put two and two together and made five hundred. If you ask me, somebody had tipped the police off, thinking there was something funny going on. The officers weren't exactly arrested, but just asked to help the police with some enquiries, as they put it.'

''Bout the murder, you mean?' Mary broke in, wide-eyed.

'We can't be sure it was murder,' Tom replied tactfully. 'I know we all think that's what it was, and the police are still keeping an open mind on the case. But nobody's got any evidence that would stand up in a court of law. It does look pretty suspicious, but there was absolutely nothing to pin on our friends from Potsdam.'

'An' they were expelled?' asked Roger.

Tom shrugged. 'Maybe. But they might have left of their own accord. It could be that the authorities asked them to leave in order to avoid a dangerous incident.'

Roger gave a sarcastic laugh. 'Shuttin' the stable door after the 'orse 'as bolted, if you ask me. The dangerous incident, as 'ee put it, 'as 'appened already.'

'Don't mean that at all, dearest.' Mary picked up a raw carrot in her fingers and chewed it thoughtfully. 'What 'e means is, they was asked to go 'ome 'fore our government 'ad a diplomatic incident or –'

'I know, woman. Only jokin'.'

Katie felt something soft brush against her legs. 'Hello, Mole. Where have you been?' She bent down to tickle him under the chin.

'Our champion boy, Mole. Should 'ave seen that rat 'e caught this afternoon,' Mary announced, like a proud mother extolling the achievements of an adored child. 'Almost as big as 'im, it were.'

'I know,' Roger chuckled. He dropped his voice and looked round at their plates, 'Don't tell the wife I said so, like, but that rat don't 'alf make good sausages, either.'

Mary pulled a face at him as she joined in the general laughter.

Sergeant Donald was in a benign frame of mind as he sat at his desk in the police station at Ashburton, lighting his pipe. True, there had been a minor domestic incident during the weekend, a husband and wife quarrelling with each other hammer and tongs until the neighbours started complaining, and he had been called round to intervene before it reached the threshold of physical violence. Apart from that, the last week had been one of the most peaceful he could recall for over a year. Those German characters had pushed off, presumably back to their own country. With a little luck they could put George Stephens' unfortunate death down to the accident that most of them had thought it was all the time, and they could forget the whole affair.

Any such hopes were dashed as Constable Fox walked in.

'I was in the Red Lion last night. Saw Isobel Cuthbert, and

she says she's got some news for you. She would have been up to come and tell you herself, but her Alf is nursing a bad back and she sends her apologies but she can't leave the place. She's only got a couple of the younger barmaids helping out. But next time you drop in, she'll add to what she told you last time. Says it can wait, she doesn't think it's urgent, but it might help.'

'I think I can manage that tonight. Anything else?'

Fox shrugged. 'Not really. Except for one theory that the whole thing was set up by us British.' Seeing the puzzled look on Donald's face, he continued. 'I was buying some groceries yesterday, and Mark Phipps behind the counter told me that one of his customers thinks our chaps are behind it. Someone in army intelligence, or what-have-you, wanted to get George out of the way because they knew about his being the Kaiser's son, and they were convinced he was a German agent. But they didn't want any suspicion to be attached to them – or us, should I say, in Britain. And they knew that it would be pretty embarrassing for the government if anybody pointed the finger at them. So they found out about these officers on Dartmoor, and decided to use them as a cover, to make everybody think they had murdered George. That way, our hands are clean.'

Donald looked at Fox and burst out laughing. 'It shows great imagination, I'll say that for them. You don't believe it, I trust?'

Fox grinned. 'Not for a moment. And I don't think there are half a dozen other people around here who would take it seriously.'

That evening Sergeant Donald cycled to the pub. He had barely walked through the door before a beaming Isobel waved to him from behind a busy bar.

'With you as soon as I can, Sergeant. Just let me fetch Lily to hold the fort.' She went out through the back and a young girl followed her in to continue serving as Isobel led the way to an empty table.

'Been doing my homework for you since last time,' she announced proudly, before dropping her voice. 'This business about Count Andrewitz up at Little Tor Farm Cottage, I mean. I thought I would have a talk with Lily's parents. Do you know Lily behind the bar?'

He nodded his assent.

72

'She's the salt of the earth, that girl. So are her mother and father. The sort of people who would do anything for anybody. Well, they've lived here for ages, like the rest of us, and they met Marianne when she was last here with her husband. That must have been a few years ago, and Lily was only a youngster then. Now, I repeat that none of this is to be traced back to me, if you can help it. If it comes to giving evidence in court I suppose that's different, but we'll meet that one when the time comes.' She looked doubtful for a moment, but he nodded reassuringly. 'She – Marianne, I mean – told them that she suspected George Stephens was up to no good, or at least her husband thought as much. And orders came from, let's say, a higher authority, for her husband to keep an eye on him. They knew where he lived in London, and that he'd been coming to stay regularly in Devon. Don't ask me how, but they'd been watching him pretty carefully for a long time. Makes you wonder, doesn't it?'

Sergeant Donald's eyebrows moved quizzically. 'It certainly puts this business in a different light. You know about these rumours that he was thought to be the son of the Kaiser?'

'I know about that, yes. And that's probably the higher authority, for all we know. Marianne couldn't tell any of us directly, of course. Her husband would have made it pretty hot for her if she said too much, but I'm sure that's what she was getting at.' She laughed and tapped the side of her nose. 'Good thing for you that us women are such gossips, isn't it? As long as we're careful about it.'

'Where would we be without you, Mrs Cuthbert?'

'I'll answer that when you take me on as your assistant. Seriously, though, it's all looking more and more suspect, isn't it? And you can see why I'm anxious that this doesn't get around. Well, not all at once.'

'No doubt everyone around is beginning to talk.'

'Oh yes, of course. They always do, and I daresay the truth will out in its own good time. But sooner or later, they're going to say that this fellow was murdered on Kaiser Bill's orders, and that he's got secret police in every nook and cranny on Dartmoor.'

'They're saying that already, aren't they?'

'Yes, and a whole lot more. And if anyone thinks I've been spreading stories, it's not going to do me a lot of good, is it?'

'I agree with you there. The good name of your establishment to consider.'

Isobel frowned. 'Not only that. I don't want to go the same way as George Stephens. Not that it's likely, but those who protect themselves stay around longest, don't they, and if somebody's up to mischief, I'd rather not be on the other end of it.' She moved as if to get up, then sat down again. 'What's the story behind these guns discovered out at Poundsgate?'

'Nothing much. One of my colleagues was told about something peculiar going on at Little Tor Farm Cottage. He found two or three rifles there, and from the condition of them it looked as if they hadn't been used for ages. It doesn't seem that they had any connection with Count Andrewitz and his friend. No, I reckon some reporter got hold of the wrong end of the stick.'

'And not for the first time.' She chuckled. 'No end to these gossips, is there? Oh, one other thing I could mention. I'm pretty sure the Count and Countess are separated, like I said last time. They certainly spend most of their time apart, if not all of it. And if that's the case, perhaps Marianne's got nothing to lose by confiding in one or two people about her husband's activities, particularly if she doesn't regard him as a husband any more. That's only guessing on my part, so it's up to you to decide how important it is.'

Glancing at the bar, she rose to her feet. 'If you'll excuse me, Sergeant. Lily needs a hand and I think we're going to be in for a busy evening.' With a grin, she added, 'these gossips find it thirsty work. I'd better keep my ears open and find out what else they're saying, hadn't I?'

Chapter 9

On the last Saturday morning in August Paul received a postcard at home. On one side was a photograph of Westminster Bridge, and on the other a brief handwritten message, reading,

Mother admitted to Charing Cross Hospital on Thursday. Condition as comfortable as can be expected. Thank you once again for all your kindness and support.
With kindest regards, Charlotte Waters (Mrs).

At once he thought it sounded ominous, as if her mother had all but given up the will to live. He mulled over it for the rest of the weekend and took the card to the office on Monday to show Charles.

'Do you think I ought get in touch with her – Mrs Waters, I mean? I don't really see what I can do, but if our previous guesses were correct, her husband probably isn't going to be much support in a situation like this.'

'I wonder if we might be maligning the fellow, you know.' Charles looked carefully at the handwriting again. 'But the fact that his wife has written to you like this after only one meeting suggests that she regards you as a close friend. She's just lost her brother, admittedly an estranged one, and may very well be about to lose her parent as well. And she obviously trusts you a good deal.' He tapped his fingers gently on the desk, his brow furrowed in concentration. 'I'd say that this is a thinly-veiled call for help, wouldn't you?'

'But she hasn't left an address. All I know is that their town house is in Pimlico, and under the circumstances I can hardly send a letter or a card to her through her husband? He'd open it in no time.'

'And then tear it up before she saw it, no doubt. Mr Pargeter might have an address for her through the management contacts, and if not, he's bound to know someone who has. Unless –'

Charles shrugged. 'If she really does need your help, perhaps she'll get in touch again with you more directly.'

'I had the same thought myself. It's not as if she really knows me that well. She's obviously a very reserved kind of woman, and I suppose with her family history she's been used to keeping things very much to herself. I would hate her to think I'm interfering, but –'

He sighed as he turned his attention to a file on his desk. Inside it was a report about recent amendments to the legislation concerning employers' insurance contributions, which Mr Pargeter had asked him to study in preparation for a meeting with a new client that afternoon.

'So you've found me at last?'

Ethel lay in her hospital bed, her tired blue-grey eyes looking in the direction of, rather then directly at, Charlotte who sat on a wooden chair on her right. One of her hands was resting on her mother's bony hands, clasped together on her top blanket.

'Yes, mama. Canon Richardson told me you were here.'

As good as his word, the Canon had asked around a few parishioners and found out about Charlotte. On being given her address, he had postponed another appointment and called briefly at her house the previous week to make his number with her. It was fortuitous, as only a day later her mother collapsed in the street and was helped to her feet by a passing policeman. Her injuries were superficial, only minor cuts and grazing, but it was thought only wise to admit her to hospital for tests.

The Canon was exchanging a few words with another patient in the ward whom he had recognised. He made his way towards Charlotte and Ethel, then coughed politely.

'Perhaps you would like me to wait outside, my dear,' he whispered to Charlotte.

'No, please.' She turned towards him, an imploring look across her face. 'I think I'd rather you stayed.'

There was a pause while Charlotte racked her brains for something to say, but Ethel beat her to it. 'How are my grandchildren?'

'They're very well. Thomas and David are –'

'Why didn't you bring them here today with you, my pet? I've never seen my little grandchildren, and we should get to know each other, shouldn't we? It might be too late next time.'

'But mama, you'll be all right.' Charlotte patted her clasped hand, as if to reassure both of them. 'You're in good hands here, and you'll be looked after properly.'

'I don't need looking after.' She sounded irritable. 'Was all right in my house, wasn't I?'

'Well, you'll be home soon, and then you can come and stay with us. We've never had you under our roof as a guest before, have we? You'd like the house in town if you saw it, and we can go and spend weekends in the country. James has got a marvellous house in Aylesbury, and you can sit out in the garden as long as it's warm enough for you. Maybe we could take you for a little walk or two when you're strong enough. And Thomas and David would have a chance to get to know their grandmother, as you said just now. They're lovely boys, and you'd be proud of them.'

'Yes, but it's too late, pet. I don't think I'll be here long,' Ethel murmured, her frail voice devoid of expression. 'I've been around long enough. Your brother was lucky enough to die at the right time. He wouldn't have wanted to see your father declare war on us.'

Charlotte looked at her and blinked.

'My father?'

'You heard what I said.'

'But – my father – he was – I –' Patience, Charlotte, she counselled herself. 'Oh, mama!'

'Pull yourself together, child. You always were an argumentative little thing when you were small, you always thought you knew better than anyone else, and I can see you haven't changed much. He may not have been my husband, but he was your father. And never forget your brother might have been an Emperor.'

'But, mama –' She stopped suddenly, recognising the futility of trying to argue.

'He might have been an Emperor. In Germany. But they were after him, weren't they?' Her eyes glinted. 'You should consider yourself fortunate they didn't come looking for you as well, my girl.'

Charlotte took her hand away from that of her mother, as if she had been stung. She shook her head as if bemused and looked at the floor, her face a picture of misery. Canon Richardson felt it was time to try and ameliorate the situation.

'If there's anything we can do, Mrs Stephens?'

Ethel's eyes turned in his direction. 'No thank you, Reverend. As my daughter said, I'm in good hands.' For the first time since they had entered the hospital, they felt they glimpsed the shadow of a smile playing around her mouth. 'I'll be all right. But if you don't mind, I'd like to sleep for a bit now. And thank you for coming.'

Charlotte stood up and gave a forced smile as she bent over her mother to kiss her cheek. 'We'll be back in a day or two, mama. Look after yourself.'

'I will. And remember, I want you to bring your boys next time.' Murmuring gently as if speaking to herself, she added, 'If I'm here.'

Before returning home after work, Paul decided to take advantage of the sunshine and go for a walk in Kensington Gardens. Looking at the trees in full leaf, it struck him that soon their autumn tints would be appearing. When George had tried to enthuse him with the beauties of Devon's landscape and the glories of each season merging seamlessly with the next, he had never taken it seriously. Now at last he was beginning to see something in his words. Were his eyes and senses at last responding to the great tapestry of nature before him, or had George's death opened a previously sealed vein of sentiment? He must be getting middle-aged.

He was lost in his thoughts when he heard a cry and was aware of a smartly-dressed woman walking briskly towards him. At once he recognised Mrs Waters.

'Mr Jenkins! I thought it was you. Did you receive my card?'

'I did. In fact I meant to contact you. Only I didn't have your address, and I was going to ask our office superintendent, but I hadn't yet got round to it.'

'My fault. I know I should have written it on the card, but –' She clutched the handle of her parasol tightly. 'Perhaps we could sit down and talk?'

He motioned her to a nearby seat.

'So your mother has been in hospital for nearly a week?'

She nodded. Her face looked like a mask, as if years of

78

suppressing her feelings had helped her to conceal any sign of emotion from the world outside.

'Soon after I came to see you, a clergyman called to see me. A Canon Richardson. He had known her fairly well for quite a long time, and some friends had put him in touch with me. He took me to visit her yesterday.'

'And how is she?' Rather more diplomatic, he thought, than asking her first about their meeting.

She looked expressionlessly ahead of her. 'She seemed quite comfortable, chatted quite a bit and asked if she could see my little boys next time I go. But as she said, there may not be a next time. The doctor spoke to me about her before I left, and told me she has liver damage, caused by years of – well, I think you can guess. And he doesn't think she will last for much longer. It could be a couple of months, or it might only be days.' She smiled bravely at him. 'Maybe it's all for the best.'

'I am sorry.' He felt helpless at being unable to offer more than the usual short message of sympathy.

'After all this time, I can't tell whether her son's loss – my brother's loss – really meant much to her. I had the feeling her mind was wandering, and wasn't sure whether she had taken it in, or whether she's convinced herself somehow that it's not true and he will come back one day. I suppose the three of us were really in our own separate worlds for so long. We were still a family, and after all blood is thicker than water, as they say.' She wrung her hands together. 'I feel guilty about saying it, but – I know I ought to feel more than I do, but we all seemed so independent of each other, and now it's too late...'

Her voice faltered and gradually broke, crumpling up in tears. He patted her softly on the hand while her body heaved in sobs, until she pulled herself together.

'What must you be thinking of me?'

'It doesn't matter,' he reassured her. 'It's only natural. You've had to go through a lot recently.' No sooner had the words left his lips than he wondered whether that was a tactful remark to make in view of possible marital problems, but he tried to reassure himself that he knew nothing for certain about matters between husband and wife. As if it was any of his business – yet.

'But it wasn't too late, was it? At least we did meet each other again.' Her eyes looked a little brighter, though with the forced gaiety of one making the most of a sorry situation. 'She seemed fairly lucid. Wanted to know how I was, and asked about her grandchildren. I said I would bring them to see her next time, but –'

But I wonder if your husband will let you take them, he asked himself, trying to suppress a ripple of anger. He was only guessing at the situation, but with almost everything she said, he became more convinced.

'The police got in touch with me,' she went on. 'They confirmed his address, which was the same as the one I had, and passed me over a few of the things he had left behind. Well, probably everything, I suppose.' He looked at her, trying not to appear guilty at having withheld the information himself, but it was evident that she did not hold anything of the kind against him. 'Only a few books and things, nothing very valuable. I don't think George had ever been much of a collector or hoarder.' He resisted the temptation to question her further on the matter.

After biting her lip reflectively for a moment she stood up.

'I am grateful, Mr Jenkins. You have spared me a good deal of your time, and – you have listened to me.' Her voice falling to a whisper, she added, 'It means so much.'

'Not at all.'

She smiled bravely again. 'I mustn't keep you any longer. And I should be on my way as well. There's just one thing.' He looked at her, encouraging her to continue. 'She's still firmly convinced that George's father was the Kaiser, and – well, I know her mind was wandering a bit, but she now wants me to think that I'm his daughter as well.'

'And you're –'

'I can't be. I still don't really believe that George was his son, either.' She shook her head with determination. 'It's all in the past, isn't it, but – no, I think she's just had this idea fixed in her mind all these years, and nothing anyone can say will alter it. I suppose she still believes it, or else she wanted to persuade herself so badly that it was true that she really has convinced herself. And I had meant to ask her about my father, or should I say the man I always believed to be my father. He may be dead, or he may be alive and well somewhere and just not want to know about us any more. But if only I knew the truth, no matter how unpleasant, it would help to complete the family picture.

80

And I could draw a line under all these ghosts, as I see it.'

She looked away, her attention distracted by a grey squirrel running past within a few feet of them before climbing up the nearest tree and disappearing from sight.

Paul held out his hand. 'Promise me to let me know how your mother gets on. And if there is anything else I can do to help, you know where to find me.' As an afterthought, he added, 'Should I have an address, so I can contact you?'

She shook her head. 'No. I think perhaps it's best if I don't. But I will write to you at once if anything happens.'

Without another word she turned, and he watched her vanishing form sadly. Poor woman, he thought. She really does need friends.

Lying alone in bed that night during the long hours that sleep would not come to her weary mind, Charlotte thought sadly to herself how much Paul's supportive, kindly manner reminded her of poor Oliver Fanshawe. Dear Oliver, who had been her devoted friend and admirer since she was a girl of sixteen or seventeen. Always sending her flowers, taking her to the theatre or music hall at least once a month, and asking her for her hand in marriage. Such a sensitive, sympathetic, attentive man, with a brilliant business brain, he was not only good-looking but also modest about his not inconsiderable abilities. She knew instinctively that he would make the best of husbands and fathers that she could ask for, as well as an excellent brother-in-law. He and George had got on so well, and she always thought that he was exactly the person George needed to be drawn out of himself. When he proposed to her she had accepted him without a moment's hesitation.

It all came to nothing. He had railed bitterly, and rightly so, when his father informed him that as the eldest son he would be expected to spend a year in India, looking after the family's mercantile interests at their office in Delhi. He had accepted with good grace and gone out on ship a few weeks later, having extracted a promise from Mr Fanshawe Senior that he would be allowed to return and settle in England twelve months hence, with a handsome allowance and a house of his own where he and Charlotte would set up their first married home. But she had always had a nagging feeling that he was not really robust. That hacking cough and pale complexion in winter, aggravated by London fog, alarmed her. How would he possibly flourish in India? Sure enough, his letters from overseas had soon ceased, and were followed at length by one from his sorrowing mother to say that he had been taken ill with consumption and had barely begun his journey back to England before he succumbed. His body was brought home and buried in the church near their home at Croydon, and his conscience-stricken father had taken to his bed soon afterwards with an undisclosed illness, dying a few weeks later.

How she had wanted to attend Oliver's funeral and say goodbye as best she could, but his mother had refused to let her know when or where it was taking place until after it was over. As soon as she knew, she had taken her own floral tribute to lay on the grave and sit weeping one bitter winter afternoon by his headstone. In a mood of numb depression some weeks later she had been introduced to James. They had got on well, and on a subsequent meeting a few days later he had taken her out for dinner at a hotel in The Strand. He seemed honest, worthy, upright, if a little dull and self-important. Moreover it was evident that his prospects were good, and towards the end of the meal when he asked for her hand in marriage, she had said yes without hesitation.

Nobody could ever be like poor Oliver, she had thought. But there was something in Paul's manner which reawakened memories of him. No, she *must* fight those memories. Paul was happily married, and she had a husband, who might have his faults, but he was her husband for better or worse. And they had two fine young sons. Over several years, for the sake of them all, she had dismissed all those cancerous thoughts of what might have been. And this was not the time to pull them back from the abyss.

Chapter 10

At the beginning of October Paul received a letter, and recognised the handwriting on the envelope at a glance.

> *Dear Mr Jenkins,*
> *It is my painful duty to tell you that my mother passed away peacefully in her sleep on the 26th of September. She was aged 55, and had suffered from liver disease for some time. Though it grieves me to lose her, I am glad to have had the chance of meeting her again so we could be reconciled in her last days. It was clear that she had lost the will to live, and I cannot but be thankful that she is at last gone to rest. Her funeral will be on the 10th of October at 2.30, at All Saints, Kent Road, Bermondsey, and Canon Richardson has kindly agreed to officiate. Please don't think you have to attend, but if you could come, it would be good to see you.*
> *With deepest gratitude once more,*
>
> *Sincerely,*
> *Charlotte Waters*

Charlotte's relief that her mother's years of suffering were over was tempered by disappointment with her husband's churlish attitude. He had been away for several days on political matters, including the appointment of a new secretary and treasurer for his constituency association. Then a number of businesses had suffered badly as the result of a major fire in a street in Aylesbury, and he had been asked to intervene in a rather heated exchange between the trade association regarding the matter of rebuilding their premises and finding temporary alternative accommodation.

Finally, Sir Gregory Hall-Adamson had invited him to his home one evening for a chat. Though he had been careful to dress it up as a cosy conversation about the state of Parliament and constituency matters over the last few weeks, it was clear that the main purpose of the invitation had been for the old boy to tell him not to worry about the rumours about his brother-in-law's real father. Sir Gregory was nothing if not a born diplomat, and he had broached the matter by quoting gossip in the Lords as his source. James knew that he was jumping to conclusions by suspecting that Charlotte might have been behind it. He had seen them from a distance, deep in conversation at the garden party that afternoon. Yet he knew that he could hardly bring himself to reproach her for it, though nothing would have pleased him more.

To be fair, he admitted, she had had enough to worry about lately. Not only had she just lost her brother and mother in quick succession, but she and the boys had had to stay in London. Thomas had been very ill with a sore throat, fever and various other symptoms, and for an anxious forty-eight hours she feared that he might have developed diphtheria or some other dreadful illness against which there was little defence, until the doctor arrived and he responded rapidly to treatment. When James arrived back he was tired and overwrought after being told about some financial scandal in which the member of a neighbouring seat had been involved, and made it painfully evident that his wife's family problems were the last thing in which he was interested at present. If he had any sympathy at all, she thought bitterly to herself, he had a rather strange way of showing it.

'It's no good going around with a long face like that,' he told her sharply as they sat in their front room overlooking the street, he peering over his paper while she tried to concentrate on a piece of knitting. 'Your mother's gone, your brother's gone, and that's that. We all have to go. Don't forget I never knew my father, and my mother went down with the Titanic. But life goes on for the rest of us.'

'I know, James,' she whispered, fighting to keep back the tears. 'But some of the things she said the last time I saw her –'

He groaned. 'Such as?'

'Well – she said that – what she seemed to be trying to tell me was that, not only was the Emperor my brother's father, but he was mine as well.'

James put his paper down and glared at her. 'And you believe her?'

'I just don't know what to believe any more. That's the trouble.' She kept her eyes firmly on her knitting, hardly daring to face her husband in case the tears would fall at once. 'I never really believed it in the case of my brother, and certainly not where I was concerned, but – after all this time, I just can't be sure.'

James rolled his eyes upwards and sighed. 'It's not my problem, is it? It's perfectly obvious that your mother's mind was wandering. You never believed the German Emperor was your father in the first place. And if you never really thought so, what on earth makes you suddenly start thinking there's any truth in it now?'

'I know.' She nodded weakly. 'I shouldn't.' The shadow of a smile flickered across her face. 'I won't say any more about it. And certainly not when we're at the funeral.'

James snorted indignantly. 'What do you mean by that? When we're at the funeral?'

'Why, yes. You're coming, aren't you?'

'I shan't be there. For one thing, the next three days are going to be taken up with this work on the defence estimates. I have to produce a report, there will be a debate in the house, and the opposition are snapping at us, trying to find any excuse to put a spoke in our wheels. This little storm in a teacup involving McRandle and his suspect shares isn't making life any easier. And on top of all that, with all these rumours about your brother and the Kaiser, you know full well of all people that I can't possibly appear at the funeral with you, until the furore dies down. Have you thought what the scribblers would make of it?'

Charlotte put her knitting down and faced him squarely. It was as if several years of acquiescence to his every whim had to be swept away, and at last she had to make a stand for herself. Gone were the unshed tears as her eyes blazed with fury.

'Now just you listen to me, James, you're not going to let your work or your pride stop you coming to pay your last respects to your mother-in-law!'

'I married you,' he snarled. 'Not her. You knew full well when you met me that I had my sights set on the House of Commons.'

'And is your career really going to suffer if you accompany me to the funeral? For a short service of remembrance lasting about half an hour, maybe less, and a few refreshments at the house afterwards for the other guests? Come on, James, I don't think I'm asking much!' Another thought struck her. 'And if people ask me why you aren't there, what do you think I am going to tell them? That you haven't got time to say goodbye to a close member of the family? The only surviving member of your wife's family at that?' She returned his glare in full measure. 'They're not going to believe that. Suppose they think that we've separated or something. Have you ever thought what that could do to your precious career? Look at how it all went wrong for your friend Lennox-Smith. You said that he would have probably been promoted to the cabinet by now, if it hadn't been for his divorce case.'

James was momentarily taken aback. The mention of Maurice Lennox-Smith, his best friend at school, had been a salutary example. Having entered the Commons at the tender age of twenty-four, he had been tipped for a meteoric rise until his passion for gambling to finance a sybarite lifestyle, in which other men's wives and visits to gaming tables on the other side of the Channel, had played a prominent role, had stalled him. Maurice had always been one to play with fire, and he had thrown it all away. There was no danger of James doing anything as foolish. The idea of jeopardising his marriage, and those of other people, seemed distasteful to him, and gambling, he maintained, was for fools.

Even so, in their five years as husband and wife, Charlotte had never spoken to him quite as forcefully as that. What on earth had come over her? Or had he perhaps taken her a little too much for granted?

'Very well,' he sighed, picking up his newspaper again. 'I will do my best to make alternative arrangements, if I can.' He glowered at her. 'And we will let that be the last word on the subject tonight.'

October the tenth dawned cold and cheerless, with the hint of an early autumn mist, and by midday there was a thick drizzle. How appropriate, Charlotte thought sadly as she and James led the boys, all dressed in black, into All Saints. It was a grey postscript to a grey life.

Thinking back on her argument with James, she was astonished at herself. For so long she had played the downtrodden wife, but she had never been so angry with him. Lying in bed that night, the fear had struck her that he might take it out on her and go his own way regardless, refusing to attend the funeral. Looking at his morose expression, it was clear that he had only come under duress. He would do anything to protect his public image as a good family man and member of the House of Commons, she thought bitterly. Still, it was the last thing he could do for the memory of that poor frail woman who had been her mother. And at least he had paid for a magnificent wreath of lilies of the valley to be placed on the coffin.

As they stood in the church singing *Abide With Me*, she allowed herself a furtive glance at the congregation. There was Paul Jenkins and, she presumed, his wife. In the same pew was another couple whom she did not recognise. Was that his colleague at the office and his wife, perhaps? There was the sister from the hospital, she knew, and a few others to whom she could not put a name, but there would doubtless be a chance to meet them afterwards.

After the service she shook hands with Canon Richardson, who politely declined her invitation to return to their house with them for tea and sandwiches. James stood behind her tight-lipped, the boys almost overawed by the sight of so many strange faces all at once, Alexander trying to bury his face in his father's coat. Paul, Charles and their wives stopped to say hello, as did Louise, Alfred and Ralph Hillman, all of whom had been informed by the Canon about Ethel's demise.

As they talked she felt her spirits lift a little. All these people were virtual strangers, yet they were so keen to help her and rally round, almost like an extended family united by two events of such sadness. Ralph excused himself but the others returned for tea. James, she was relieved to see, slipped easily into his role of affable MP and good family man. She passed the odd glance at him, noticing that on at least one occasion the mask slipped for a moment, and she could see from his expression that he would have far rather been somewhere else. Too bad, she told herself as she watched the boys. They had got over their shyness in next to no time, and by now they were showing every signs of making short work of the cake. At length she had to tell them firmly that they could have no more than two slices each – and then not until after they had done their duty and been round offering some to each of the guests in turn.

Dick Priestley unlocked the front door of his cottage at Saltash, seated himself in a comfortable chair beside the window, and lit his pipe pensively as he looked out down the river Tamar, the weak afternoon sunshine creating ever-changing patterns on the water. One more day's fishing would see the season out, he promised himself, and then he would go back to Poundsgate for a couple of weeks, maybe more. He hadn't seen Eleanor and Edward for a while, and although they were in Hampshire this week, he liked to keep himself satisfied at regular intervals that they were still coping with the farm properly.

His daughter had turned out very well, and he was proud of her. They had lived in one of the less salubrious areas of Glasgow when she was born, and when she was a child he, his wife – Jessica, dead ten years now, God bless her – and the doctors had feared that Eleanor might have been born with a weak heart. She was always a sickly baby, and it was possible she would need an operation which was still relatively new to medical science and could be almost as much a risk as not doing anything. Many a time they believed it would be a miracle if she lived to be twenty-one, with her shortness of breath, her sudden spells of dizziness, and numerous other ailments. But a move south to Devon had done the seemingly impossible. Now she and Edward were the parents of four strapping lads and two fine girls, all healthy, and she seemed as strong as any man. Even so, he liked to keep an eye on her and make sure that there was no sign of a recurrence of her childhood troubles.

And there were one or two disquieting stories in the papers. He had read of the suspicious death of George Stephens with no more than mild curiosity. But this piece about Count Otto von Andrewitz and Count Max von Linevitch being asked to leave Little Tor made him uneasy. They had been very helpful to him, particularly after that trouble over the fire. He felt he could rest easy now about that fire. After all, it was several years ago, and the police must have closed the file on it by now, with more important things to think about.

But their sudden departure from his property gave him food for thought. They must be up to something, but what? All this talk about the Anglo-German arms race, and rivalry which some people thought could only end in a major European war, he'd been inclined to dismiss as scaremongering. An unlikely alliance of big business interests in the City of London, trade union leaders, and restraint on the part of more cautious voices in the government would probably make sure that Britain kept well out of it. But lately he was starting to have second thoughts. Surely some of the prophets of doom knew what they were talking about. Prepare for the worst, as his father had told him when he was a small boy – you never know when the worst might creep up behind you and take you unawares.

At any rate his hands were clean, he knew. If they had been engaged in intelligence work, that was their own business. He could hardly be implicated, and there was nothing anybody could pin on him.

For a moment he was torn between a desire to stay put in Saltash for a few months longer, or even lie low somewhere else in England, until it all blew over. But what was the point? Pull yourself together, he told himself. You've got nothing to feel guilty about. Isobel Cuthbert could be relied on to tell him everything. He hadn't been into the Red Lion for some years, since the fire, in fact. He had the distinct feeling that he wouldn't have been welcome inside its four walls while the memory was still fresh in everyone's minds, but – well, what's done is done. And in spite of what the insurance company had said, nobody could prove anything.

Two days later Dick walked into the bar of the Red Lion. He felt rather pleased with himself at having chosen a quiet moment. Only five other people were there, all in their twenties or early thirties at the most, and none of them would have recognized him from Adam. Deeply engrossed in discussing a bowls match, none of them as much as glanced at this apparent stranger.

From behind the bar, Isobel looked at him in amazement. Fancy that, only the other day she had been telling Sergeant Donald what a rare sight he was around these parts, and here he was again. While she wasn't sure if she could really trust him after that fire, she was the first to admit that, like everybody else, she didn't know enough to be sure he was as responsible as they all thought. In law the man was innocent until proved guilty.

'Long time no see, Dick!' She smiled warmly at him as she

placed a ready hand on the bitter tap and he nodded, putting a handful of change on the bar in front of her.

'Must admit I've missed the old place, Isobel.' He perched himself on the stool. 'And how's yourself?' He glanced around him. 'The inn still looks much the same as I remember it.'

'I should hope so, too. Why go and change a good thing for the sake of it, eh?'

'My thoughts exactly.' He nodded and sipped his pint in silence for a moment.

'Have I missed anything special while I've been away?'

Come off it, Dick, a voice said inside her. You know something. If a couple of complete strangers had taken over your place while your back was turned, you'd hardly be as calm as this.

She looked at him carefully. 'You didn't hear about those German officers on your farm?'

He hesitated for a second. 'Well – I did see something in the paper. I was in Saltash at the time, and Eleanor and Edward are still in Southampton. I'm not expecting them back for a few days.'

'And does the name George Stephens mean anything to you?'

'George Stephens. You mean the chap they found dead near here a few weeks ago?'

She nodded. 'And they think there might be a connection between him and those officers.' Lowering her voice, she explained at length, watching his expression throughout. Either you're a cool customer or else you could be in trouble before long, she thought to herself. But his face remained impassive throughout. Not even a flicker of surprise crossed his features.

After a pause, he asked casually, 'Do you really think they were keeping track of this fellow?'

'Your guess is as good as mine. But it looks funny, doesn't it? Not exactly funny – but you know what I mean. More than coincidence.'

For the first time he looked slightly apprehensive. 'And you wouldn't be saying that people think I might have something to do with it?'

She shook her head. 'I'm not to know, Dick, am I? But you must know something about them, otherwise how would they have been staying on your farm in the first place?'

'One of them's a friend of Edward,' he answered, looking at his drink.

'And you don't know him?' Though she found his secretive attitude irritating, she cursed herself silently for her persistence.

'Met him once or twice, that's all,' he muttered crossly.

Very well, she thought, have it your own way. If you're not going to tell me, too bad.

'Another thing, before I forget to mention it. There was talk of weapons being found somewhere in the area after they'd gone. I don't know if it was your cottage, or somewhere else in Poundsgate or Holne. But something pretty odd is going on, and the police are interested, as you'd expect. So I'd tread carefully if I were you. You know how people will talk.' At this she laughed. 'Everyone knows how I talk, don't they?'

He tried to force a laugh as well, and took another sip of his pint as Alf appeared alongside his wife.

'Hi, Dick. We'd 'ave put the flags out if we'd known you was comin'. Thrown a party, maybe. You stoppin' for long?'

Dick shrugged. 'A few days, maybe. Haven't decided for certain. It'll give me time to see the old farm again. I might stay around for harvest festival, just for old times' sake. Perhaps even Christmas as well, though it depends on what Eleanor and Edward and the youngsters are going to be doing.'

'That's a nice little cluster o' grandchildren they given you, Dick. You oughter see more of 'em, you know.'

'I ought to. Thought we might all spend Christmas together for a change. Haven't done that since they were very small, you know.'

Isobel grinned. 'Put a bit more weight on you, Dick, give you a white beard, and you'd cut a fine figure as Father Christmas. We could use you at some of the kids' parties round here when the time comes round. We've got the red cloak and all that, tucked away in a trunk in the storeroom upstairs. All we've got to do is find a few reindeer and we're in business.'

For the first time since he had walked in, he smiled warmly. 'I used to help out at parties for the youngsters in Ashburton years ago. It would be fun to do it again, wouldn't it? Tell you what, let me know when you want me and I'll do it.'

That's better, she thought as she served another customer.

Now that's the Dick Priestley I know. All the same, I think I'd be treading pretty carefully if I were in his shoes at the moment.

Finishing his drink, Dick was about to leave as one of the other patrons ambled towards him and held out his hand in greeting.

'Andrew! Didn't know you were still around these parts.' He and Andrew Langstone had known each other since they were boys at Ashburton school together.

'Could say the same about you, Dick. Been up to the mid-lands for a time, helpin' brother and his wife with their business in Staffordshire, but I moved back here last year. I always swore I'd come back to this place when I could. And how you been keepin'? They say you found a good spot o' fishin' in Cornwall, like.'

'Not so bad. But that's over for the season.'

'Did you ever go fishin' on the Teign? If you're in this area, that's the river for you. Not just for the sport, like, but also Fingle Gorge. Terrific place to walk, and you never seen views anythin' like it. Tell you what, why don't you come with me for a day or two next summer and see what you think of it.'

'You're on, Andrew. It's a deal.'

'Good.' Andrew looked carefully at his friend's face for a moment. Their friendship went back a long way, and unpalatable though the truth might be, some things had to be said. 'And if I might be so bold, Dick –'

'You as well?' Dick was instantly on his guard.

'I don't know who else you mean, but I'd be dead careful if I were you.'

'Meaning?'

'You know what I mean.' Andrew put his drink on the bar and held his hands out, gesturing with the palms facing upwards. 'Look, I'm not bein' nosey, just speakin' as an old pal who would hate anythin' to happen to you. But you're back at the farm, right?'

'That's right.'

'Well, this business about those guests of yours has left a bit of a nasty taste around the place.'

'Guests of mine?'

'You know very well who I mean.' There was a tone of impatience about his voice. 'Your friends in uniform from across the sea, right? People round about are startin' to put two an' two together and makin' a hundred, if you get my meanin'.'

'And what are they saying?'

Andrew sighed. 'Spyin' and all that. None of us was born yesterday, and there's bound to be talk after what happened to young Stephens.' He lowered his voice. 'Now don't get me wrong, Dick. I've known you for years, and I don't believe for a moment that you've had any part in it. I'd swear on the family's grave that whatever may be goin' on, you're innocent. But other people round 'ere might not give you the benefit of the doubt, right?'

'Right. Thanks, Andrew.' Dick felt mildly apprehensive, but he knew his friend was right and had no wish to sound ungrateful.

Andrew finished his drink and got ready to leave.

'Right, see you around Dick.' He patted him on the shoulder. 'No hard feelings, eh?'

Chapter 11

'You 'eard the latest, Roger?' Mary called out as she brought her kettle to the boil and looked across to Roger, who had just come indoors and was taking his boots off. 'They say Dick Priestley's come back.'

'Dick Priestley? Back from Cornwall? Almost a stranger in these parts now, ain't 'e?'

'Must 'ave somethin' to do with those goin's-on at 'is cottage.' Mary poured boiling water into the pot and rummaged around in the drawer for a tea cosy. ''E 'asn't been seen 'ere for – well, over a year. Then there 'e is, bold as brass, an' 'e suddenly walks into the Red Lion an' wants to know what's goin' on.'

'Can't blame 'im. Well if I wanter know what's bin 'appenin 'round these parts, it's the first place I'd be goin' to. What Isobel don't know ain't worth knowin'.'

'But 'as 'e chosen the right time to be back, Roger? What with they German friends of 'is pushin' off sudden like from Poundsgate? If they are 'is friends, that is.'

'Like 'e might know somethin'?' George walked over to the sink to wash his hands. 'Like 'e an' Counts what's-their-names was actin' together?'

'You never know, Roger. If 'e's anythin' to do with the death of George, 'e could be 'ad up as an accessory to murder.'

'Dick Priestley?' He shook his head as he dried his hands. 'No, not Dick. I know 'e prob'ly got 'imself into hot water over that fire, like, but 'elpin' a couple o' Fritzes to commit murder? 'E did serve in the wars in Africa when 'e were younger, so 'e wouldn't do anythin' that weren't patriotic, like. No – get away!'

'I 'ope not, for 'is own sake.' She reached for a couple of mugs and poured out the tea. 'Sergeant Donald 'is goin' to have some questions to put to him, you mark my words.'

'Aye, there's that. But if Dick is guilty, like, 'e'd never 'ave come back, would 'e? Look, Mary, if it 'ad been me in 'is shoes, I'd 'ave made meself right scarce 'til all the fuss died down.'

Mary looked out of the window thoughtfully. 'You're probably right. Still, we should know soon enough. You know 'ow fast word travels 'round 'ere. What shall we 'ave for supper? Fresh baked bread, a good chunk o' cheese an' mutton soup suit you, me dear?'

Roger smacked his lips in eager anticipation.

Dick Priestley walked back pensively, gazing at the moonlight. There always seemed to be a special magic about it when it was like this – bright moon, autumn clouds darting like horse-drawn chariots pulling across it in an inky blue-black sky. As he unlocked his front door and lit the gas lamp in his sitting room, he looked around himself carefully. For a moment he thought of sending Eleanor and Edward a telegram, asking them to come back at once, then though better of it.

In spite of what he had been told at the inn, he decided there was no point in alarming them unnecessarily. Isobel seemed to know rather more than he hoped she would, though he thought it unlikely she was aware of everything. How much did Andrew have up his sleeve, or was he just giving him a friendly warning? Would it be better to make a clean breast of it, go and tell them the full story? Perhaps not – while he could trust them not to go telling the wrong people what they may have found out already, it seemed pointless to stir things up in haste. It was bound to emerge in its own good time.

If the police questioned him about his German tenants, his conscience was clear. That misunderstanding about the fire and the insurance business – well, nobody was going to hold anything against him because of that, surely? It wasn't as if he hadn't done his bit for King and country, or Queen and country, as it had been at the time of that campaign in Khartoum under General Kitchener, until he had been invalided out of the army after a particularly virulent attack of fever. Still, he had paid full heed to his doctor's words and kept fit ever since. Ten, even fifteen miles walking the moors at least once a week, come rain or come shine, had made sure he remained well. The occasional indulgence, like a pint of bitter or a good pipe, never did him any harm. A little of what you fancy does you good.

And as ever, there was plenty to be done. Eleanor kept telling him he ought to write his memoirs before he got too much older and started forgetting things. Just like a daughter to try and organize his life for him, but he had to admit she had a point. Not necessarily for publication, but because it would be good if there was some sort of record of his life to pass down to future generations. He'd travelled throughout France and Spain as a young man, and tried his hand at tea planting in Ceylon for a couple of years. Then he had served with the army in northern Africa, been invalided out after a dose of suspected malaria, and opted for a more peaceful life farming on Dartmoor. During that time he had taken an active role in the county archaeological society, and helped to compile records of stone hut circles. How many people in the Holne and Poundsgate area of his age had never been out of Devonshire, let alone overseas?

The archaeological studies – now, there was food for thought. He had given a few talks to local clubs and societies, without getting round to writing up his notes into a more permanent record. That was something else which historians in succeeding years might thank him for. The society had asked him at intervals to get his work into some kind of order so they could file it, and perhaps adapt it for publication in a future series of their trans-actions. It might even be deposited in the county museum or local history archives with his name on it. 'Notes on prehistoric Dartmoor, by Richard Priestley'. He rather liked the sound of that. Men may die, but there was no reason why something of what they contributed to mankind shouldn't survive them.

His eye wandered along the bookshelves, and he reached across for a copy of Conan Doyle's *The Hound of the Baskervilles*. Since its publication eleven years previously he had read it three or four times. A little contrived, perhaps, but a cracking good story all the same. Now why didn't he sit down and try to write a blood-curdling tale with a local setting like that? His English teacher in his far-off schooldays had always told him that he ought to persevere with his stories, as he seemed to have a talent for it. But after writing a couple of adventure tales which he submitted to 'Blackwood's Magazine' as a young man, only to have them rejected, he had abandoned the idea. Why not try again, and see if the old wordsmith's muse is till there, he thought?

Still, first things first. Tomorrow he would take a brisk walk around the farm, check all the outbuildings, have a look at the stores, and check the culverts which were prone to overflowing in wet weather. If it remained fine, he might go and have a look at the Ashburton market, as long as somebody could give him a lift. Or perhaps he'd go for a good long walk on the moors. There was nothing like the atmosphere of Dartmoor at the onset of autumn. The heather might have finished blooming for another year, the bracken dying, the buzzards and skylarks silent once more. Still, a stroll by the river was always a sight to be seen, with the thick foam crashing over the rocks on the river bed. Or the chance of watching a flock of lapwings, creating their ever-changing patterns overhead.

But first, tonight, he would write to Eleanor and Edward. It would be good to see them again and have them back at the cottage for a few days.

Before that, though, perhaps he ought to make sure that everything was left in apple pie order in the cottage. Andrewitz and his friends always made sure things were neat and tidy when they went, and he'd never had any trouble before. Eleanor had moved everything of value and taken it with her for safe keeping. Little was left on the premises apart from the basic furnishings, a few books and framed prints of no great importance. He picked up the lamp, wandered casually through the kitchen and utility room, up the stairs and into the bedrooms.

In the second bedroom it struck him that something was different.

The bed was not in the same position, surely? That was it – it was now lined up against a different wall. And there was some kind of a long thin case underneath it. Dark blue, or black cloth – it was difficult to tell by gaslight – and slightly scratched. He knelt down to move it on to the floor, and fumbled with the rusty metal catches, his suspicions hardening as he worked them loose. Eventually his efforts were rewarded. An army rifle! That certainly didn't belong to him. He'd disposed of all his guns a long time ago, and he doubted whether it belonged to Edward either. What did Isobel Cuthbert say about discovery of firearms after the two Counts had left? How else could it have got there? Of course there was a chance that Edward might know about it, but it would be most unlike him to leave such a thing in an empty house.

No, it must have been Count Andrewitz, or his friend. Could they really have been responsible for the death of George

Stephens, or was there some other connection? His blood ran cold at the idea that he might have been holding open house for a calculating murderer. It hardly bore thinking about...First thing tomorrow morning, he would report it to the police. Perhaps he should even take it to the station and hand it in. If it was discovered in his possession, he had little doubt that his plea of innocence would be accepted as perfectly genuine, but after that fire he certainly couldn't take that for granted.

A brown envelope next to the case caught his eye. Tearing open the flap, he tipped the contents on the floor. There were a couple of sweet wrappers, and a punched railway ticket for a single journey from Paddington to Exeter dated 23 July 1913. Most intriguing of all was a heavily creased sepia photograph of a woman with two small children, presumably a boy and a girl, taken in a rural setting which might have been anywhere, with three or four words on the back scored out in black ink and rendered illegible.

He put the wrappers in his pocket to dispose of later, and replaced the ticket and photo in the envelope. As he dropped it on the bed, a noise outside made him start. It was a calm night with barely a breath of wind, and he was sure something or someone was outside. Who on earth would be calling on him at this time of evening? Very few people knew he was back from Cornwall, anyway.

He listened for a moment. Silence. Carefully he closed the case and pushed it against the wall. As he walked downstairs he was sure he could hear footsteps outside. Again he stopped and listened. Silence again. No, any sound was just in his imagination. He went back to the sitting room. Where was that newspaper he had brought with him?

Five minutes later his eyelids were drooping and he dropped the paper as he sat in his chair. A noise at the door woke him with a start. Of course, he suddenly realized, he hadn't thought to check the front door was locked after him. He was positive somebody was creeping around outside, and he would rather like to know who. Getting quickly to his feet, he made his way there just in time to see a figure burst through the door.

It was the last thing he ever saw.

A single revolver shot shattered the calm of the cottage as his lifeless body fell to the stone floor.

The ripple of excitement around Holne that had followed the death of George Stephens was nothing to the shock and sensation following the discovery of Dick Priestley's body. It was a postman passing by the next day who noticed the broken down front door and contacted the police.

At the bar of the Red Lion, most of the regulars and staff found it hard to talk of anything else. Several of the customers had their own theories. Dick had been a secret German agent, perhaps in the pay of the Kaiser; he was actually George's father, or uncle; he had been eliminated by a crack squad of German police, or even by someone in British counter-intelligence which nobody was meant to know about but everybody did anyway.

Roger Strong found it impossible to believe that violent death had come to their community and snatched away one, if not two, people whom they had known so well.

'Can you credit it, eh, Mary?' he asked over lunch the next day. 'Forty or fifty years, we've bin livin' in our cosy little back-water. Round these parts, like, if lads goes scrumpin' someone else's apples, it counts as a major crime. An' now this fishy business with George an' Dick. Don't like it one little bit.'

'Don't think any of us likes it, dear.' Mary was more anxious than she liked to admit. She was torn between a desire to examine the news from every possible angle and chat about it until midnight, and a determination to try and forget all about it. Bad things always happen in threes, they said, and she for one didn't dare to speculate on who might possibly be next.

'It's them two Germans meddlin' that done it,' he scowled, as he cut himself another chunk of cheese and bit into it savagely. 'Mus' be. Always thought they was up to monkey business. Look at France an' the people in Paris when we was young. That Bismarck got 'em all where 'e wanted 'em. Even eatin' their cats an' dogs an' elephants out of the zoo before 'e'd finished with 'em. 'E trained 'is army up well. An' now 'e's gone, plenty left to do 'is dirty work. Playin' with fire, like. An' what our George were playin' at, Lord knows.'

'Come on, Roger. Got to be fair, 'aven't you? None of us knows for certain that poor George were anythin' to do with it. Till we got proof, you got to give 'im 'is benefit o' the doubt an' that. An' now we might never know.'

99

Charles and Alice Shepherd, and Paul and Joan Jenkins, were sitting down to their annual dinner with Oliver and Matilda Pargeter at their house in Baker Street. Mr Pargeter was a Methodist and his wife had lost her father at an early age through cirrhosis of the liver, and there was a marked absence of anything stronger than barley water and coffee in their household. Nevertheless Charles and Paul were prepared to overlook one evening's abstinence from the joys of the grape in view of the excellence of their French cook's cuisine. His roast, said everyone who had ever dined with the Pargeters, was second to none outside the major hotels in London.

Nevertheless they knew that serious matters would take the place of the usual inconsequential small-talk tonight.

'So what do we know of this fellow Priestley who's just been shot dead on Dartmoor?' Oliver asked as he tucked his napkin into the front of his shirt in anticipation of the mulligatawny soup.

'Not much I'm afraid, sir,' Charles answered. 'I've been following this one in the papers, but they've no idea who killed him. But it seems he doesn't spend a lot of time in his cottage nowadays, and he'd barely returned there from his bolthole in Cornwall and somebody gets him. And they think there's some connection with his murder and poor old George.'

'And the police seem to be coming round to the idea that George's death was no accident,' Paul broke in. Seeing Oliver raising his eyebrows, he continued, 'They're looking at a connection between Priestley and those Germans who left in rather of a hurry. And some idea that they were keeping an eye on George.'

'So you think this spying business for the Germans may have something to it after all?'

'Difficult to say, sir,' Charles added, watching Paul to see if he had anything more to add. 'I don't think it that likely. In fact I never did. I think I could see George selling antiquarian books or pictures in Devon, and he seemed to harbour some ambitions of doing so. That hardly stretches the imagination. But espionage...' He shook his head. 'Unless there was a different side to him that we never saw, I still can't believe it.'

'There were those things in his flat,' Paul reminded him. 'You know, those German invasion novels, and the passport.'

'Which we thought might have been tampered with.'

'Yes. As if somebody had added some things to it with all those stamps, to make it look as if he had been travelling a lot more than he really had. There was a handful of books about Germany as well. And the police told us they found a map of Kiel harbour on him, or something of the sort. That's the one they're said to be enlarging at the moment for strategic reasons, isn't it?'

Oliver looked startled. 'I think that's the one. Talking of harbours and the like, do you remember that recent case of the naval officer on the Hampshire coast?'

The others all shook their heads.

'I knew some friends of the chap who told me about it, and then it was in the paper just afterwards. During the summer a young officer was having a picnic with his wife and children. It was a lovely day so he dozed off in the sunshine while the others went to play, and he woke up to hear these German voices. He thought he was dreaming at first, until he got up to investigate. So he looked through a fence and saw these two men with a very elaborate-looking telescope. Not the kind of thing you normally take when you're going for a walk in the country. And then it dawned on him that they had it trained on Portsmouth harbour.'

They whistled in amazement.

'And what did he do?' asked Charles.

'He whispered to his wife and children not to say or do anything, then he went down the hill and informed the village constable. The stupid man didn't appear to be bothered, until the officer told him in no uncertain terms that he had a good mind to report the matter to the naval authorities at once. The constable eventually agreed to phone his superintendent, and the men were caught and interrogated. They were detained in custody for a while and then released on condition they left the country at once.' Looking round at them, he added, 'It shows you have to keep your wits about you.'

'Didn't you find something out about George's sister?' asked Alice, then turning to Oliver. 'Charlotte Waters. We met her and her husband at her mother's funeral. She seemed a very pleasant woman. And she must have a lot to put up with at the moment.'

Joan nodded sympathetically. 'Poor thing, I felt really sorry for her.'

Oliver frowned. 'James Waters' wife, isn't she? Anyone who's married to a man like that has problems enough.'

'Oh, Oliver!' Matilda reproached him. 'He's not that bad, surely? Young, ruthless and keen to make a name for himself in the House of Commons, I dare say. But aren't most of the newer intake like that?'

'Yes, dear, I suppose there must be some worse examples of the parliamentary lizard. But I'm sure you wouldn't want somebody like him for a husband.'

Joan felt compelled to add, 'I certainly didn't care for him. What little I saw of him after the funeral. It looked like he was putting on an act for the sake of appearances, showing us all what a delightful caring family man he was. But I don't think he fooled anyone.'

Matilda smiled a little uncertainly, keen to give him the benefit of the doubt, and took another mouthful of soup. 'Maybe he was a bit overwrought.' Turning to Oliver, she remarked, 'Still, you wouldn't want Sophie Clark for a wife.'

Paul turned to her with a puzzled look. 'Oswald Clark's wife?'

'Yes. James Waters and Oswald Clark are almost like brothers in the House. But Sophie, she's – well, it's not for me to spread stories, but her name has been closely linked with one or two of her colleagues.'

'Say no more,' Oliver broke in gently.

'Say no more, indeed. I don't know whether she's had James within her clutches, in more ways than one, but there's at least one broken marriage that can probably be laid at her door. And that façade she puts on with all her work down the East End.'

'The angel of mercy bit?' Paul asked. 'And no hiding one's light under a bushel?'

'That's right.' Matilda's tone was uncharacteristically sarcastic. 'Doing her good works and making sure the whole world knows all about it. All the time, she's carrying on with other men while her husband's back is turned. You never can tell, can you?'

'However, that doesn't address the central issue,' Oliver remarked, feeling that the conversation was turning into a potentially troublesome direction and felt it only right to rake over the marital misdemeanours of others. He glanced at Charles and Paul. 'Having a suspicious – well, probably suspicious – death among my office staff, and now the murder of somebody who might have connections with him, no matter how tenuous, means that there could be implications for both of you. Not to mention everyone else at Smith & Hanbury.'

They nodded.

'It goes without saying, but we have all got to be extremely circumspect from now on,' he went on, regretting that he had to take advantage of a social occasion at home to adopt such an authoritarian manner, but aware that circumstances made it necessary. 'Should any representatives of the press wish to communicate with you, either on or off the premises, I feel that you should refer them to me, without volunteering any more information. Is that clear?'

They murmured expressions of assent. 'By and large I think our press are pretty responsible where these matters are concerned, but it would be wrong to take any chances. At best, two lives have been lost in rather melodramatic circumstances. At worst, with matters involving this country and our cousins across the North Sea looking somewhat fragile, there might be wider issues involved. Tread carefully, gentlemen, and I have every confidence that we shall come through this unscathed.' He took up his spoon again. 'And now, before this excellent soup starts getting cold, I think we might regard the subject as closed for the evening and turn our minds to something else.'

Charles looked thoughtful. 'Did you read about that Frenchman who was flying over the Mediterranean a few weeks ago?' Seeing the interest on their faces, he continued. 'It was all over the papers. This chap following in Bleriot's footsteps, or airstream, I suppose I should say. He managed to fly over the Med, making a flight of nearly six hundred miles in less than eight hours in strong winds. And he still lived to tell the tale with enough fuel in his tank. The fellow must be a national hero throughout France by now.'

'This aviation astonishes me,' said Oliver. 'When I see those frail flying machines, I can hardly imagine anybody travelling safely to the next county in them, let alone across the sea. Twenty years ago, you had to travel abroad across the water by ship, or you didn't travel at all.'

'Not so frail,' Paul broke in. 'What about the dirigibles? Or, Good Lord preserve us, these Zeppelin airships?'

Charles nodded. 'Like that German machine that crashed a few years ago?'

103

'That's the one. Or destroyed in a storm, or something. The Germans evidently had plenty of faith in it, for in no time they subscribed a king's ransom to put the damage right again.'

'That's where it's going, isn't it? I think the future lies in the air.'

Charles smiled. 'If I was ten years younger, I wouldn't mind having a go at learning how to pilot one of those contraptions myself.'

'And I would be the first to wish you well with them,' remarked Oliver, who felt that as his guests' senior at work, as well as the host and master of his house, he should be rather more than a passive observer of the conversation. Watching Matilda's face carefully, he added, 'And if there is a war with Europe, heaven forbid, I think much of it is going to be fought in the air.'

'You don't really think there will be, do you?' she asked him anxiously. 'War, I mean.'

'Some say there will, some say there won't. Goodness knows, we've come close enough to it in the last few years. That trouble at Agadir a year or two ago, for example. Germany trying to pick arguments with France, claiming her commercial interests are being threatened, for no good reason at all. But thank heaven, there's always been somebody to drag us back from the brink.'

'Or else we've just been lucky,' Paul remarked.

'Well, yes, luck comes into it sometimes. Just as long as the Kaiser and the old boy in his palace at Vienna can stick to their petty territorial squabbles in the Balkans, and if our politicians can resist the temptation to meddle, I think we'll be all right.'

Chapter 12

Sophie Clark brushed a speck of dust off her coat as she slipped quietly out of the back entrance of the house at Hawthorne Gardens. The Louis Quatorze in the hall was chiming nine o'clock. Oswald was engaged in some late-night work on an armaments committee and would not be back much before midnight, so she had told him she was going to see her elder half-sister Elizabeth, still convalescing from pneumonia. The servants would lock up if necessary.

Right on cue, a Hansom cab rolled up outside the front door and stopped. She recognised the driver, who was familiar with her regular visits to the Kensington Hotel and knew better than to ask any more than his job demanded. The ten-minute journey gave her ample time to collect her thoughts. At first she had hated having to lie to her husband and their household, but from childhood she had always found it easy telling tall stories. It came of being an only child, she supposed. Her dear mama would have liked more, surely, but an operation had made that impossible. Not until she was eighteen and about to get married herself had she been told the true nature of her mother's complaint. Anyway, she now managed to pull the wool over dear Oswald's eyes. He had his parliamentary career, and if he did lose his seat next time there was always Paris. And there was always Elizabeth, or one of her many cousins who could be relied on as a convenient smokescreen for any clandestine assignations in London if necessary.

Of course, Count Otto von Andrewitz might not need her any more by then. But she would find others. Anyway, the last two years had been good. Though there were risks in her secret association with him, both had covered up their tracks effectively, and unless one of them was unduly careless, nobody need ever know what they had been up to. And where she was concerned, he had proved himself twice the man that poor Oswald could ever be. Thank goodness she had never been able to have children herself. How they would have got in the way of all her…good times.

Within minutes she was safely in the Kensington, where a passionate embrace from Otto, as usual, all but made her forget for two or three hours that she was married to someone else.

'Nobody saw you coming, I trust?' he asked her once he had escorted her silently up the stairs and as they seated themselves in his second floor apartment, appreciatively eyeing the champagne. It was the first time they had seen each other since April, and there was so much to find out – as well as lost time to make up for.

'Only our dear driver. We're perfectly safe.' She watched the expression on his face as he poured them both a glass and handed one to her.

'To our next little assignment, I think.' They sipped in silence for a moment.

'Is there anything else you can tell me?' she asked carefully after a pause.

'Our friend Mr Richard Priestley in Devon will not trouble us any more.' Seeing her about to probe further, he shook his head and gave her a look which warned her against it. 'You will know all about it in good time, my dear Sophie. We have been watching the family and it seems most unlikely that his daughter and son-in-law will be interested in returning to his farm cottage, but if they do, we have the means for meeting the occasion. Have you ever been to Dartmoor, by the way?'

She shook her head.

'A place full of wild beauty and mystery.' His eyes gleamed with an intensity that made her shiver. 'Perhaps rather more mystery than some people imagined. Now, you probably have something to tell me?'

'I will be in a position to do so very soon.' She lowered her voice, more from force of habit than from any genuine fear that their privacy might be at risk. 'Oswald is at one of his committee meetings tonight, and I think they will have some reports before long. There may be some armaments figures, details on the naval building programme, intelligence about fleet manoeuvres, and possibly even part of the estimates for defence expenditure to be presented before the house in the forthcoming session. I don't know how much of these I can actually obtain for you. But I think I will at least be able to help with the names of some of the private secretaries involved.'

'And their addresses?'

She nodded.

'Anything else?'

'There may be some committee minutes, and not merely the full minutes which will be published by the Stationery Office for public consultation. But the private papers which are for the eyes of the ministers and some of the civil servants alone. If Oswald brings them home with him, I think you can trust to my discretion. For convenience, we might call them the Wellington.'

'After the Duke? I agree.' He smiled gravely. 'That will be a start. And do I have your word that Oswald doesn't suspect anything?'

She laughed gently. 'Dear old Oswald! Good gracious, Otto, not a thing. With the amount of Courvoisier he gets through every evening at home, it sometimes amazes me he can get up to bed afterwards. Let alone do anything after that. Not that I wish to betray any secrets about my private life, of course.' They both smiled, in the knowledge that she no longer had any to betray.

'Tell me about his friend James Waters.'

'Oh, Waters! That conceited donkey. Thinks he's going to be a minister at cabinet rank in the next government as long as he does what everybody tells him to. I've met him a few times, and he's got far more brains than Oswald. But he's so vain, he'd probably take his own hand in marriage if he had the chance.'

Count Andrewitz smiled a little coldly. 'You say he is more clever. So you have to be careful of him?'

'No more careful than I am already. He suspects nothing.'

'And his wife?'

'Oh, that little mouse Charlotte. Of course not. She's not in the least interested in what goes on, and never has been.' He handed her a cigarette and lit it. She inhaled, pausing to collect her thoughts. 'She's a sweet little woman, but quite stupid. There's no reason to suppose that she might start taking an undue interest in anything that doesn't concern her. Unlike that even more stupid brother of hers. Talking of whom –'

'You must not ask me yet!' he snapped. She had never seen him look so angry with her before, and the sight temporarily unnerved her a little. 'You will know all about it when the time is right, but we still have a few more matters to see to first. Max and I have some further business.' His voice softened again. 'You knew that Mrs Waters' mother died in hospital a few weeks ago, didn't you?'

'Yes. Charing Cross Hospital, at the end of last month, wasn't it. Oswald was at the funeral, as a friend of James, but I didn't go. It wasn't really for me to be there.' A sudden thought struck her, but she suppressed any sense of shock as she did her best to disguise a question as a statement. 'You had nothing to do with her death, of course.'

He smiled cynically. 'No, you can absolve me of blame in that case. She died of natural causes, with a little help from her friend the demon alcohol. And I think Mrs Waters herself is safe as far as I am concerned. It is evident that she presents no threat to us, and I don't think anything need happen to her. Unless –' He took another sip of champagne. 'I suppose she was her mother's sole beneficiary. And I wonder if Mrs Stephens left her anything in her will.'

'I would have to make some discreet enquiries about that, Otto. As you know, she lived in that poky little house in Southwark, with only a bottle of gin for company.' Her voice softened momentarily out of pity. 'I don't imagine there would be any financial bequests or property involved. But there may be some personal possessions. Odd little keepsakes, family heir-looms, jewellery even.' She looked at him carefully again. 'Are you thinking what I am?'

The knowing smile played around his lips again. 'You will have to tell me.'

'You know very well. Would it be the jewellery.'

He feigned an air of inscrutability. 'She may have some little trinkets, even precious ones, given to her in the past by certain male admirers. Perhaps her late husband gave her some. Or perhaps somebody else did.'

Having an idea of what he was getting at, Sophie nodded knowingly. 'I think I have ways of finding out. Mrs Stephens and her children must be the only family, unless there were any uncles or aunts. I'm sure Charlotte and George were the only children. You will allow me a little time, of course, to pursue my enquiries.'

'But naturally. Find out for me what you can, have a little

patience, and you will be rewarded amply for your trouble. And now, let us change the subject. What do we know about the situation in Ireland since we last met?'

'Ireland? I think the government are suitably preoccupied with that. I can arrange to send you one or two written reports before long.'

'Very well. *The Times* and the *Daily Telegraph* have had much to say about the Irish crisis, and maybe you will have access to something more.' He could not suppress a faint scowl. 'And perhaps I should ask of you about the antics of your friend Mrs Pankhurst and her suffragettes.'

'My friend Mrs Pankhurst? No, Otto, I don't think so. I would never be party to the suffragette cause, and I think you might credit me with more sense of womanly dignity than that, please. Unless you have this perverted desire to see me chained to the railings.'

He laughed coarsely. 'I would sooner see you chained to the bed post, my dear. Perhaps I should have brought a chain with me tonight for the purpose.'

'You men are so disgusting sometimes.' She allowed herself a forced smile. 'But then these suffragette activities are like the home rule crisis. Everything like this helps to keep Mr Asquith and his administration suitably preoccupied.'

'Too preoccupied to concern their heads with matters further afield?'

'Quite so.'

'I am glad to hear it. You are much more tolerant of these eccentric women in England. In Germany, any suffragettes would soon be thrashed to within an inch of their lives. Nobody, least of all His Imperial Majesty, would stand for it.' He refilled their glasses. 'And unlike your husband, I do not think I will be rendered helpless by copious amounts of brandy. Not too helpless for what I have in mind.'

'You will have your little sport with me, won't you, Otto,' she laughed prettily.

'Yes. You English ladies are great sports, so they tell me. And I am sure that none can compare with you.' He glanced towards the bed and she nodded, smiling coyly. Sometimes she felt that it was worth living dangerously just for a night – or even a couple of hours – of what she knew was about to happen. Otto was rather good at it, and as she loosened her long red tresses to let them hang freely over her shoulders, she realised how she had missed him.

Ten minutes later they lay naked together, savouring the afterglow of their passions. They first time they had physically connected, a little more than a year ago, she had felt mildly guilty about being unfaithful to Oswald. But on the second occasion she had appeased her conscience with the reflection that several of his parliamentary colleagues were known to have cheated on their wives, even if they had kept quiet about it. To say nothing of His Late Majesty. As for Oswald himself – well, men would be men, and if anybody was to bring her incontrovertible proof of his adultery, she believed that she would like to rise above it and not be heartbroken, like some of the other Westminster wives. Had he ever known another woman's embrace in bed since their wedding? She was not aware that he had, but if he had – would it be the end of her world?

She smiled to herself. 'When was the last time you took another woman to bed, Otto?'

'Why do you need to know?'

'Oh, I don't need to. Just curious.'

He kissed her on the cheek. 'One day your curiosity will be the undoing of you, my dear. But as you ask – not since I was last in Berlin, several months ago.'

'I see. And was she as pretty as me?'

'Of course not. No other woman could compare with you.'

She returned the kiss and laughed coquettishly. 'You silver-tongued devil, Otto!'

It was his turn to smile. 'And when was the last time you bedded somebody other than your husband?'

'You know very well. I've never taken another man but you, apart from Oswald.' She paused, hesitating. 'Well, not another man.'

His eyes gleamed. 'You mean – a woman?'

She nodded.

'Tell me more!'

'I've got you excited, haven't I?' She giggled wickedly. 'Well, I had you excited already, but even so. I was once seduced by one of my mother's maids.'

'And how old were you?'

'I was a sweet innocent girl of but seventeen summers. It was when I was on my own in the house one afternoon – or rather, my parents were out, and I was all alone except for the servants and this maid.'

'So what happened?'

She laughed again. 'Trust you to want to know all about it! Nothing out of the ordinary. I was sitting in my room reading, and she came in to see if there was anything I needed. She looked rather tired, so I told her to come and sit down beside me for a while. Then she kissed me on the lips, told me she loved me, and the next thing I knew, she was brushing my hair and helping me out of my clothes. Then she undressed herself and we lay on my bed, doing the usual things women sometimes do together. Women who love women.'

As she chuckled to herself, watching his expression, she could sense that he was longing for her to tell him some of the more intimate details. But if she made it plain she was not going to talk about it any more, he would just have to let his filthy imagination run riot.

'Just the one occasion?' he asked.

'Yes. To this day, I still don't know whether my mother and father ever found out about it. They never said anything to me. They must have been too shocked to dare face up to what a naughty girl I'd been.' She chuckled. 'But the maid left rather suddenly a few days later. I didn't know she had gone until I asked where she was, and was told she had left. I tried asking one or two of the other servants if they knew the reason why, and they seemed as if they did but weren't going to say anything. Maybe someone had been spying on us. But a few months later, I met Oswald and married him.'

She watched his face intently while she was speaking, aware that he was aroused by her admission. If indeed admission it was.

'You are not making this up, my dear? Not playing games with me?'

'I might be telling you a pack of lies.' She laughed. 'All right, I am. There's not a word of truth in it whatsoever. I just wanted to see what your reaction was going to be, you old rogue.'

'And what would your reaction be if I was to procure the services of a young maid and ask her to join us in this bed for a little *jeu de trois?*'

She could not suppress a faint grimace. While she had to admit that the temptation of exploring previously uncharted territory had its appealing side, she did not feel inclined at present. For a moment, she began to wonder if her little joke might have gone a shade too far.

'I'd say you were a typical man, darling, and I'm sure it's doing wonders for your libido, but personally I don't care for the idea.'

'You don't think it's healthy to indulge in such sport with the ladies?'

By the tone of his voice, she was reassured that he, too, was only teasing her. 'No I don't. And I only want you. Now shall we stop talking about it, and keep things strictly *entre nous*. Have we time for any more?'

At Little Tor the farm and cottage stood empty in the increasingly bleak autumn-merging-into-winter season, while the leaves and bracken turned every shade of russet and golden brown, and the boundless beds of bell heather and ling faded for another year. Overripe, unpicked blackberries adorned bramble bushes in the hedges, ready for any passing birds to remove. Only the flowering gorse retained any hint of its summer hues, with a second flowering bloom of half-open buds, only waiting for a hint of sunshine to glow more fully. Neighbouring farmers and landowners around Holne, Poundsgate and area looked with some trepidation at the inhospitable skies, tapped their barometers or took note of the temperature faithfully every morning, and rubbed their hands grimly in anticipation of a bitterly cold winter.

The property at Little Tor, everyone knew, was going to be sold. Edward and Eleanor Bridgman had instructed an agent to send the remaining livestock to Ashburton market and put the property on the market. It had been common knowledge that their interest in the place was only half-hearted, and that there had been an element of keeping up appearances for the sake of Dick Priestley. They had no loyalty or allegiance to the area, and with his death they felt totally free of any further obligations. That he had met his death in such a manner had, of course, done nothing to make them feel differently about it – quite the opposite, in fact.

'Daresay I wouldn't 'ave minded that place for meself, like, if I'd bin a bit younger,' Roger remarked to Mary over lunch one day. 'Not at me time o' life nowadays, though. Too big a place. An' course, we're settled 'ere. But it wouldn't 'ave bin such a bad little prospect once. Sorter place Tom an' Miranda might make a go of, if they wanted it.'

Mary shuddered. 'This time last year, possibly. But you got to think of it from their side, Roger. Poor Dick Priestley bein' shot an' killed on 'is own doorstep. It'll be 'aunted now, and I'm not meanin' to make a joke out of it. Other folks laugh at you if you tell 'em you believe in ghosts, but there's no knowin'. An' now, who'd want to be steppin' into dead man's shoes?'

'You're right, love. Not me for one.'

'So you wouldn't wish it on Tom an' Miranda, would you?'

'No, not really. An' they're no nearer findin' out who's responsible?'

'No word yet. Police say they searched the place pretty thorough, but they found no weapon, no clues, no nothin'. The place 'adn't been disturbed. No signs of burglary or anythin'. An' as for those ideas they 'ad that Edward wanted to speed 'im on 'is way 'cause 'e were wantin' to take over – a right load o' nonsense if ever there was. Anyone could 'ave told 'em that. No, the more I think about it, the more I'm sure it's all part o' this business with poor George. Might 'ave bin the same person got 'em both. An' I don't like to think of it more than I 'ave to.'

Roger snorted in derision. 'None of us likes thinkin' of it. So let's change the subject and be talkin' of somethin' else. Like what are we goin' to do for Christmas?'

'That's more like it.' Mary smiled, pleased to be able to turn her attention to matters more wholesome. 'A lovely spruce in the next room all smothered in tinsel, an' a huge turkey with all the veg an' trimmin's. An' plum puddin', with a great big sprig o' holly an' berries on it, if the birds leave us any this winter. Carol singers comin' round, *Once in Royal David's City* an' all our other favourites, an' the largest dish o' my mince pies you've ever seen. Right, who are we goin' to invite round to dinner this year? Must 'ave someone to share it all with.'

Charlotte Waters sat in her front room, cursing her luck. She really had hoped that James would forget all talk of trying to involve her in Sophie Clark's good works. Not because she begrudged helping those less fortunate than herself, but Sophie Clark, of all people....James had invited her and Oswald to dinner, and between them they had talked Charlotte into promising to help. She knew she was powerless to protest, and as she had stood her ground over persuading James to attend his mother-in-law's funeral, she knew it would be churlish to say no. After all, she could hardly refuse on the grounds that she found her colleague an overbearing, affected madam.

Sophie had more or less invited herself over for a cup of morning coffee – 'as I really do think it's time we got to know one another *properly*, my dear'. James was away on parliamentary business, and Oswald had gone for a couple of days to speak on behalf of a candidate at a by-election, so she was on her own. Having taken a good look at the papers he had left behind in their London house, particularly some minutes of his last meeting with colleagues on defence and armaments estimates for the coming year, she was feeling more than a little pleased with herself. There were plenty of notes she could present to Otto on their next secret assignation, and perhaps that was not all.

Eleven o'clock, Sophie had promised to come round, and it only increased Charlotte's irritation when the clock in the hall began to strike the hour and the doorbell rang simultaneously on cue. One of these people you can set your watch by – trust the woman to be so punctual, she said to herself as the maid showed her in and took her coat. Sophie grasped Charlotte's hand with what seemed an exaggerated display of effusiveness as she showed her in to the front room and another maid brought in coffee.

'*So* glad we can meet properly at last,' Sophie gushed, with a smile that struck Charlotte as rather false, and looked around her. 'I say, what an absolutely *marvellous* room you have. You *really* must tell me who the paintings are by – oh, and about the porcelain shepherdess in your cabinet in the corner. Dresden, is it? Or Meissen, I never know which. You must tell me later, Charlotte dear. I shall insist. But first, we really must get down to business. I shall be going down to Stepney to see about supervising the kitchens next Thursday afternoon, and I would be pleased if you could help me then. I shall be leaving soon after luncheon – say, at around two. You will of course come with me in my cab. Would you be available?'

To her relief, Charlotte did not have to tell a little white lie.

'I regret I can't, Sophie. I have an appointment with my doctor that afternoon.'

Sophie's face fell, less from concern about her friend's state of health than from the chance that her plans might be disrupted.

'Oh, you must!' She gave a resigned shrug of the shoulders. 'Never mind, it's too bad. I shall be doing the same a fortnight after that, and you can join me then. What do you say?'

Charlotte took a deep breath, and hoped her reluctance would not give her away.

'Maybe. I can't promise this far ahead, but if I am available I'm sure I could come.'

You must make every effort. I insist on it. And think how pleased James would be if he knew you were coming to help.'

'All right. I'll do what I can.' Charlotte tried not to sigh, and took a sip of coffee. She knew when she was as good as beaten.

After a short pause, Sophie decided to change the subject. 'I was so sorry to hear about your mother.'

'Thank you. Yes, but it was all for the best. She had a difficult time of it, what with – what with that business about my brother.' She was a little surprised, but pleased with herself, that she could speak about it without giving way to emotion in front of others, particularly those whom she felt might not be that sincere in their sympathy.

Sophie longed to steer the conversation into delicate matters, but hesitated to make it too obvious. Almost in desperation, she tried to sound casual, as she looked at a striking item of jewellery pinned to her host's white blouse. 'That's a lovely brooch.'

'It is rather attractive, isn't it?' Charlotte glanced down at it and smiled guardedly. For goodness sake, woman, don't stop there, Sophie thought to herself. Playing for high stakes, she decided to be a little more bold. Focusing on it, she said, 'What's that design?'

'Design? Oh, nothing much. Some sort of cross, I suppose. My mother left it to me. There were one or two others, but I liked this one the best.'

Sophie tried not to overdo her enthusiasm in attempting to

learn a little more about its provenance. Guesswork probably told her everything else she needed to know.

'How's Oswald these days?' Sensing possible troubled waters ahead, Charlotte was racking her brains for any suitable small talk.

'Oh, Oswald's all right. Full of this by-election campaign in Somerset. In fact, he's away for a couple of days, so he can go and make one or two speeches in support of the candidate. The fellow's defending a majority of about eight thousand, so it probably won't make a lot of difference. I wanted to go with him, actually, because I've never seen Somerset. They say Exmoor is lovely, although probably not at its best at this time of year.'

'My brother used to like the moors. Well, Dartmoor really, though I suppose Exmoor isn't really any different.' She stared sadly ahead of her. 'I haven't been to Dartmoor since I was a child. The three of us used to go there sometimes when I was small, though I don't think I really appreciated it at the time. My little sister attitude, I suppose, always wanting to do something different from what my mother and brother wanted. But it would be nice to go back sometime. Just as soon as things are a bit less busy here, unless I wait until next summer. I might like it better now, and I suppose it would be a good way to say goodbye to my brother, wouldn't it? You know, seeing the part of England he always loved the most.'

Part of her, she could feel, was beginning to think she had misjudged Sophie, and that it was impossible not to confide in such a woman whose brash exterior was perhaps redeemed by a kind heart. 'He always loved the moors as a child. It never meant much to me, I'm afraid. But we change with time, don't we? Maybe I would see something in it now that I never did before.'

They sat drinking their coffee in silence. Charlotte was now having second thoughts, and reflecting that she must have said rather more than was wise. Being friendly to the wife of her husband's colleague was one thing, but starting to exchange confidences with a woman whom she suspected of being an intriguer in addition to her other misdemeanours was quite another. Was Sophie merely showing a friendly interest in her, or did she have any ulterior motive? Much as she hated jumping to conclusions, she could not help feeling that the woman who was notorious for her interest in other people's husbands rather more than her own was up to something sinister. Whatever her own brother had been up to on Dartmoor, if anything, she would rather not know. Maybe there was nothing to know after all, and certain individuals might be twisting facts out of all proportion in order to suit their own ugly little theories. But if Sophie Clark was playing with fire, she for one wanted no part of it, and she was quite sure that neither did James.

Who could she ask? Unless she had any proof, there was no point in asking James. To him, women's intuition and fantasy were probably one and the same. Would Sir Gregory Hall-Adamson know anything, or be able to reassure her that her imagination was running wild?

As for Sophie, she was beginning to curse herself for having taken everything for granted. Dear stupid, timid little Charlotte was not quite the goose she had believed when she set out that morning. She had prided herself on being able to get her to talk freely about certain matters of interest. Still, time was on her side. If they were to meet regularly in connection with the charity kitchens, she would surely be able to break down Charlotte's resistance bit by bit until both were the best of friends, sharing secrets without a second thought. Patience, Sophie, one step at a time. Meanwhile, she felt she had found out one or two extra little tit-bits for which Otto would be grateful.

That evening Sophie journeyed in her regular cab to the Kensington. She had taken the precaution of locking the notes she had scribbled down in her jewel box, stored safely at home, and looked forward to being able to arrange a suitable time and date when Otto could relieve her of them.

On entering the hotel she looked around at the entrance suite, but there was no sign of him. She sat down in a vacant chair to wait a few minutes, trying not to betray her agitation and hoping nobody would recognise her, even under her veil. Though it would be most unlike him to send a messenger, maybe he had had some change of plan which would make it necessary for him to break with precedent. She sat tight for another quarter of an hour, feeling more self-conscious by the minute, but still there was no sign of him.

Looking around her carefully, she went up to the reception desk with some trepidation and asked for Joseph Lewis. Rather a good alias for him, she thought. The receptionist checked his book carefully before turning back to her.

'I'm sorry, Madam. Mr Joseph Lewis vacated his room this morning.'

'Did he leave any message for Mrs Madeleine House?' Another rather clever incognito, she had decided.

After looking behind the desk, the receptionist shook his head.

'And there was no word as to when he would be returning? Or where he had gone, even?'

'I am sorry, Madam.' The man spoke in the expressionless tone of one who had said the same words many times before. 'It is not the policy of this hotel to reveal the future plans of our guests, even if they do wish to inform us prior to their departure.'

With as much dignity as she could muster Mrs Madeleine House, alias Sophie Clark, turned her back and swept out to order another cab for her journey home.

So Otto had gone, but where? Presumably laying low somewhere else in the area, or back to Berlin, without telling her first, she thought angrily on her return. The impertinence of the man! He might have had the courtesy to let her know in advance, unless – what if he had had to go in a hurry? What if he had been forced to leave the country? Had the hotel management stumbled somehow on his main purpose for being in London? His incognito was not watertight, and it would only take one person with a little too much knowledge to expose him as an imposter. What if he had been arrested, and taken it on himself to confess the nature of his business in the capital? Would it lead to the discovery of her role as well? One false move, and she was finished.

Sophie, you fool, how could you let yourself get in such a humiliating position, she said to herself as she felt the tears of shame and bitterness welling up inside her.

Chapter 13

'It doesn't make sense!' Eleanor muttered angrily to herself for the tenth time that morning. She and Edward had come back to the cottage two days after the police had informed her of her father's murder. At first she was stunned at the suddenness of it, before the shock had given way to tears. Now there was only bewilderment and anger, that a gentle old man, apparently without an enemy in the world, should have been struck down in his own home like this. Just one glance at his personal possessions, his books and notes, reminded her of the breadth of his interests and how he had sometimes spoken to her of how he planned to devote his remaining years to pursuing them. It only took a bullet from a gun to destroy it all. A savage, incomprehensible, waste. Not to mention the tragic, unexpected loss...

'The police are looking into the matter,' Edward said helplessly.

'The police! What can they do? All these stories of a couple of Germans around the area, that young man from London being found dead in suspicious circumstances, and what have they done about that?' Her voice softened. 'All right, I shouldn't be too hasty. But...' She stared out of the window. 'I know it won't bring my father back, but you'd have thought that by now they would have arrested someone.'

'Give them time, dear.' Edward knew better than to argue with his wife. Maybe the effort to distract her attention by finding something else to occupy her mind was the answer. 'In the meantime, shouldn't we try and get some of this stuff tidied away?'

'What stuff?'

'Well, some of these papers, furniture, books and things. Whether we sell the farm and cottage or not, you're going to want to take a certain amount back when we go home, aren't you?'

She nodded, and got up from her chair to close the window.

As she did so she caught sight of a postcard on the floor and bent down to pick it up. She glanced at the view, a black and white photograph of Piccadilly Circus, partly obscured by a smudged postmark. Turning it over, she looked at the German stamp above her husband's name and address on the right, and skimmed the almost illegible scrawl on the left, with the name 'Grenville' underneath.

'When did this arrive?' She glanced at Edward quizzically.

'About a week ago.' He shrugged, trying to sound nonchalant, but she could see the hesitant expression in his eyes as he tried to avoid facing her directly.

'We haven't seen your brother for a long time. What's he been up to?'

'Travelling around. Sometimes he's in England, sometimes he's in Germany. He's doing some research for the University of Leipzig, but don't ask me what it's about. You know he only keeps in touch on an irregular basis.'

Eleanor put the card on the table with a sigh. It had long since ceased to surprise her how little Edward knew about the mysterious activities of his elusive elder brother Grenville, and there was no point in probing any further. Now who were the people with whom the hapless George used to stay, she asked herself. A word with them on the whole murky business might not come amiss.

A visit to the Red Lion that evening and a chat with Isobel Cuthbert gave Eleanor the answers she needed. Without telling Edward, she decided that she would visit the Strongs the following day. Knocking on their door mid-morning, Mary came to answer the door, she introduced herself and they shook hands and exchanged facts over a cup of tea and Mary's freshly-baked scones.

'You don't think I'm jumping to conclusions, do you?' Eleanor asked a little apprehensively.

''Bout some connection between your pa's death an' George? No, not for a moment, my dear.' Mary patted her guest's hand reassuringly. After her anger and misery the previous day, Eleanor had mastered her feelings regarding her father's murder, and Mary was a little taken aback by what she saw as her rather detached attitude towards the callous shooting of her father, but accepted that some people acted less emotionally than others. If it hadn't been for the anger she had shown when describing events at the cottage, she would have put it down to shock. 'Too much like coincidence. I mean, such goin's-on in our quiet little patch? Not natural, is it?'

'My husband says the police are working on it, but –'

'Sergeant Donald's a good man.' Mary detected a note of cynicism in Eleanor's voice, which she was anxious to dispel. 'If there's things goin' on as shouldn't around 'ere, 'e'll get to the bottom of it. If 'e don't, it won't be for lack of tryin', don't worry.'

There was another knock at the door. Mary got up to answer, and Maud breezed in.

'Don't think 'ee've met?' Eleanor and Maud exchanged introductions as Mary explained the reason for Eleanor's appearance.

'It's funny your being here like this,' Maud said as she took a sip from the tea put in front of her. 'I was going to London to stay with my cousin, and I though I might make a few enquiries myself. You know, George's friends at work, to start with.'

Mary shot her a warning look.

'Now you be careful, young Maud. I know you're a grown woman an' all that, but Roger an' I don't want you goin' round playin' detective. Once you get started, you never know what you'll be leadin' yourself into.'

'Of course I'll be careful, Mary. But I was due to pay Adam and Polly a visit before Christmas anyway, and it occurred to me – well, if I could find anything out while I'm there...'

'Very well.' Mary shrugged her shoulders. 'I can't stop 'ee. But jus' you be careful. I think you should be leavin' it all up to the police. When all's said an' done, that's their job, that's what they're paid to do. But if you must, then there's no more to be said.'

'Adam and Polly live near Ealing,' Maud explained to Eleanor. 'Adam's the eldest son of my father's sister. He and Polly have been married for a couple of years and I'm the god-mother of their little girl Lizzie. She's a delightful little thing, but I haven't seen her at all since her christening. They let me have a turn in holding her at the font. It was her first birthday in September, and she will be grown no end.'

'But 'ow will you find out where everyone is, like?' Mary

broke in. 'I mean, none of us knows where George worked. Or where 'is friends are. Or 'oo they are, even.'

'Sergeant Donald will know.' Fond as she was of Mary, Maud felt a twinge of exasperation with her negative attitude, her philosophy of letting sleeping dogs lie, and above all her readiness to look for obstacles. 'If not, he can tell me who will. If not – well, maybe I won't be able to discover anything more. But I think I owe it to George.'

Mary looked at her carefully. 'Nice young man, 'e was. But you were jus' friends, you know.'

'I *know*.' Maud sighed. 'I'm sorry, Mary. We were friends and nothing else. We might have got married if we'd known each other better, we might not. But if I'm going to London anyway, it seems a good opportunity to make the effort, at least.' A supportive nod from Eleanor convinced her that she was right.

'Very well.' Mary knew when she was outnumbered. 'Good luck, but jus' make sure you take care, that's all.'

Two days later Maud sat in the drawing room of Adam and Polly's house at Castlebar Hill, Ealing. Thrilled at the sight of her 'auntie Maudie' from the wild west, as Adam kept on describing their relative's home territory, Lizzie had proudly recited every nursery rhyme she knew and a few which she didn't but made up lines for to fill in the gaps where her memory proved imperfect. At last she had found it impossible to keep her eyes open, and had been carried upstairs half-asleep to bed clutching her doll, so the grown-ups could talk. The Marchants had listened carefully to Maud's account of events, and their fears that their young cousin was brokenhearted after the strange death of the man who might otherwise have been her husband proved quite unfounded. So were their apprehensions that she might be trying to cast herself in the role of unofficial detective.

'But even so,' Adam said slowly, pouring the three of them a glass of port before making himself comfortable in an armchair next to the fireplace, 'you can go and talk to these people in London that George worked with, you can meet his sister, but what do you imagine you will gain by it? What's the point?'

'I feel I owe it to George's memory.' She shifted uncomfortably in her chair, aware that the reason was buried deep in her subconscious and that it was hard to explain precisely to anyone else. 'I know the police will sort everything out in due course, but – well, I don't think I ought to sit back and do nothing. And if only I can do something to help the others – you know, his friends, his sister...'

'Adam's right, dear,' Polly added, seeing her cousin temporarily lost for words. 'Talk to them by all means. But without meaning to hurt your feelings, I'm not sure you'll achieve anything. And don't forget that there have been two mysterious deaths. None of us want you to be the third.'

'It won't happen like that.' Maud shook her head firmly.

'Very well, you know your own mind.' Polly did not enjoy arguing for its own sake. 'I'm not doing anything myself for the next couple of days, and I insist on coming with you.'

'But –'

'Polly's right,' Adam broke in. 'We know you're not a child, but if we let you go travelling around London unescorted, and something happens to you, just think how we'd feel.'

'We'd never be able to forgive ourselves, would we?' Polly added.

'Thank you. All right,' Maud conceded, cross with herself for sounding faintly churlish when she realised that they were right.

'Good. That's settled. Now while you're here, would you like to join us in a night out at the opera? There's a choice of Gilbert and Sullivan or Wagner at the moment and I'm simply dying to go to one of them. Or even both, but one can wait for a few weeks. They'll probably be playing until into the new year.'

'I'd love to.' Maud knew nothing about either, and she was conscious that her musical education left much to be desired. Until her first evening on this visit to Polly and Adam when they had showed off their most recent acquisition – a gramophone and a small collection of the large heavy discs to be played on it – the national anthem and a few of the best-known carols had been her limit. A night of genuine metropolitan culture was not to be passed over lightly.

Meanwhile, tomorrow morning there was the little matter of a casual visit to Smith & Hanbury. Sergeant Donald had given her the address in Bayswater, although not without mixed feelings. Plucky young lady, he had thought to himself as he wrote it down for her, as long as she isn't biting off more than she can chew.

As she went to bed, more misgivings assailed her. Only then did she realise that it was perhaps hardly the height of good manners to call at the premises without an appointment or even a word of warning. Nevertheless, if she kept on thinking of all the difficulties in her way, she would never get anywhere.

The following morning Maud and Polly took the train to Bayswater and walked to the office together. By the time they approached the front door, Polly felt more proud of her cousin than she was prepared to admit. She could never have foreseen herself doing such a thing at a similar age. No, she would have sat back and let everybody else get on with it. Even so, a small still voice of apprehension told her that there was still a chance something could go horribly wrong and there might be a further tragedy if she was not careful.

Knocking on the door and standing at reception, Maud's voice could not conceal a momentary quiver as she asked to speak to Mr Charles Shepherd or Mr Paul Jenkins on personal business. After five minutes, though it seemed like longer, Charles appeared and they introduced themselves.

'Miss Watts?' He held out his hand and she grasped it a little nervously before shaking it.

'I'm so sorry to come here without warning. But – if it's convenient – sometime – I wondered if I could ask you a few things about George Stephens.'

'Maud's my cousin – well, by marriage,' Polly broke in, as she placed a protective hand on Maud's shoulder. 'She lives in south Devon and she was a friend of George, as well as the niece of the people he used to stay with. And we know this may be taking something of a liberty, so we do apologise. I know we should not be interrupting your work, but she would be eternally grateful if you could spare her a few minutes of your time in due course.'

'Oh, naturally.' If Charles was taken aback, he was too much of a gentleman to let it show. 'I admit I am a little preoccupied with one or two things at the moment.' He looked at Maud with a kindly expression. 'Are you staying in London, Miss Watts?'

'For a few days,' she blushed, suddenly feeling rather foolish without realising why.

'I would be pleased to meet you at lunch today. And perhaps

Mr Jenkins can accompany us, if you like.' She nodded. 'Shall we say about midday, if that would suit?'

Maud and Polly took a train to Trafalgar Square and spent the next hour at the National Gallery, looking at the Renaissance paintings. Maud had always been fascinated by the pictures of Raphael and Titian, but this time she felt unable to concentrate on them properly. She could hardly wait until the time came to meet Charles and Paul, and for the first time she was suddenly looking forward to going back to Devon, with this whole slightly unreal episode behind her. Still, she had gone too far to back out of it now.

After meeting at Smith & Hanbury all four of them adjourned to a nearby cornerhouse. After her initial nervousness, Maud breathlessly recounted her version of the story, with occasional moral support from Polly. Charles and Paul listened carefully, nodding occasionally, until she had finished.

'And do you know about George's sister?' Paul asked. When she shook her head, Paul filled her in on the subject of Charlotte and James Waters.

'I don't know if you would gain anything by meeting her,' he added. 'She appears very genuine, but seems like a rather private person. My impression is that she might find such a meeting rather intrusive.'

'You will forgive me for asking, I trust,' Charles added, 'but your motives might be misinterpreted. I hardly need add that everything is at a rather delicate stage, particularly with the murder of Mr Priestley.'

'Do you think that everyone around Holne is living in fear of their lives?' asked Paul.

'Oh no,' Maud reassured them. 'But they're a bit uneasy. You know – as if they're looking at each other and wondering all the time who the next victims might be.'

'I suppose the death of Mr Priestley is going to bring matters to a head,' Charles remarked. 'The police are probably questioning everyone in your area as we speak. And his son-in-law and daughter will probably be the first.'

'Wouldn't like to be in their shoes,' Polly added.

'Oh, I don't think anybody suspects them of the murder,' Maud cut in. 'They were in Southampton when it happened. But it's a grim business for Eleanor, having to make the journey to

Devon because she's lost her father like that.'

Paul drummed his fingers on the table in concentration. 'Does the name Oswald Clark mean anything to you?'

Polly rolled her eyes. 'That Member of Parliament? Isn't he something to do with James Waters? Two of a kind, if you ask me.'

'Exactly,' Paul went on. 'I haven't got much time for either of them. I've met Charlotte Waters and she's charming, but her husband's an unfeeling brute if ever there was one. That's my feeling, anyway.' He gave them a brief account of his meetings with her. 'And as for Clark's wife – Sophie. There's something pretty peculiar about her. And I've got a hunch that there's more to her than meets the eye in this whole business. Don't ask me why, but when there's trouble around, there's a fair chance that she's involved.'

'One other thing,' Maud asked shyly, trying not to look at the table. 'Did George ever mention me by name?' As soon as the words had left her lips she blushed. Trust her mouth to run away with her.

Paul thought carefully, trying not to smile and embarrass her further. 'I don't recall him doing so. But he was a very private sort of person, just like his sister. He never even mentioned Roger and Mary Strong by name. If you wanted to get anything at all out of him, you really had to question him. We all took the line that he would tell us everything when he was ready. But of course he never did.'

He glanced at the clock on the wall.

'Please, you must excuse me. We are in the middle of some pretty important business at work for a client, and I do have to get back. How long are you in London for, Miss Watts?'

'About a week.'

He produced a pocket book, removed a card bearing his name and address, and passed it to Maud. 'Do contact me again at home if I can help with anything further. Or call into the office, if it's more convenient.' He and Charles stood up to shake her hand and that of Polly. 'Thank you for meeting us. It seems funny, but we have learnt a good deal more about him from you.'

'And thank you for sparing the time, Mr Jenkins, Mr Shepherd.'

'Something on your mind, old man?' James asked, looking

anxiously at Oswald. Both had felt the need for a short stroll after a particularly taxing session in the House of Commons, and were standing on Westminster Bridge. Oblivious to the hum, the dusk, the sounds and senses of central London winding down gently at the close of an autumn day, they took no notice either of the mist of fine rain that had been enveloping the city since around midday. Instead they gazed at the dark oily river Thames beneath them, looking ever blacker as dusk fell around them. 'Not still troubled by the talk of those naval estimates for the year ahead, are you?'

'Not really.' Oswald turned briefly towards James, then continued to gaze moodily at the river again. 'There were times when I had my doubts as to whether the voters would accept it, whether I mightn't have some awkward explaining to do to my constituency. But I think they will. They know we've got to defend ourselves. No.' He swallowed deeply. 'It's Sophie.'

James thought for a moment before continuing. He was aware that rumours had circulated among their fellow-parliamentarians about her behaviour for a long time. That she had avoided being openly associated with any scandals was probably a matter of luck on her part. But he thought it best not to act to his friend's discomfort by making any unsolicited reference to them. 'What's up with Sophie? She's not ill, is she?'

Oswald shook his head. 'No, not exactly. But there's something rather furtive about her these days. I asked her the other day about the charity function she was involved with.'

'The work she was asking my wife to help with?'

Oswald gave a mirthless chuckle. 'I might have known she'd try to get Charlotte involved. She gave me a rather odd look, and then changed the subject. Started talking about how she wanted to go away for a holiday in Paris, or Venice, or somewhere. I know she loves travelling abroad and visiting the cities of Europe, but it did seem rather unlike her.' He spoke slowly, as if thinking hard about every word before letting it escape. 'I wonder whether she's – up to something.'

Knowing what he did of Sophie, James would have been more surprised if she was not, but he too chose his words with care. 'Is it anything you wish to talk about?'

'It's very kind of you, James.' Oswald smiled, a little sadly, for the first time that afternoon. 'You know Sophie, and you know she's tended to look outside her wedding ring a bit. I'm not blind and I can accept that, I suppose. I've been just as busy with matters here at Westminster as you have, so maybe I'm to blame in some way. Maybe us Members of Parliament aren't cut out to be good husbands.'

James grunted. Perhaps this was a little close to home. Seeing a thoughtful expression in his eyes which Oswald correctly construed as partly guilt, he instantly became apologetic.

'I'm sorry if that seems tactless. None of us are perfect, after all. But Sophie seems – how do I put it – rather more evasive these days. As if she's got more to hide than usual.' A look of resignation swept across his face. 'Let sleeping dogs lie, I suppose. These things tend to sort themselves out if you give 'em time, that's my motto.'

Oswald was too patient by half with that flighty wife of his, he thought. He would never have put up with such a cuckold himself. Still, in Charlotte he'd married the right woman for the problem not to arise. But if Oswald was prepared to be patient and let the matter resolve itself, fair enough.

Strange how things come around, Sergeant Donald mused as he knocked on the door of Little Tor Cottage. The last time he had been here, it was to make enquiries about George Stephens. Now it was to speak to Eleanor and Edward about Dick Priestley's murder. Edward answered at the door and showed him into the kitchen, where Eleanor made them all a cup of coffee.

'First of all, madam and sir, may I offer my deepest condolences.'

'Thank you,' Edward muttered, while Eleanor nodded woodenly.

'You had the results of the inquest?' The verdict, of murder by person or persons unknown, was a foregone conclusion on which it was pointless to elaborate. Despite an intensive search, no weapon had been found at or near the scene of the crime.

They nodded again.

'You were in Southampton when it happened, I believe?'

'That's right,' Edward volunteered. 'We had a telegram, and arrived here three days later.'

'And have you any idea of who might have done this?'

'Sergeant Donald, my father did not have an enemy in the

world,' Eleanor broke in sharply, while Edward nodded silently.

Donald hesitated for a moment. 'There was some trouble with a fire on the farm around seven years ago?'

'What has that got to do with it?' she asked. There was a defensive note in her voice which made him feel he had touched a raw nerve.

'Well – was it an accident, or was somebody out to get him? Could somebody have been seeking revenge on him?'

Eleanor got up from her chair.

'This is all quite pointless! The fire was an accident. It started in a bale of straw and some bags of foodstuffs, nothing more. You think that there was more to it than that?'

'They did say –'

'You mean to say you believe those rumours?' She clenched her fists, making an effort to control her anger while Edward looked on helplessly, knowing that to intervene might only provoke her even more. 'That he was trying to cheat the insurance company and that he had started it deliberately? Oh yes, I know exactly who was responsible for putting that nasty little rumour about. Old Joe Reynolds and his son, who used to farm at South Tor just over the hill. You can see it perfectly from here on a summer's day. Joe never liked my father, and always had it in for him. He died a couple of years later and the family sold up and moved, and I don't know where on earth they've gone. Otherwise I'd tell you to go and talk to them yourself!'

'So you think one of the Reynolds family might be behind it?'

'I'm not saying anything. I wasn't born yesterday, and I'm not in the habit of making accusations which can't be substantiated, am I?' She had sat down again and was regretting her initial out-burst. 'Look, I'm sorry, Sergeant. It's your job to get to the bottom of this. But it has been a pretty difficult week for us, and – you know –'

'I understand, Mrs Bridgman. All we need to do is try and eliminate people from our enquiries, or alternatively follow up any leads there might be. If somebody in the Reynolds family has anything to do with it, the sooner we can establish this the better. Or otherwise.'

'My wife understands.' Edward patted her hand supportively as he faced Donald. 'I do, too, of course. But we can't think of any other people it's likely to be. Really, we thought he didn't have an enemy in the world.'

Donald thought for a moment. 'What other immediate family do you have?'

'We have six children,' Edward told him. 'My mother is widowed and lives in Winchester, not far from us. My mother-in-law died a long time ago, and my wife is an only child. Apart from an elder brother who died in infancy.'

'And do you have any brothers or sisters, Mr Bridgman?'

Edward hesitated. 'I have two sisters, both married. And – a brother.'

A note of unease in his voice made both Donald and Eleanor look at him carefully.

'So where do they live?' Donald asked casually.

'Is this relevant, Sergeant?' Edward tried not to sound as impatient as he felt.

'Well – you understand we do need to build up the full picture, in a manner of speaking. It all helps us to get to the bottom of the mystery.'

Edward sighed. 'Very well. Hetty and her family live in Southampton, only a couple of miles from me, and Miranda just outside Birmingham. I see them all from time to time.'

'And what about your brother?'

'My brother Grenville lives in Germany.' Edward took care not to catch Donald's eye as he spoke.

'And what does he do?'

'He's – a Professor in Physics at the University of Leipzig.'

'And does he come to England regularly? Do you see him?'

'No. We haven't met for some time. He travels around Europe a great deal, mostly for research and meeting other people in the profession.'

Donald had the feeling that Eleanor looked unusually interested in this information, as if she was hearing it for the first time as well. There may be more to this than meets the eye, he thought.

He drummed his fingers gently on the table, and finished the last of his coffee.

'Thank you both.' He rose to his feet and shook hands with them both. 'You will of course keep me informed of anything else that you may think would be of relevance?'

'We will,' Edward said. 'Though we expect to be returning to

Southampton shortly.'

'Very soon?'

Edward shrugged. 'A day or two.'

'In that case, may I wish you a safe journey.'

As they saw him out of the front door, Donald was lost in thought. Grenville Bridgman. The name seemed strangely familiar.

Chapter 14

'Please, ma'am. There's a gentleman at the door to see you.' Giannetta, Sophie Clark's maid, tried to sound calm, but there was no concealing the nervousness in her manner as she stood in front of her mistress.

Sophie put down her book with a sigh. She seemed to have so little time to get down to a quiet read nowadays, and besides, would the girl never learn? 'His name?' she snapped. She could feel one of her headaches coming on, and since returning from the hotel on that last abortive mission to find Otto, her nerves had been on edge.

'Beg pardon, ma'am, he wouldn't give his name, but he said his business was of the utmost importance.'

'Very well. Show him into the drawing room and I will see him presently.'

Coming downstairs a couple of minutes later, Sophie was perturbed to hear more than one set of heavy footsteps proceeding towards the drawing room. Giannetta came towards her, ashenfaced.

'There's three of them, ma'am,' she said breathlessly. 'I couldn't stop them. One just came in, almost pushed me right over, and the other two followed –'

'Have you any idea who they are?' Sophie tried to conceal the rising sense of panic in the pit of her stomach.

'I think they're Germans, ma'am. Might be soldiers. Oh, you will be all right, won't you?'

'Of course I'll be all right!' she snapped. 'Pull yourself together, my girl! They're not going to eat me alive, are they?' Oh damn you Oswald, she thought to herself, why do you have to be in the depths of the countryside on some stupid by-election at a time like this?

Brushing Giannetta away, Sophie entered the drawing room with all the dignity she could muster.

'Otto!'

Clicking his heels together and standing with his hands behind his back, Otto scowled at her.

'Count Otto von Andrewitz!' he barked. Two thickset men with bristling moustaches, dressed like Otto in morning clothes, stood a few paces behind him in similar posture.

She glared at him.

'Aren't you going to introduce me to your friends?'

Otto ignored her request.

'Mrs Clark, I think you have some information for us.'

She looked coldly at them and seated herself in the nearest armchair, trying to assume an air of dignified confidence in herself which she did not really feel.

'Now that you have invited yourselves into my home, perhaps you would be so good as to tell me the meaning of this intrusion.'

The two others exchanged glances without a word, and looked impassively at Otto as he cleared his throat, reached in his pocket for a silver case, and took out a cigar. One of his subordinates produced a match and lit it for him. Slowly and deliberately he inhaled, and took his place on another chair, facing her coldly.

'Now, Mrs Clark, you shall tell us all we would like to know, and we will not take up any more of your valuable time.' There was a sneer in his voice which was completely new to her. Although taken aback, she vowed inwardly to rise above it and not give him or his fawning lackeys the satisfaction of knowing how shocked she was at his evident duplicity. 'It concerns your friend Mrs Waters.'

'Mrs Waters?' She decided to play for time.

'You know Mrs James Waters. And you do not play the clown with me, or else you may have good reason to regret it!' He drew on his cigar again. 'She has a most magnificent collection of jewellery, I understand?'

She found his impatient tone of voice unnerving, but it would be best to hide her apprehension beneath a chilly reserve and stand her ground. 'If you know so much about it, perhaps you had better go and ask her yourself?'

He smiled coldly. 'Maybe. But perhaps you can tell us first?'

'Count Andrewitz, how can you possibly expect me to know?'

'I believe she is a close friend of yours.' The ghost of a smile played across his face. 'Furthermore, I am a busy man. If you could save me the trouble of asking her, I might not need to proceed with a little plan I had, namely to inform Lord Northcliffe and his editors of the true identity and activities of Mrs Madeleine House.'

'You wouldn't – you – but –'

'Oh, but I might. Think how interested all of them would be to hear about the private life of one of their parliamentarians' wives. To lay such gossip before the public gaze would do wonders for their circulation. And the husband himself would be equally interested, would he not?'

Never in her worst moments had Sophie envisaged that Otto would stoop so low. At times her more cautious side had warned her that she was quite possibly playing with fire, but this was something else entirely. Being married to a lacklustre back-bencher with no ambitions who was not expected to retain his seat at Westminster after the election was one thing, but public humiliation and exposure as an accessory to treason was quite another.

'Mrs Clark!' He clicked his heels, walked slowly towards her, and grasped her by the elbows. She screamed, dragged herself free from his grasp, and slapped him sharply across the face. Turning round, she walked towards the door, only to find the other two Germans barring her way. She sank back into her chair and buried her head in her hands, her body wracked with sobs. After a moment she pulled herself together and looked up to see Otto standing in front of her, facing her with a look of icy contempt, his arms folded.

'I see I must repeat myself, Mrs Clark. What do you have to tell us about Mrs Waters and her jewellery?'

'All I know is that she's got this gold brooch,' she said brokenly. 'It was a sort of German cross design, and she was wearing it the last time I called on her. And she said there were some others. Honestly, that's all – that's all she told me. I could hardly ask her to let me see them all. You must believe me.'

He glared at her, then nodded. 'I believe you. And did she tell you that they came to her from her mother?' She nodded through her tears. 'Now, what about the Wellington?'

She looked blankly at him before remembering the notes she had locked in her jewel box. No, she did not see why she should give him the satisfaction of getting his revolting, calloused hands on them. They would go on the fire later that evening. 'No, I swear I have nothing! Oswald hasn't even been home since we – since –'

He looked searchingly at her, then satisfied himself that she was probably telling the truth.

'I see. So that just leaves the little matter of your own pieces. Like that rather splendid string of pearls we are looking at.'

Instinctively she clutched the pearl necklace she was wearing. It had been a gift from Otto, a particularly exquisite memento of one of their nights of pillow talk and illicit passion at the Kensington Hotel. She blushed slightly as she recalled that he had presented it to her the first time he had plied her with champagne in his room before joining her in bed. But if it was now tainted with such associations, it was one present which she would willingly never set eyes on again, let alone wear.

'You'd better have it back, hadn't you!' she almost spat as she tore it off angrily and threw it at him.

He laughed mockingly as he fingered it. 'The last time I saw this, you were wearing it around that flawless neck of yours. This, the rings on your fingers – and nothing else.' The other men roared with laughter and her face turned a deep shade of crimson. 'A fine piece of jewellery for a fine figure of a woman! My dear Mrs Clark, has anyone ever told you what a wonderful subject for a painting you would have made. A veritable Venus. Nude with pearls.' He stopped laughing and his eyes scanned the walls, coming to rest on a Highland landscape in oils. He strode over to it and inspected it carefully. 'This looks to me like the Rhine mountains.'

'It's Scotland,' she said listlessly. 'Painted in the middle of the last century. My husband inherited it from his parents.'

'A fine work of art. The great Sir Edwin Henry Landseer?'

'No. McCulloch. He's less well-known, but some of the auction houses say his work is every bit as good. He was never an animal painter, but he has more feeling for the poetry of the Scottish countryside, don't you think?' It hardly seemed to be a suitable time for discussing the merits of Scottish artists, least of all with a greedy philistine of a German army officer, but she still felt there was just a chance that some effort at conversation might soften his mood.

'McCulloch, then. I have a friend in our regiment who has a good eye for pictures. If I was to make him a present of this, I am sure he would be eternally grateful.' He nodded at the other men, who approached and to her horror began to remove it carefully from its hangings.

'You can't!' she shouted. 'It belongs to my husband. Just you leave it where it is!'

'But what if he was to come home to find a large space on the wall where it used to be? Would it break his heart? You could always tell him that it had been stolen. He must have insured it? Or perhaps Mrs Madeleine House could provide a different explanation.' He looked at her with a hollow smile, as if intent on prolonging her agony. 'Very well.' A further nod at the men and they straightened it up on the wall again, with a calculated display of roughness, before he walked slowly towards the mantelpiece. Two gold candlesticks caught his eye and he picked one up, caressing it with his fingers as he admired the shape, then turned to her. 'Are these valuable?'

'I don't know! They belong to Oswald as well, and he's the expert on them, not me.'

'I collect candlesticks, you see. I have a magnificent display in my own home at Berlin. And I think these might go rather well there. They are quite an unusual shape, which I have not seen before.'

'Take them, then!' Suddenly she realised she was beyond caring about material possessions. If only they would just go away and leave her alone.

'No, perhaps I should not be too demanding. And I think that is all, Mrs Clark. We need not waste any more of our time. And perhaps we should see ourselves out of your charming residence.' All three of them walked towards the door, then he turned round.

'You will not, of course, mention this little meeting to anyone else, least of all Mr Clark. It is unnecessary to add that nobody would ever believe you, except for that silly servant girl of yours who let us in on our arrival. And it would be very sad if she was to be found floating face down in the river Thames. Even sadder if she was not found.'

She glared at him, her lip quivering, as he reached for the door handle.

'One last thing.' He turned to face her again, and gave her a sharp smack across the face. The shock, combined with the physical force of the blow, sent her sprawling on the floor. 'An English lady does not conduct herself in such a manner towards a German officer. If she does, she soon finds there is a price to be paid for it.'

The ribald laughter of all three as they left rang in her ears. On their previous meetings the aura of evil surrounding him had excited her, but now she realised it made her flesh creep. She threw herself on a sofa, buried her face in a cushion and wept.

At his table in a corner of the saloon bar of the Red Lion, Sergeant Donald drained his pint of bitter and sighed deeply. Having served a group of five regulars who had just arrived, Isobel Cuthbert did her tour around the tables, picking up the empty glasses to wash.

'So what's the latest, Sergeant?' she asked.

He shook his head. 'Not as much to go on as we'd like.'

'This matter of Dick Priestley, you mean?'

He nodded. 'You'll understand I can't say too much at the moment, but...'

She looked at him carefully with a knowing expression. 'I know. Those Germans who were at the Cottage a few weeks ago. You don't have to tell me.'

Ever the soul of discretion, she continued on her way and left him to his thoughts. The last thing he wanted was a journey to London – or anywhere else, unless it was within cycling distance – to question the officers again. With a little luck, it would not come to that. His superiors at Exeter would surely find a way around that. But he knew that, unless they could be prevailed upon to help the police with their enquiries, his chances of solving the murder – or murders – were about as likely as King George and Queen Mary suddenly walking through the door and calling out that the drinks were on them.

One theory had barely crossed his mind until now. Joe Reynolds and his son – now there was a thought. It was strange how Joe and Dick had always bitterly disliked each other. There had been some kind of family rivalry between the Priestleys and the Reynolds ever since he could remember. Something to do with one of them taking too keen an interest in an unmarried daughter, he was given to understand. Soon after coming to Holne as an eager young policeman, he had heard salacious tales of a Miss Reynolds, a flighty young thing from all accounts, being too free with her favours with the lusty swains of the neighbourhood, finding herself in the family way and having to leave the area in rather a hurry. Whether there was any truth in it or not, he had never managed to establish. Not even Isobel Cuthbert had known the full story, and if Isobel's remarkable fount of knowledge as to who was carrying on with whom – and jolly well shouldn't be – couldn't furnish the answer, then nobody could.

Village gossip was all very well as long as it didn't harm anybody, but when people could be hurt, or when it erupted years later into something as savage as cold-blooded murder, that was a different matter. And as long as it didn't reflect on anything to do with his job, it wasn't really his business. When his mother had said that either you were married or you weren't, and anything else was a bore, he thought she had the measure about right.

Tomorrow was another day, he reflected. Soon Maud Watts would be back from London. What a plucky young miss, volunteering to try and find out something like that, particularly as she had never been away from home before. With a little luck, he wouldn't have to wait long to hear about it from her.

Much as she was enjoying her time in London, Maud felt it would show a lack of manners on her part for her to outstay her welcome or impose on Polly and Adam longer than necessary. She also knew that Roger and Mary – especially the latter – would become worried if she stayed away for too long. Moreover, though she had not learnt as much as she would have liked from Paul and Charles, she was grateful for the information they had given her. It was clear that Charlotte Waters would be unlikely to welcome her intruding into her private life, and she did not intend to make the effort.

All that remained for her to do, she decided, was to write to Paul thanking him and Charles for taking the trouble to meet her and Polly, and asking them to tell Charlotte anything they thought she might find useful.

'If you must go as soon as all that, you are coming to the

opera with us on the last night before you go,' Polly told her firmly. 'Adam and I promised ourselves we would make sure all three of us had an evening out at the theatre, and we won't take no for an answer.'

It was an offer Maud could hardly refuse. But in view of her reasons for being in London, she had to tell them ruefully that perhaps Wagner was not the answer. She felt it would be inappropriate to see something German, and the others told her she was right. There were no such reservations in choosing Gilbert & Sullivan's *The Mikado* at the Gaiety, Aldwych.

Despite occasional embarrassed glances from Adam during the show, Maud had laughed at the performance of the Lord High Executioner until the tears rolled down her cheeks, and as they came out of the theatre afterwards she was only mildly surprised to find herself singing "To make the punishment fit the crime" under her breath, and hear at least two other appreciative patrons doing the same.

'You should have gone onto the stage yourself, my dear,' Polly teased her. 'I'd have done so myself, if only I had the voice for it. Carol singing at Christmas is about my limit.'

'I can just see her as Yum-Yum, can't you,' Adam broke in. 'And I'd be the Executioner.'

When they arrived back at Ealing by cab, Maud was more tired than she cared to admit. Almost as soon as she had undressed, climbed into bed and her head hit the pillow she was asleep, dreaming that she was back at Holne and had been volunteered to take the female lead in a musical with the local operatic society. On their opening night she was horrified to find herself on stage dressed in her everyday clothes, with no orchestra to be seen anywhere in the village hall, and worst of all, she had completely forgotten her words. Disappointment was mingled with relief as she woke to find Lizzie, holding a doll in one hand and tugging at her eiderdown with the other.

Chapter 15

After spending most of the afternoon wondering what to do next, Paul wrote a brief note to Charlotte Waters asking her if she would contact him at her convenience. Five minutes after posting it, he wondered whether he had done the right thing in view of the fact that her husband might intercept it. Shrugging off the possibility – what was done was done – he banished it from his mind until walking into his office a couple of days later to find her waiting in reception.

'I had your letter, Mr Jenkins. Could I meet you at your house this evening?'

'Yes, of course. If – if Mr Waters won't object.'

She smiled with what struck him as a new spirit of self-confidence.

'Should we say that sometimes I have to make up my own mind on these things.'

He went into his office, feeling pleased for her sake that she had evidently developed a mind of her own. If it put that insufferable husband in his place, it was not before time.

Soon after six-thirty that evening a cab drew up outside his house, and he went outside to meet her and escort her indoors.

'So what is the news, Mr Jenkins?' she asked as they sat in the drawing room.

'Paul, please.' He felt it was time to drop the formalities.

'Then you must call me Charlotte.'

'Thank you, Charlotte.' He cleared his throat. 'Does the name Dick Priestley, or indeed Mr and Mrs Edward Bridgman, mean anything to you?'

She shook her head.

'I had a friend of theirs from Holne come up to see me recently.' He proceeded to outline the details of Maud Watts' visit and the murder of Dick Priestley.

'And you think this could have something to do with my

brother's death?'

'We shouldn't jump to conclusions. But I think you'd find it hard to find anybody that doesn't. The local police certainly think there is a connection.'

'Oh dear. James won't like this at all, I'm afraid.' Her features broke into a grin, and he was quite startled to see her relax so much. This was not the worried, tense woman he had met a few weeks ago. 'My husband is convinced that all this is going to hurt his career. As if it was his fault!'

'Well, wouldn't it attach something of a stigma to his name?'

'I can't see that it would. At first I thought it might, possibly in the short term at least. Then I talked to one or two friends, people like the previous member in the constituency, who can't see that it would make the slightest difference. But the way James went on about it the other night, you'd think that he was in danger of being arrested for murder himself. As if he was intelligent enough to commit the perfect murder.' She blushed slightly. 'It isn't really for me to be speaking like this about my husband. He works very hard indeed in the Commons and in his constituency, and he has been a good husband to me. And he is a good father – well, he would be if only he wasn't so determined to make them frightened of him. Maybe he'll see the error of his ways in time. But he can be so pompous. If I couldn't see the funny side of it sometimes, I think I'd have gone off my head a long time ago!'

He smiled, secretly agreeing with her while realising it would be impertinence to make any disparaging remarks about James, tempting though it was.

'And what do we know about these German officers?' she asked.

'They seem to be the obvious suspects. There's some rumour of a possible revenge killing – as regards Priestley, I mean – but they don't think it very likely.'

'Local people?'

'Yes. Some time-honoured family feud.'

She laughed. 'Feud or feudal? They do tend to live in the middle ages, these rural communities, don't they?' After thinking for a moment, she went on. 'Do you know Oswald and Sophie Clark? Or know about them, I mean.' He nodded. 'I don't think I would be too surprised if she was involved somewhere. It's

141

difficult to put my finger on it, but frankly I don't trust her. There's much more than meets the eye in her case, I'm sure. Oh, I know I shouldn't be telling you all this, but – well, either I keep my mouth shut and none of us get anywhere at all, or else I tell somebody and accept the consequences. And if I can't rely on you, then I can't trust anybody, can I?'

Seeing the look of reassurance on his face, she went on. 'For one thing, there's her devious attitude whenever she speaks to you. Not only that, but there are rumours, and I must emphasise that's all they are at the moment, of her having an affair with somebody.'

'But you don't know who.'

'I have absolutely no idea. But some of the other members' wives are starting to talk. I heard things at a reception recently.' She smiled. 'Of course, I shouldn't be listening to gossip. But that woman has had a reputation for a very long time. And if you closed your ears to gossip all the time, you would never learn anything.'

'I can well believe it. About Mrs Clark, I mean. How does Oswald put up with her?'

'Everyone asks the same question. Some people say that he's in his cups too much of the time to notice what's going on around him. There's another theory, that she's got a lot more money than he has and that he can't afford to send her packing. Her grandfather came from the fringes of landed gentry some-where in Suffolk. He was in the banking business himself, and with a family pedigree like that none of them have ever wanted for anything.'

'Or maybe he just wants a quiet life and can't be bothered with dragging her through he divorce courts,' Paul suggested helpfully.

'You may be right. I've only met him briefly. He seemed a good enough chap. Not very clever, but pleasant enough. And I think he deserved someone a bit better than that Sophie.' She almost spat the name out in disgust.

They sat lost in thought for a moment, with only the ticking of a grandfather clock to break the silence. Presently there was a knock on the door, and a butler brought the evening newspaper in to Paul. He glanced quickly at it and then went to put it on a side table, but she dissuaded him from such a cursory inspection.

142

'Have a look, if you like,' she urged. 'You never know if any of our friends might be in it, do you?'

He reached over and scanned the pages swiftly in turn. Suddenly his jaw dropped.

'Great Scott! Talk of the devil, eh?' He folded it back on itself and held it in front of her, pointing to a small paragraph, headed

M.P.'S WIFE: CONDITION CRITICAL

Underneath it stated that Mrs Oswald Clark had been admitted to Charing Cross Hospital after being taken seriously ill.

'No speculation as to the illness?' Charlotte asked, reading it through a second time. 'She always seemed pretty healthy to me.'

Paul read through it twice and shook his head.

'Well, whatever it is, I am sorry,' she said sympathetically. 'Much as I may dislike the woman, I don't wish her ill.' She stood up. 'I mustn't stay too long. Now, are you in contact with these people in Devon?'

'Yes. With your permission, I will write to them forthwith.'

'Thank you. They will obviously want to know of any developments. And now, Mr Jenkins – Paul – I should summon a cab and go home. Thomas wasn't too well this morning.'

'Nothing serious, I hope?'

'Oh no.' She shook her head reassuringly. 'It was his birthday yesterday, and he just ate too many slices of chocolate cake at teatime. You know, boys will be boys.'

Charlotte stepped out of her cab and into her house again five minutes later, to find James seated at the desk in his study writing. On hearing her enter, he put down his pen and grunted as he looked up coldly at her.

'Who have you been visiting this time?'

'Mr Jenkins.' She removed her coat and gloves, trying not to look too defiant as she glanced at him.

'Still playing private detectives, I suppose?'

'If you must put it like that, dear, then we are.' Her voice softened. 'I'm sorry, but you know how important it is for all of us to sort this matter out.'

'Very well.' He shrugged, and picked up his pen again.

'Oh, I nearly forgot,' she continued as she drew up a chair

next to him. 'While I was there, we saw something in tonight's paper. What's this about Sophie Clark being admitted to hospital?'

He hesitated momentarily, replaced the cap on his pen and faced her squarely.

'What I tell you is not to go further than this room – for the time being.' There was no disguising the note of sympathy in his voice, a note which she heard all too seldom, and her heart instinctively went out to him more than it had done for a long time. 'Sophie was found unconscious in her bed last Friday night by her maid.' Charlotte gasped with alarm. 'Oswald was away on this by-election campaign, as we know. Giannetta, I think her name is, went upstairs to her bedroom at about ten o'clock that night, as she hadn't asked for any supper. She discovered her lying in bed with an empty glass on the floor beside her. Luckily she had the presence of mind to summon a doctor, and they took her to hospital at once. It seems she tried to take her own life, and if they had delayed any longer she would probably have succeeded.'

'Surely not! So is Oswald back?'

'They were going to send him a telegram, but he was due to come back to town anyway on the Saturday, and I understand she is due to go to a nursing home to convalesce once the doctor thinks she is well enough to be moved. She could be there for a while.'

'And do they think there's any permanent damage to her?'

He shook his head sadly. 'Too soon to say. They think she swallowed some kind of acid, and there is a chance that her throat or vocal cords might have sustained serious injury. If it's as serious as that, it is possible she might never speak again.'

'Poor Sophie!' Charlotte blinked, staring at the floor and fiddling with her hands in despair. 'And do they know what drove her to it?'

'Oswald didn't say anything about a note or letter, which is usually the first thing they look for in a case like this. But Giannetta says that a gang of men visited her that afternoon. Without making an appointment, apparently. Of course the poor girl was in a really awful state about it by the time James was back. But she says one of them arrived on the doorstep without announcing his name, and two more followed. There was no way she and Sophie could have done anything to keep them out of the house.'

'Did they stay for long?'

'Only a few minutes. But Giannetta said she heard raised voices while they were there, and Sophie was in a very distressed condition after they left. Not physically, so much as mentally. It seems one of them hit her and she was more shocked than injured, but she was extremely upset, as you can well imagine.'

'Was anything stolen?'

'Oswald doesn't think so. He and their manservant looked over the place, and nothing seemed to be missing.'

'And has he got any clues as to what this was all about?'

'Nothing at all. Oh, Giannetta said she thought Sophie was wearing a pearl necklace when they arrived, and that she wasn't when they left. That may mean something, I don't know.'

They gazed speculatively at each other.

'I can't believe it,' Charlotte said at last, on the verge of tears. 'Someone we know so well. And a thing like this happening to her. I know I didn't really like her, but –'

'She could be a little outspoken, I know, but with the best of intentions. She had her faults, but she was a very capable woman.'

Charlotte was tempted to add that she knew what Sophie had been capable of, and was immediately ashamed of herself for entertaining such uncharitable thoughts at a time of crisis. At the same time, her mind was racing over everything else she had learnt recently from Paul. It was surely stretching the boundaries of coincidence too much to think that the incidents could not be related. No, she must work this out for herself before confiding in anyone else, particularly her husband, and risk making a fool of herself.

James, she told herself, was beginning to mellow a shade. Ever since she had asserted herself that evening, he appeared to have changed, almost imperceptibly, for the better. But how ironic that it should have taken such a horrific sequence of events to effect such a change.

A contemplative silence was broken by the sound of raised voices, footsteps and an agitated tap on the door. James was about to call out a brisk 'Enter!' when Mr Crompton, looking unnaturally flustered, turned the door handle and was almost knocked off his feet by a skinny, dishevelled, unshaven man in a tattered suit and torn overcoat.

James and Charlotte opened their mouths in amazement, but no sound came out, as he sank to his knees in front of her.

'Oh Charlotte!' he cried out.

'Who on earth are you?' She recoiled in horror.

'Your brother Edward. Surely my own sister recognises me?'

James looked at her blankly and at him in fury, while Crompton stood by the door, looking on in an agony of indecision. He glanced at James, who mouthed 'Stay' at him as he nodded.

'What do you mean, your sister? I've never seen you before in my life.' Her astonishment had given way to anger, but she knew she owed it to them to keep calm.

The visitor rose to his feet, a little unsteadily. The overpowering stench of his unwashed, damp clothes, and spirits on his breath, assailed their nostrils, but they said nothing as he made his way towards a chair and half-sat, half-collapsed on it, putting his right arm over the back for support as he faced her.

'I'm your brother Edward, like I told you. You must remember me.' His slurred voice had a whining, peevish quality which irritated them almost as much as his unkempt appearance.

'I had one brother, and he is dead.'

'You mean George, our elder brother.'

She decided it would be safer to humour him for the present. 'Who sent you here, and how did you find me?'

'*They* told me where you lived. I've been abroad.'

Her patience, she knew, would not last much longer. 'Perhaps you would like to start at the beginning.'

'I went to sea when I was young, didn't I. Stowed away to Africa, looking for a job, and didn't like the place. No work there. I came back on board ship to England. To find my family.'

James was tempted to intervene, but a look from Charlotte deterred him. She felt they might as well test him on whatever family knowledge he might have, or claimed to. Where he had acquired it, they might never know.

'So where are the rest of the family?' She tried to sound bright and welcoming.

'I don't know. Came to ask you, didn't I. If I can't ask my own sister –'

'Did you find our mother?'

'So now you admit it.' Despite the faint note of triumph, he was having increasing trouble in articulating the words. '*Our* mother.'

'Yes, but I said, did you find her?'

Her looked blankly, staring in her direction with vacant eyes. James decided they had wasted enough time.

'I don't know what your real name is,' he growled, advancing towards the man, 'but it is quite obvious that somebody has put you up to this ridiculous little charade. My wife Charlotte only had one brother, and you are not him. You heard her when she told you that her brother is no longer alive. Would you like to tell us exactly who you are, and what you are doing here, before we send you back to go and crawl under the stone where you evidently belong?'

Even Charlotte was startled at his angry sarcasm, merited though it may be. Crompton looked on impassively, well trained in the art of showing surprise as little as possible.

'How did you find my address?'

'I knew where you lived.'

She was evidently not going to get a coherent answer to that one. 'Very well,' she sighed, 'where did you live before you went to search for work in Africa?'

He stared at her as if he had not heard, and James could contain himself no longer. Pointing at the door, he glared at the man and hissed, 'Out!' The man did not move and James advanced on him, his finger still pointing. 'Get out of my house before I call the police.'

The man staggered to his feet as Crompton walked cautiously towards him, he and James gently edging him towards the door and cutting off his line of retreat elsewhere, so he had no choice but to go out and towards the front door. As they opened it, they saw a policeman on the pavement standing near the bottom of the steps. At the sight of them he nodded grimly.

'Evening, Mr Waters. I see our friend has paid you a visit.'

James looked at him, startled, but the policeman continued, 'We've had our eye on him for a while.'

'On account of what?'

'He's been acting rather strangely. Looking up at houses in, shall we say, a suspicious manner.' And when we saw him heading along this street, we decided to follow him.'

Charlotte had come to the door by this time, watching in astonishment as the constable took their uninvited guest by the collar and looked round for a cab.

'If you'll excuse me madam, sir. I'd better take him back to the cells so he can cool his heels for a bit, and I'll be back with you presently for a statement.'

Charlotte and James stood watching until they were out of sight, before returning indoors.

'Thank goodness for that!' she commented as they closed the door.

James shook his head, muttering darkly.

'They've had their eye on him for some time, the man said. There's more to it than one isolated case of acting strangely. I don't like this one bit, Charlotte.'

Later that evening the policeman returned for full statements from James, Charlotte and Crompton.

'There is not a lot I can say at the moment,' he told them apologetically when they had finished. 'All I can mention at this moment is that we have been trailing him for a matter of weeks, and we have our own theory as to who or what he might be.'

'Don't tell us,' James muttered, more tired at the end of a long day than he cared to admit. 'Something to do with being a German agent?'

The policeman looked at him quizzically. 'As it happens, Mr Waters, you may not be that wide of the mark. Would you mind telling me what makes you say that?'

Between them James and Charlotte outlined the events surrounding George's death, and what had followed. Charlotte added the sum total of her recent knowledge, explaining as much for her husband's benefit as for that of the policeman.

'What I don't understand,' James concluded, 'is why he should have presented such a sorry figure. You would have thought that anybody involved with such sensitive work would have had the sense to make himself more presentable. Better dressed, and more well spoken than that specimen. But then that may be part of the disguise.' He gave a mirthless laugh. 'Not that I've had any experience of such types.'

The policeman nodded. 'Well, it does fit in with what we have so far. Some of this is entirely surmise on my part, but we did think he was being used as a catspaw, and what you've just said points us further in that direction. I thought it was too much of a coincidence not to have some bearing on those deaths in Devon.' Getting to his feet, he thanked them for their time and promised to keep in touch.

As Maud cycled along the road to Little Tor Cottage, wrapped up warmly against the chill November wind and watching carefully for any icy patches which were a legacy of the night's bitter frost, her eyes scanned the view as she contemplated the changes of the last few weeks since her previous journey that way. The wind-buffeted beech trees, which had been the most prominent feature of these hedges ever since she could remember, had then been in full leaf, just starting to turn from green and yellow to brown and gold. Now their branches and trunks were almost bare, the leaves forming a wet, muddy carpet of sorts along the hedge. A few yellow flowers dotting the gorse bushes were the only light colour to be seen. Even the sky looked dark and threatening. Just across the hills on her left, a metallic grey expanse of cloud suggested that more heavy rain was on the way.

In her coat pocket was a letter from Paul Jenkins describing his last meeting with Charlotte, and also the strange turn of events concerning Sophie Clark. Thankfully Sophie was now much better, and had left London to convalesce in a nursing home on the coast of Kent. The doctors were satisfied that there would be no permanent injury to her throat, and she was expected to make a full physical recovery by Christmas. She had had a lucky escape, but was still in too fragile a state to talk about the events which had precipitated her suicide bid.

'This is extraordinary,' Eleanor remarked, when she had read the letter. 'If my husband was here now, he would agree with me. He'd have to.'

Maud looked questioningly at her, but Eleanor read her expression and spared her the need to ask further.

'We had a bit of an argument about it, I'm afraid. All rather stupid, and I suppose neither of us was to blame. Or maybe both of us were just as much as each other, if you like. He told me I ought to mind my own business and leave everything to Scotland Yard and the police. I told him that if I did, then we'd be waiting until kingdom come. I know it sounds a trifle impatient of me, but I do think I had a perfect right to say so. After all, it was my father who paid the price for being in the wrong place at the wrong time.'

Maud felt guilty for intruding, albeit unintentionally, on such a private issue. 'I'm sorry.'

'Oh, please stop apologising. Absolutely no need. I'm still shocked about it, but all the grieving in the world isn't going to put things right or bring him back, is it? But I said I was going to stay at the cottage for a few days to see if anything else comes to light. It's going to eventually, but – well, I shan't stay here longer than I have to. Edward had to go back to attend to business at home, and whatever happens, I promised I'd be back there by mid-December.' She shuddered as she looked around her. 'One thing I can say for certain, I'm not going to spend Christmas here.'

'Wouldn't be much fun on your own,' said Maud, more from a desire to fill the space than anything else.

'It certainly wouldn't. The little ones have a governess, but I don't want to be away from them for too long. You don't need me to tell you that Christmas is a very special time of year, particularly if you have children. And who knows, we should get to the bottom of this soon. Edward has spoken to an agent with a view to selling this place. But if there's any more high-powered investigation to be done, I imagine that will hold things up on the legal side.'

'Do you think it will be difficult to sell?'

Eleanor sighed deeply and looked at Maud. 'You probably know more about the state of the market than I do. After all, you've lived in this part of the country all your life, haven't you?'

'Yes. But I don't know anything about – about business, and all that.'

'Of course not. Silly me. But there are so many factors we've got to take into account. What the state of the agricultural market is like. How farms are selling at present, or not. Whether the general uncertainty about matters in Europe is making people reluctant to purchase. And whether anyone is prepared to buy a place where the previous owner has been murdered on the doorstep. I'm not sure I would, frankly. Would you?'

She shut her eyes, as if to blink back tears. 'It's not as if Edward and I are in desperate straits. We don't really need to sell at once for the sake of it. But just look at the place, and think of all the land attached to it. The farm is in good heart, as far as we know. But if it's left to go to seed, and the cottage itself stands empty for too long, it's going to go to rack and ruin, isn't it? Then nobody's going to want to live in it, unless they can buy it at well below the market price, and spend a king's ransom doing it up. So there's no point at all in us holding on to it for sentimental reasons. Edward is planning to go and talk to a couple of agents, and we can take it from there.'

They sat in silence.

'Well, I've talked enough, haven't I? Thanks for coming to see me, Maud. I'll be here for another week or ten days, I would think. And I hope to goodness something else comes to light during that time.'

As she went to see Maud out of the front door, they listened to the sound of rain on the roof.

'Another shower. Did you walk, Maud?'

'No, I came on my bicycle.'

'Did you come from the Strongs' farm, or from home?'

'My own home. Walking's a bit too far in this weather. It's a good three or four miles.'

Eleanor shivered and rubbed her hands.

'Are you sure you wouldn't like to stay to lunch? Or at least wait until this shower's over?'

Maud thought for a moment, then shook her head.

'Thank you, but I really ought to be getting back.'

'Very well. Mind how you go, though. This rain after last night's frost could make the roads pretty treacherous. I think we're heading for a cold snap, and if it wasn't raining, after those clouds earlier on, I'd swear that snow was on the way.'

Chapter 16

In a corner of the bar at the New Imperial Hotel overlooking Plymouth Hoe, Marianne Andrewitz sipped from a cup of coffee and stared blankly at the table in front of her while she took mental stock of the last thirty years or so. At the age of forty-nine, she felt the time had long since come when she was entitled to do exactly as she liked.

Two weeks before her twenty-first birthday, as Marianne Bennett, she had married the handsome young Otto Andrewitz. Her father had been an attaché at the British Embassy in Berlin, and she had been there much of the time with her parents. A reception one evening during the military manoeuvres led to an introduction to the soldier who not only had good looks but also a bright military career ahead of him. Though she barely knew him, her father thought this looked too good a match to turn down, and despite her mother's reservations, within weeks they were betrothed to be married. As a sheltered young girl she was hardly in a position to know what she was letting herself in for.

What a grey dismal life it had been! Too late the innocent English rose had found out that the lot of a German army wife meant absolutely no right to a life, let alone a mind, of her own. The occasional visits to her family in England were over all too soon. For a cruelly brief period she had known happiness when giving birth to a daughter, Sylvia, after fourteen months of marriage. Nevertheless the experience left her incapacitated in bed for several weeks, followed by a major operation which left her with no chance of bearing any further children. Otto made it clear that any daughter, no matter how pretty, was a disappointment. When little Sylvia caught diphtheria and died at the age of three, he seemed quite unaffected. With plenty of ladies of the night close enough to the barracks at Bonn, it was not surprising. An unpleasant bout of illness and extended sick leave from military duties for him – venereal in origin, she suspected, judging by furtive hints from their physician,

Dr Erhardt – had left him temporarily weakened and with little inclination to argue when one of her cousins offered them accommodation in a farmhouse in Dartmoor. He had been reluctant to go, but motivated more by pity for her than by concern for him, Dr Erhardt told them that it would be in his best interests to accept the offer.

By the time they had been married for twenty years, Otto no longer bothered to conceal his infidelities from the wife with whom he had not slept with for a long time, while she had no desire to share a bed with him ever again. For the sake of appearances they still accompanied each other to England. Once there, he divided his time between London and Dartmoor, while she spent more and more time with her unconventional cousin Thea in Oxfordshire. A lifelong spinster and unashamed liberal who made no secret of her support for votes for all women at the age of twenty-one and Irish independence, she told her friends that she would give anything to be ten years younger so she could join Emmeline and Christabel Pankhurst and their followers in the suffragette campaign. She had a similarly unbecoming taste for indelicate stories and practical jokes, and woe betide any guest in the same house party as her who did not think to inspect their sheets for an apple pie bed last thing at night. At the same time she was unfailingly generous to anybody worse off than her, and every Christmas she used to provide the local church with a well-stocked hamper to be shared out among the poorest of the parish. Dear Thea – the court jester with a heart of gold.

A skilled watercolour painter who had sometimes exhibited at the Royal Academy, Thea's influence and teaching skills gave Marianne a new interest in life. Turning her hand to drawings and paintings of flowers and animals, Marianne had sold a few pictures herself. As Otto paid her a regular allowance she hardly needed the money, but it gave her a new feeling of confidence which she had not known since she was a young girl. Thoughts of divorce crossed her mind, but she could hardly be bothered. If Otto can go his own sweet way, she told herself, I can go mine. Why waste time dragging each other through the courts in order to regularise a state of affairs which in effect had existed for some time?

So it was that this particular week in November 1913 found her and Thea staying in Plymouth for a few days. Thea had become interested in marine painting and had decided to execute a series of studies of sea and coastal scenes around the south Devon coast. If the weather remained satisfactory, they might take an excursion out to Dartmoor, where the rugged landscape would also no doubt provide inspiration for further pictures.

Then on their second night at the hotel, Thea had had a visit from Joe Hayes, a distant cousin of hers stationed at the barracks in Devonport, to say he had heard rumours that Otto was in the south Devon area. Somebody had seen him around Buckfastleigh or Ashburton. Marianne had not had sight of him herself for nearly three years, and while the maintenance was still being paid into her bank account every quarter as per his written agreement, mild curiosity suggested to her that she ought to make further enquiries. She no longer really cared what he was doing, but some sixth sense told her that she might as well find out. After all, if differences between Britain and Germany did reach the point of no return, she might find it necessary to take legal advice to safeguard her position in order to avoid being classified as a German citizen, an alien, or something even more unpleasant. Should war break out, nothing would give her greater pleasure than to sever her last remaining ties with Germany, but it would be foolish of her to let herself be taken unprepared.

On discussing plans for the next few days with her cousin at lunch later that day, they pored over Thea's ordnance survey map of the area. Always the more adventurous one, Thea suggested they think about staying at a guest house or some similar accommodation in one of the towns on the borders of the moor so they would be in a position to go round making house-to-house enquiries.

'Honestly, Thea, you must be off your head,' Marianne told her over afternoon tea. 'It's sheer fantasy.'

'You always were an old stick-in-the-mud, Marianne,' Thea chided. 'Look at it like this. Time is on our side, we have absolutely no obligations to anybody else. And what have we got to lose?'

Marianne was lost for an answer.

'See what I mean? Just think of it. We will be a couple of eccentric middle-aged ladies, looking for a man in one of the more remote rural regions of southern England. It could be fun.

154

Call it a treasure hunt.'

'It won't be a treasure hunt if I find that stupid man.' Marianne pulled a face and Thea almost choked on her muffins with laughter.

'Darling, that is no way to talk about your husband. After what he's put you through, you should be able to come up with something far more indelicate than that. And even if we don't find the beast, we will probably find enough scenery for plenty more pictures. I simply must have something new to put in the local exhibition next year.'

'I thought you were planning to do some travel abroad then.'

'That was my first idea. I had planned to go round Europe, but if the situation looks difficult I decided I might go to America instead. After all, I'm sure I can afford it, and I want to see something of the place before I'm too old to enjoy it. But I may put it off for a year or two. That society exhibition at home is going to be the largest they've had for some time, and I don't want to miss that. So I will look for inspiration in the scenery and mists of Dartmoor, or somewhere else on the British mainland, and you will search for your unlamented husband.'

While her head tried to tell her otherwise, her heart and her cousin's promptings won the day. By the time they retired to bed that night, Marianne had agreed that they would cut short their stay at the hotel in Plymouth, take a train to Ashburton next day, and look for accommodation while they tried to find Otto. Of course, the fact that he had been seen – or might have been seen – in the area made the whole scheme look more ridiculous and far-fetched. But she had spent almost a lifetime being sensible, and it had got her nowhere. It was surely time to kick over the traces a little.

Late the following afternoon, Marianne and Thea were unpacking their cases in a small two-bedded room on the edge of Ashburton. Marianne had had to pinch herself several times that day to reassure herself that this was not some mad dream. Almost single-handedly, Thea had packed their things at the hotel in Plymouth that morning, booked them out of the hotel, hailed a cab to the railway station, bought them two one-way tickets to this remote small town almost in the middle of nowhere. She had made enquiries about accommodation and found them this little guest house run by an expressionless, dumpy woman – whose name she still had not caught properly – who seemed almost eighty years old and saw nothing unusual in two ladies asking for rooms and bringing their own luggage. True, that wooden mask had seemed to slip a little when Thea asked for one room instead of two, but on reassuring her that they were cousins, she shrugged and nodded her assent.

'So what is your plan of action?' Thea asked as she hung a coat up in the wardrobe.

'I hadn't really worked one out,' Marianne admitted a little glumly.

'Now, come on, dear. You mustn't forget that's one of the reasons why we're here. Leave it to Thea, who suggests that we do is go and have a look at this town tomorrow, and try making a few enquiries. Starting with the police. Maybe the staff at one or two of the inns. Find out if they have any news of your husband.' She sat down on the bed, suddenly convulsed with laughter. Marianne's puzzled expression seemed to provoke further paroxysms of mirth.

'It just occurred to me,' she said through her tears once she had regained her composure. 'What if I was to tell them that we had come here looking for a husband?'

Marianne pondered this gravely for a moment, before seeing the funny side of it herself.

'I suppose we are, aren't we. Looking for my husband.'

'Not that you really want to find him. You never know, you might bump into some handsome young Adonis of a strapping farmhand or a rat-catcher to sweep you off your feet, and you'll forget all about your wonderful Otto. Perhaps he will leap out from behind a remote barn, and the two of them will fight a duel to the death for your hand. One with a sword from Berlin, the other with a gleaming scythe for the corn. Or whatever they fight each other with here.' She chuckled wickedly. 'I wonder if they still fight duels in the countryside.'

Marianne tried not to smile. She had been feeling a little tense and short-tempered, wishing she had not allowed Thea to involve her in this unlikely venture, but she was beginning to shed one or two of her inhibitions. Besides, her cousin's sense of humour, far-fetched though it might be, was starting to prove infectious.

'They probably still have duels in the German army, for all I know. I suppose it's one way of relieving the world of a few fools.'

The next morning dawned unexpectedly bright and clear, if chilly, for November. Marianne and Thea ate a perfunctory breakfast, despite Mrs Towne's insistence – they had at last found out their hostess's name – that if they were going out exploring, then the least they could do was to make sure they did so on a full stomach, particularly at this time of year. By mid-morning they were looking in shop windows in the town as they made their way on foot to the police station, where they found Constable Fox on duty.

When Marianne introduced herself his eyes glinted.

'Can't say your name isn't unknown around these parts, ma'am,' he said, 'or should it be Countess?'

'Please don't stand on ceremony for my sake. The name Countess means nothing to me,' she almost whispered, adding for reassurance, 'we have been separated a very long time.'

'Then, ma'am, the truth of the matter is, my superior Sergeant Donald would be very pleased to make your acquaintance. He's gone out on his bike to see someone this morning, but I am expecting him back later on today. About lunchtime if everything works out.'

He disappeared briefly, to return with three cups of tea, and invited them to sit down while he summarised the chain of events from George Stephens' unexplained death, the appearance of her husband and his friend at Tor Cottage, the death of Dick Priestley, Eleanor Bridgman's appearance, and what little he knew of Maud's meeting with George's colleagues in London.

'A pretty tangle, you might say,' he concluded as he finished his tea. 'And I suppose this is all news to you ladies?'

Thea nodded, while Marianne looked mildly stunned, trying to take it all in. For a moment Fox wondered whether she had something to hide. The ones who seemed the most innocent, he had learned from experience, were sometimes those with the guilty secrets. Still waters run deep, and all that.

'Is there a chance you could come back later?' he asked. 'If I let you go away without seeing Sergeant Donald, he'd never speak to me again, but you won't want to hang around in here all morning until he gets back, will you?'

157

Thea looked at Marianne. 'Come on, let's go and explore the town.' Turning to Fox, she held out her hand to him, and promised they would return in due course.

'So that's not what you expected, is it?' Thea put her umbrella up as they stepped out on to the pavement to find that sunshine had suddenly given way to a cloudburst.

'I don't really know what to expect these days,' Marianne murmured. 'He hasn't bothered to keep in touch since I last saw him. The money is still coming through regularly, so I know he's alive, and frankly that's all that really concerns me at present. He could be the other end of the world for all I know – or care.'

'When did you last see him?'

'It was in the spring of 1910. Mother was very ill with preumonia, you remember, and after I'd visited her in the nursing home at Guildford, she told me I ought to make one last effort to see if I could patch things up with him. I thought at the time it was rather strange, as she was the one who had always been so unenthusiastic about our marriage in the first place. Father pushed me into it, more or less.'

'Maybe she saw it as a sacred trust to your father's memory.'

'I rather thought the same myself. It was silly really, because Otto and I had long since gone past the point of no return. But I'd never had the heart to tell her everything, and now she was lying ill in bed, obviously not going to recover, it would have broken her heart if I'd decided to tell her about it then. So, like an obedient daughter, I got in touch with him and we arranged to meet for dinner one evening at a restaurant in Mayfair.'

'And it didn't go too well, did it?' Thea knew only vaguely of the outcome, but had yet to hear the full story.

'It was an absolute disaster. If it hadn't been for the thought of mother, I would never have considered it. Or else I'd have contacted the restaurant and asked them to tell him I couldn't be there after all. Maybe I should have, but I simply couldn't go back on my word after promising her. So we had drinks and he ordered the meal, and I told him we ought to think about going back to Germany and starting all over again. He just laughed at me and started telling me about his latest amorous conquests.'

Thea could not suppress a mirthless smile. 'From what I've heard about Otto, that sounds a little too dignified for him.'

'You're right.' Marianne shook her head. 'Yes, I suppose that's not really the way to put it. Those little tarts in Berlin had their price, and he'd sleep with any of them for the going rate. But after a while I had had enough of his foul-mouthed reminiscences, so I just got up, collected my coat, asked for a cab, and went back to my hotel.'

'Glad you came to your senses. And then you took the train back to Banbury and to me. I could see you were pretty upset at the time, and I didn't want to question you before you wanted to talk.'

Marianne grimaced. Time, as everybody had told her, had been a great healer, and it no longer stirred her emotions to recall what had happened. Now she could look at the end of her marriage in a detached, even faintly humorous light. 'It could have been worse, Thea. Much worse. What if he had turned round and said yes, let's make another go of it, after all?' She shook her head again, as if to try and rid herself of the memory of it. 'I was an absolute fool to risk it. When I was there in the early days, I used to cross off the days in my diary until I could escape from that God-forsaken place. If he'd played the penitent husband three years ago and I'd agreed to give him another chance in spite of everything he'd gone and done, another six months and they would have had to put me in an asylum. Not that I'd notice much difference, except that the food would be even worse.'

Thea grinned as a sudden thought struck her. 'Did you finish your food before you left the restaurant?'

'No, I don't think I did. Why do you ask?'

'You said you were a fool, Marianne, and you were! Really, you could have made the most magnificent exit. If it had been me, I'd have picked up my plate, stood over him and had great pleasure in pouring the uneaten remains all over his horrible head.'

The mental picture of her self-important Otto seated at a table in public with filets de boeuf, assorted vegetables and gravy running down his face and neck and under his collar was too much for her. Thea was delighted to see her cousin's slightly careworn features give themselves up to unrestrained mirth, the first time she had seen her really laugh for a long time. Soon both of them were helpless.

Once they had regained their composure and dried their

tears, they pondered their next move. Ashburton looked singularly uninviting in the cold and wet, and after spending the best part of an hour at a tea shop, staring at the street from the comfort of a table and two chairs, they retraced their steps along pavements and puddles back to the police station, to find Sergeant Donald waiting for them.

'I heard from my colleague that you were on your way.' He held out his hand to each of them in turn. 'We've just been reopening an old case that we thought was long since closed. Still, that needn't concern us here and now.'

Over the next twenty minutes the situation gradually began to fall into shape for both Donald and Marianne. He built up a firm picture of a German army wife left by her husband who evidently went his own sweet way, while she really wondered if he had been an accessory to murder. When he suggested a visit either to Eleanor Bridgman or to Roger and Mary Strong, she needed no prompting.

'If all three of us are going,' he said, 'I think we can find ourselves some transport.'

'I needn't come,' Thea volunteered. 'Don't worry about me. I can always go out sketching.'

'In this weather? And how will you get back?' Marianne demanded. 'No, you'd better come with us. You can take your pad and pencils out tomorrow, if you must.'

Five minutes later Donald returned, having procured the services of a workshop owner at the end of the road who would be prepared to drive them to Great Tor Cottage and back to Ashburton again, for a small consideration. He decided to see the Strongs first, as he wanted to sound them out on the case on which he had been working that morning. He felt mildly guilty about invading them unannounced with two strangers in tow, and made a mental note to bring them some kind of present another time, as a token of goodwill.

Mary Strong was her usual accommodating self. Donald, Marianne and Thea had barely arrived in her kitchen, all wondering whether they weren't trespassing on her hospitality, but she brushed their objections aside as she told them to find themselves a chair each and put the kettle on for tea. A large dish of scones, generous pots of jam and butter followed onto the

160

middle of the table, and in no time they were all chatting like old friends. Thea felt she was beginning to fall in love with Devon, its unique landscape and the easy-going character of the people who lived there. She wondered whether settling in the county for a year or two to paint might not be a better alternative to travelling overseas, particularly if the international situation continued to look so threatening.

'It is a surprise to be meetin' 'ee after all this time, Marianne,' Mary said between mouthfuls, once they had exchanged news and views. 'Some relation to poor ol' Dick, they say?'

'Not exactly. My father Isaac was an old army friend of his, you see. They'd been at Sandhurst together and stayed in touch, so after that Dick was always Uncle Dick to my brothers and sisters and myself. Only an honorary uncle, I'm afraid. But as a result, everyone thought we were cousins or something.'

'There's just one thing I wanted to ask you about, Mary,' Donald said as she poured them second cups of tea. 'Do you remember that business of Grenville Bridgman?'

She put down the teapot and concentrated for a moment. A gleam came into her eyes. 'Vaguely, like. Would this be Eleanor's mysterious brother-in-law?'

'That's the one. After all this time, it seems she's never met him. You would think that Edward might have had some opportunity of introducing them. Anyway, someone at Exeter has just reopened the file on that business about twenty years ago. You remember he was the one we wanted for questioning in connection with the armed robbery cases in Plymouth and Exeter, and the Howells murder case, that jeweller and his wife.'

'Rings a bell, Sergeant, now 'ee mention it. Nasty business.' She shuddered at the memory. 'Never caught 'im, did they?'

'No, that's right. We never managed to trace the wife, but a man's body was washed up in the river Exe a little later. We thought it might have been Mr Howells, but he was so badly decomposed that it was impossible to identify him. He was about the same height, but that was all we had to go on. They closed the case after that, but now Exeter are looking at it again.' Donald dropped his voice. 'It seems they think there may be some connection with George Stephens.'

Mary turned round to face him. 'What connection could there be?'

161

Donald averted her gaze. 'We're keeping an open mind on it. One of the many things I'm not allowed to say too much about at present, I'm afraid. But I think we may get some interesting developments about it soon.'

'None of us ever believed Grenville were drowned. We all think 'ee made 'is getaway. Anyone asked Eleanor?'

'I intend to shortly.'

'Well, I wouldn't leave it too long if I were you, Sergeant. She's packin' 'er things an' goin' back to Southampton soon, or so they say.'

Chapter 17

Charlotte pushed her breakfast plates aside. Any appetite she might have had on waking up that morning had rapidly been dispelled by one item in the morning post. Listlessly she picked up her unsigned, undated letter and read it for the third time. Her initial feeling of shock on seeing it at first had now given way to disbelief. The scrawled handwriting on the envelope had been unfamiliar, but her surprise as she looked at her name and address on the front were nothing to what she felt as she opened it.

Dear Mrs Waters,

It has come to my notice that you have a small quantity of jewellery which you inherited from your late mother Mrs Ethel Stephens a few weeks ago. I wish to pass on my sincere condolences on your loss, and at the same time I have to advise you that I have been personally entrusted with the duty of inspecting these pieces. You must understand that I am not permitted to divulge my reasons at this stage. Will you be so good as to arrange to come and meet me at the Duke of Cumberland Hotel, Park Lane, at 7.00 on the evening of 2nd December next, bringing these items. If this is not convenient, you will kindly write to Mr Wadsworth-Johns, c/o The Hotel, and advise him. I will then contact you with a view to arranging a further date as soon as possible.

Should you wish your husband, James Waters, Esq., M.P. to accompany you, there will be no objection. Nonetheless I am sure you must know it will not be in your personal interests, or those of your husband, to ignore this command.

You will bring this letter to the hotel with you on your arrival.

'Oh, this is preposterous!' James exploded when he read the letter on his return to the house that evening. 'Some kind of blackmail threat against us? Some sick fraudster's idea of a joke? Entrusted with the duty of inspecting your mother's jewellery? I've a good mind to go straight round to the police and show them this filthy piece of paper!'

Charlotte looked at him apprehensively. 'Do you really think that would be safe?'

'Safe? For heaven's sake, Charlotte. We still haven't had a satisfactory explanation from anyone yet concerning that tramp who called himself your brother bursting in on us the other evening, beyond what that policeman told us what he thought but couldn't prove. Now, either there's some connection between that and this damned piece of nonsense, or else I'm a Chinaman. It's increasingly obvious that some madman is on our trail. Some infernal anarchist, after people in public life, I suppose. It's been happening in France, and now the contagion seems to be spreading. Why on earth they should be after me, as a very lowly member of Parliament, I'm hanged if I know. But...'

'Well, you are a junior minister.'

'Yes, but why oh why should they bother with someone of my rank, when there are plenty of senior ministers of far more importance to their twisted little devices? Unless it's got something to do with your brother and what's been going on in Devon.'

'You really think that's got something to do with it?'

'What other possible explanation can there be? Ever since poor George died, well –' He paused, looking at the table, deep in thought. While realising that he had not been as sympathetic as he ought, he resented the way in which events appeared to be spiralling out of control. And to be confronted with a letter which looked like something out of a cheap adventure story... 'Anyway, this nonsense has got to be nipped in the bud.'

'If you think we can trust them –'

'Trust who?' He sighed deeply. 'Charlotte, this is the work of some utter crackpot who has got to be caught! And the sooner the better.'

'Yes, James. But it's some crackpot who has managed to find out our address, and who appears to know that Mama left me a few trinkets and things. And if this letter is to be believed, he's going to stop at nothing to get his hands on them. If it's one person, which of course we're not to know. There might be a gang – it could be several of them, for all we know.'

'And if so, you're prepared to let them have your things?'

'If it's a choice of giving away a few jewels and things, and having somebody watching us all the time, I think I know which I would choose.' She shrugged sadly. 'They are rather lovely pieces, and they were just about all Mama had left. They're of sentimental value, but they're only material objects. If the price to pay for keeping them is to be constantly under threat, so be it.'

James pondered this for a moment.

'All right,' he said at last, his voice betraying more reluctance than he intended. 'I accept that. We will keep this appointment, or at least see if there is anything to it. I think it sounds like some preposterous adventure, or even a sick practical joke, but if that's the way you want it, we might as well. But I think we might arrange to have reinforcements nearby, in case of anything getting out of hand.'

'Reinforcements? Really, James, we're hardly talking about another siege of Sidney Street. What do you want – an entire regiment armed with rifles stationed along the pavement?'

'Don't be so ridiculous, Charlotte!' He shook his head. 'I don't mean anything of the kind. Now I'm sorry, but we are certainly not going into this alone. We'll talk about it tomorrow.'

Charlotte made a mental note to write to Paul Jenkins, asking him to contact Maud Watts or anybody in Devon he thought fit. Puzzled but ready to oblige, he duly wrote to Maud on receiving her letter. Maud informed Eleanor, whose suspicions were hardening by the day, and contacted Marianne. On 1 December a party consisting of Eleanor, Maud, Marianne and Thea boarded the train at Ashburton for Paddington, planning to look for hotel accommodation in the capital on arrival and meet Paul on the following morning.

Soon after six o'clock on the evening of 2 December they appeared in a procession. Charlotte and James walked into the hotel first, and headed for the bar. Eleanor, Maud, Marianne and Thea followed a moment later, feeling rather self-conscious as they walked in and joined Charlotte and James at their table, all ordering drinks. Clutching a bag containing two brooches, a necklace and two sets of earrings in her handbag, Charlotte shivered inwardly, praying that she and James were doing the right thing by not ignoring the letter. But with an implicit threat like that, she knew they could hardly have disregarded it.

After making a certain amount of awkward small-talk in order to pass the time, while keeping an eye on the clock as the hands moved towards seven o'clock, James and Charlotte walked out to the reception area. She passed her husband the letter, who glanced at it grimly for one last time before handing it to the porter on the desk. After frowning at it, the porter looked at them.

'If you will wait a moment, sir, madam, we will find someone to escort you to the room.'

Presently an attendant appeared.

'Mr and Mrs Waters. Would you step this way, please?'

'Just a minute.' Charlotte searched quickly in her bag and gave a mock expression of dismay. 'I think I dropped something in the entrance.' Before the attendant could offer to help, she walked away smartly and looked in at the bar. The others had been watching out for this discreet signal and averted their gaze smartly before getting to their feet and trying to look as natural as possible as they followed each other out.

The attendant led Charlotte and James along the corridor on the ground floor to a room, the others following at a discreet distance, careful not to attract attention. Once he had knocked and opened the door he withdrew.

With James at her side, Charlotte looked at the occupant of the room standing self-importantly in front of the table, and showed him the letter, taking care to hold it carefully in order to prevent him from snatching it away.

'Good evening, Mrs Waters, Mr Waters. Count Otto von Andrewitz, of the 1st Potsdam Grenadiers.' He gave a small stiff bow. Charlotte was relieved that he did not proffer his hand to be shaken.

'I was sorry to hear of the death of your mother.' She nodded equally stiffly, silently muttering an expression of gratitude which she felt was out of place. 'And now we will proceed to business. Let us not waste time. I understand you have brought something to show me.' He looked at the bag and she put her hand inside, putting the pieces carefully on one side of the table, ensuring that she and James were standing closer to it than he was.

'May I take a look?' Before they could stop him, he had picked up the brooches and was inspecting them carefully through his monocle. He did the same with the necklace and ear-rings, before putting them down and producing a small envelope from which he produced a couple of small pieces of paper. Reading them through carefully, he frowned and put them on the table.

'As I thought, these pieces were the property of His Imperial Majesty Kaiser Wilhelm the Second,' he announced. 'If you wish to check these documents yourselves, you will see that they are receipts from Herr Hans Friedrich von Scheider, court jewellers at Berlin to His Majesty. The descriptions and marks match these items perfectly. Now it may well be that he has no further use for them after all this time. But I must respectfully insist that you allow me take them back to Germany for safe keeping pending an investigation by His Majesty's attendants.'

He moved his hand half-heartedly towards the items, but James was too quick for him and grabbed his arm. Andrewitz swore under his breath, but Charlotte took his other arm with a strength which she had never known she possessed. At once the door opened and the others walked in.

'Grenville!' Eleanor could hardly believe her eyes. Though she had never met him before, soon after their wedding Edward had shown her photographs of him as a young man. During the last few days her suspicions had hardened. He was a little shorter than his brother, and though years of self-indulgence had made him fat and coarsened his features, there was no mistaking his identity.

Meanwhile Maud, Marianne and Thea had marched smartly to the table and scooped the jewels to safety while their host was struggling and cursing. When he saw he was beaten, he stood stiffly to attention, then shook his finger at James.

'You have not heard the last of this, Mr Waters!'

'I think we have,' James smiled grimly. 'If His Imperial Majesty wishes to have these pieces back, he can sue us through the courts. We all know that our crowned cousins throughout England and Europe are always giving away trinkets, jewels, cigarette cases, and the like. He's probably forgotten all about them, and he's hardly going to want these back, even if they are his. Or should I say, were his, as they aren't any more. Count

Andrewitz, I put it to you that you simply want to acquire them yourself. Perhaps you are hoping to sell them in Berlin in order to pay off some of your gambling debts.'

The Count knew when he was beaten. He glared, but said nothing.

'And another little thing,' James continued, warming to his theme but unable to contain his sarcasm. 'You know as well as the rest of us that, if the Emperor did try to pursue this case through the courts, or get one of his toadies to do his dirty work for him, he would make himself look a bigger fool by doing so than he already has done over the years. Impossible as that may seem.'

Marianne stepped forward.

'I can't pretend I'm glad to see you again, Otto,' she said coldly. 'Or should it be Grenville? Not that it matters in the slightest, as I expect this will be the very last time.'

Now it was Eleanor's turn. While they were travelling to Paddington on the train she felt she knew the awful truth, but refrained from saying so as there was a faint possibility she was wrong. The sight of the man put her mind at rest.

'Grenville Bridgman, I believe?'

He averted his eyes from her gaze with an expression of guilt.

'You do not know me, though maybe you have heard about me. I am your sister-in-law Eleanor, and at long last we have met face to face. I think my husband will be very interested to know where his brother is, especially after that postcard you sent him a few weeks ago.' She removed an envelope from her coat and took out the card which she had retrieved from the floor of the farm that day when Edward's back was turned. 'What a pity he couldn't have been here with us tonight. But naturally we will make sure he knows all about it.'

Maud coughed nervously, then cleared her throat. 'Now we're here,' she said coldly, 'would you like to tell us what you know about George Stephens, and Dick Priestley?'

He looked at her with a momentary gesture of defiance, then sighed.

'The time has come for you to hear it all.' He dropped the German accent, and Eleanor realised that his proper English voice was remarkably like that of his brother. Had she closed her eyes, it would have been hard for her to tell which of them was speaking. 'I had to leave England in rather a hurry. There was the little matter of an altercation with a jeweller and his wife on the premises of their shop in Plymouth. A young accomplice of the town and I were involved in a burglary which went wrong. The man and his wife were in the storeroom at the time, but they caught us and raised the alarm, as a result of which the boy I was with lost his nerve and fired on the couple. He didn't mean to kill them, I'm sure, but once he had, all I could do was shoot him myself and dispose of the three bodies. I found some empty sacks in a room at the back of the shop, put them inside, and under cover of darkness I took them down to the waterfront where I threw them over the jetty. There was a strong gale that night, so in those conditions nobody would have heard anything. Then I left by train for Harwich and took a ferry to Europe, went to Prussia, changed my name, took German citizenship, and joined the army. As a young subaltern I met Miss Marianne Bennett, who is with us tonight. She was with her parents, in Berlin. We fell in love, courted, and were married.'

He glanced at Marianne, who returned his gaze with a look of icy contempt. 'When I was convalescing from illness, the doctor recommended a complete change of air, and I used to go and stay with Mr Priestley sometimes at his cottage. We met George Stephens when he came to stay on Dartmoor at Stead Farm, and he used to come and see us sometimes. We had the impression that he was quite interested in Germany, and thought that if this was the case, he might be prevailed upon to help with passing us certain military secrets from England. He was a pleasant young man, and we liked him, but he did not seem committed to the aims of the Fatherland, and our efforts did not bear fruit.'

'And what happened to him?' Maud demanded angrily.

'I had been watching his movements between London and Devon carefully for a while. Staying with my friend Count Linevitch at Little Tor Cottage gave me ample opportunity to do so, and we were well prepared for his journey to Devon in July. In the spring, the Kaiser had told me that in the interests of the Fatherland, it was imperative that we captured the young man and brought him back to Berlin. Under house arrest, you might call it, so that we could keep him under control. Though he did not say so directly in such cold-blooded terms, I took it on myself to infer from the tone of his words that as a last resort it might be necessary to eliminate him if that was not possible. His Imperial Majesty would have been displeased by such a drastic outcome, but it was a risk I was prepared to take. Under the circumstances Mr Stephens could not be left a free man in England indefinitely.

'On several previous occasions I had tried to persuade him to come back to Berlin, where we would have given him an adequate pension and found him fitting employment at court, at the legation, or anywhere he liked. All we would ask of him was that he behaved himself and did not cause any trouble. His knowledge of England would have been quite an asset, as you can imagine. But he refused, so Count Linevitch and I realised we would have to capture him. We thought that perhaps he would have realised that further resistance was useless, and with luck this time he would come quietly. If not, it might be necessary for him to die in the interests of the German Empire.'

Charlotte was shaking her head silently in disbelief.

'I know what you are thinking, Mrs Waters. It sounds cruel, but many a young soldier throughout Europe has died for less, in the service of his country. We knew that Mr Stephens often used to come to Devon by train from Paddington, and travel on to Holne on a wagonette. This time we managed to find out which train he was taking, and on which day in July, so we were ready to wait for him as he was walking back to Stead Farm. When we came across him he was sitting down, presumably resting and looking at the landscape. We did our utmost to persuade him to come with us, but he refused. There was a struggle, he tried to hit us, but as we outnumbered him, resistance on his part was to no avail. He lost his footing, tripped and fell, and struck his head on the road. If it is any consolation, I am sure this was the action which resulted in a fatal brain haemorrhage, and not a blow to the head from one of us. So once we were satisfied that life was extinct, there was nothing to be done except for us to take his body and leave it by the rocks in the surroundings which he loved the most. I am not totally without sentiment, and it seemed to be a fitting resting place for him. Count Linevitch said that it would look as if he had had an accident – which, in a sense, he had.'

Details of earlier conversations and discoveries were coming back to her as he spoke. 'The police said they found a map of Kiel Harbour, or something of the sort, in his pockets. Do you know anything about that?'

'I put that there once I knew that life was extinct. A little touch, to add credence to the spy theory.'

Charlotte had been waiting for the right moment. From her bag she produced the battered passport which had been among George's possessions, and showed it to him with a flourish.

'You said he did not come to Berlin. I've never had a document like this myself, but it looks mighty like someone has altered it. In fact, if he never went abroad, there was no reason for him to have one in the first place. And I've showed it to other people, who all agree with me. Maybe you can explain that?'

'It was another of my little touches,' he admitted, somewhat crestfallen. 'I might have known that somebody would notice, but it was worth the effort on my part. These documents can be obtained from the right sources if necessary.'

'So you admit it is a forgery?'

'It is.'

'And those old train tickets, and the like?'

'They belonged to me. Again, just little details to lend credence to the case.'

'And what happened to your Count Linevitch?'

'He has gone back to Berlin. Your Sergeant Donald came to interview us at the Cottage one day during the summer, and we thought it would be prudent to leave as soon as possible. I have not heard anything from him since. But I stayed in Devon until after Mr Priestley came back – exactly where I don't think need concern you.'

'You presumably know, Count – or perhaps I should call you Mr Bridgman – that George was my brother,' said Charlotte, accepting with some irritation the fact that he had found out much more about her private and family life than she would have liked. She felt in her bag and produced a creased, dog-eared photograph which showed a woman and babe in arms. 'This is the only picture I have of him and my mother together. She always claimed that he was the son of your Kaiser, and she even inferred that I was also his daughter. As you evidently know more about us than we seem to ourselves, perhaps you would like to tell us what you know of my parentage, and that of my brother?'

'I think I can answer your questions, Mrs Waters. How old was your brother?'

'He was thirty-four when he died. He would have been thirty-five on the twentieth of January next.'

'His Majesty came to stay in England several times while he was still a young bachelor, and he was kind enough to take me into his confidence on the subject.' Removing another envelope, he took out two photographs and compared them with the one Charlotte had produced, then showed them to her. It was clear that the mother and child in each were the same.

'I think this proves the matter beyond the shadow of a doubt. His Majesty told me that he made the acquaintance of your mother on a visit to England in the early spring of 1878, when he was a youth of nineteen. They had – shall we say, for the sake of delicacy – a rendezvous, and as a result she gave birth to your brother. But for the usual reasons of state, he was obliged to look to the great families of Germany for a bride, and in 1881 he married the Princess Victoria Augusta of Schleswig-Holstein, Her Majesty the Kaiserin. So you can see that a marriage with your mother was never to be. Still, at least she did send a few photographs of herself and her son – your brother – to him through his adjutant. And he kept them, or at least he kept this one which he asked me to produce as evidence in the eventuality of a meeting such as this. So he must have treasured her memory all these years.'

Despite her mother's protestations as to the veracity of the matter, that the man whom Charlotte had always been convinced was her brother was in fact the German Emperor's son and her half-brother was for a moment too astonishing to contemplate. Nevertheless one other mystery had to be laid to rest.

'My mother always told me that she married Anthony Stephens, a railway engineer from Streatham, in May 1883, although she claimed she never had a marriage certificate. And she said I was born nearly two years later, in April 1885. I have always supposed that he was my father. As you seem to know more about my family than I do myself, can you reassure me as to this?'

'Though I cannot show you any evidence, I am sure you can rest secure in the knowledge that Anthony Stephens was indeed your father. And that you were the only child of the marriage, of course.'

'That brings me to another little matter.' She glanced at

James, who nodded grimly. 'A few days ago, a man came and burst in on Mr Waters and myself in our London house. He claimed to be my brother, and George's brother as well, and he told us his name was Edward. Maybe you can explain that as well?'

'Indeed I can. His name is Waldemar Hauptmann, and he is the nephew of a fellow officer in my regiment. He is half-English and can switch from a German accent to English, and vice versa, with the greatest of ease. In fact he had aspirations to go on stage and join the court theatre players, but we persuaded him he could do better for himself than that. Because of his abilities, he accompanied me to England several times. At length he found himself employment in the munitions works at the docks in West Ham, a very useful post for strategic reasons, as you can imagine. Unfortunately he had developed a weakness for liquor and cocaine, and he tended to talk more than was wise, particularly when he was under the influence. I can only suppose he must have given away his reasons for wishing to work there, and this resulted in his dismissal. One evening we were having a few drinks together and playing cards in a tavern in Hackney, and I told him all about you. Then I was foolish enough to suggest that for a joke he ought to dress up in the most shabby outfit he could find, and pretend that he was a long-lost brother of yours. Between us we constructed what seemed to us a most convincing life story for him, and thought we would pretend that he had spent some years out of Europe but came home to rediscover his family. What I did not realise was that he would ever take it seriously enough to come and find you. I understand from the police that he did carry out the – little adventure. When they questioned him, it seems he admitted much of this, and he has since been ordered to leave these shores.'

That left one more question which had perplexed Charlotte increasingly during these last few weeks.

'Did you ever know a Sophie Clark, or know of her?' she inquired. 'Her husband Oswald is a parliamentary colleague of James.'

He smiled sadly.

'As if I did not know as much already. I never had the privilege of meeting Oswald Clark, but I knew his wife very well indeed. She was going to furnish me with a few little military secrets to which her husband was privy as a member of Parliament. There were various defence estimates, and minutes for committee meetings which she was going to obtain and bring me. But it never got as far as that.' A light came into his eyes. 'In another way, though, we got quite far enough. I take it you know the Kensington Hotel in Park Lane?'

Charlotte nodded.

'We had a few little meetings there, and I must say Sophie Clark was very good in bed. She is a fine, perfectly proportioned figure of a woman, and a first class lover. Her husband must be a lucky man when it comes to what you may call the marital arts.' He coughed, and smiled gently at his little joke.

Marianne rolled her eyes. Goodness knows, she had heard it all before – his drunken, lewd, self-pitying ramblings about nights on the town with cheap painted little madams procured for one-night stands in the Berlin barracks before being sent on their way, a little richer for the experience.

Suddenly it began to dawn on Charlotte that there might have been a connection between Sophie's 'accident' and the man standing in front of them.

'Her husband is very lucky,' she said coldly, staring him in the face. 'Lucky that she is still alive. She had some unexpected visitors not long ago, and it seems that she attempted to kill herself as a result.'

He turned away a little. She knew instinctively that there was nothing to be gained by pursuing the matter, but it was clear that he bore some responsibility.

If she was repelled by his callous attitude, Eleanor was equally disgusted by his coarseness, particularly in front of strangers. Fighting down a strong desire to give him a piece of her mind, she demanded, 'And what happened to my father-in-law?'

'I went back one evening to fetch a few weapons and pieces which I had left in Little Tor Cottage. While I was there I dropped a photograph of your mother which your brother had been carrying on him. It was a dark night, and I thought Mr Priestley was armed. I was afraid he was going to attack me, so I had to shoot him in self-defence. He was a good man, as well as a member of the family. It was a pity he never managed to pay his debts.'

'What debts are you talking about?'

'That little matter of the fire which almost destroyed his farm some years ago. I understand that everyone nearby thought he started it deliberately after he had been getting into financial difficulties. It was fortunate for him that I had just won a handsome sum at cards with my regiment, and I was in a position to help him make good most of his losses with an interest-free loan which he assured me he would repay in due course. Unfortunately it was a promise which he seemed anxious to forget –'

'Just a moment,' Eleanor interrupted, shaking her finger fiercely. 'Edward told me that my father had cashed in one or two endowment policies, or something. I never asked after the details, because I have always let him look after all the finances. You mean it was actually you who put the money up?'

'It was me, Eleanor, but it was a loan and not a gift. Your father assured me faithfully on several occasions that he would repay it in instalments, and despite several requests in writing from me he did nothing about it. I suppose he thought on that last evening that my patience had given way, and that it was either him or me. I had been asking him for some months for a meeting so we could discuss the repayment in person. Yes, it was an accident, and I am sorry that it ended in his shooting. If he was not armed himself, it was a needless death, and I can only offer my condolences. But that was how it happened.'

He paused for reflection. 'And if there is a war between our two countries, many more people will die.'

'You think there will be war?' James asked, unable to conceal his interest in the man's views despite his utter loathing of him and everything to which he had just confessed.

'I think it will come about before long. Maybe next year, maybe two or three years hence. And there is no certainty that it would involve England. I do not think the Kaiser wants war, and some of his ministers certainly have no stomach for it. But his son the Crown Prince is rather less cautious and thinks otherwise. The chiefs of staff at Berlin and the naval secretariat are ready for a show of arms, and have been for quite some time. Some of them have as good as staked their reputations and their careers on it. Russia is increasing the size of her armies, and France is introducing a three-year period of military service.

There is too much unrest in Germany from the proletariats and the socialists, and the opposition newspapers are preaching sedition to the masses. All this would be resolved by a short victorious campaign against one of the nations against us. History has shown us that there is nothing like a good war for rallying the state behind her sovereign, and if it happens before France or Russia is ready, then I think we will be marching as to war. And whether Albion will be able to preserve her splendid isolation, as your statesmen say, will be entirely up to your King and his government. You may tell me that you have your treaties, as do the rest of us, but your ministers will always find ways to circumvent the provisions of these if it suits their agenda. And will Mr Asquith be able to keep the dogs of war in his cabinet acquiescent? Remember that Mr Lloyd George has made some violent speeches which have won him no friends in Berlin. So he thinks a little show of arms would keep Germany in her place...'

The audience noticed that his voice was steadily becoming more hoarse.

'But it means nothing to me. I shall not live to see the outcome. You may all be wondering why I have come here alone tonight. It may seem foolish of me not to have taken the precaution of bringing a colleague as well, to make sure that there was no chance of you getting away with the jewels. But I am not a young man any more, and not as strong as I used to be.' He sat down on a chair, put his hand to his mouth, coughed violently and cleared his throat, speaking slowly in a croak. 'A few days ago, I was back in Berlin for the last time. While I was there, my physician revealed the results of a throat examination he made while I was attending his clinic as an outpatient earlier in the year. He and his surgeon have diagnosed a malignant tumour, and they do not think I had longer than about eight months to live. They offered me a tracheotomy, but I refused. There is nothing to be gained in hiding from the inevitable, or cheating the grave.'

He looked carefully at each of their surprised faces in turn. 'You will realise that I have had my life, and there is no point in fading away under sentence of death from cancer.'

Everyone watched with varying degrees of astonishment and incredulity as he put his hand in his pocket. Before they realised what he was doing he had taken a revolver out, put it against his head, and pulled the trigger.

Chapter 18

After the strangest summer and autumn they could ever remember, Roger and Mary Strong gave heartfelt thanks for the peace and quiet which had at last descended on Stead Farm and the local community. Sergeant Donald had a weight off his mind, and there was one less subject for wild gossip.

Eleanor Bridgman had gone back to Southampton to be with Edward and the family. Initially she was angry with him for having been so secretive about this brother-in-law whom she had never met until the end, yet aware that there had been some good reason for years of his reluctance to tell her the truth. However, his explanations about Grenville's violent behaviour during childhood, such as his bullying of other children at school, his revolting obsession with slaughtering pet animals and birds, and his warning later that he would hunt Edward and Eleanor to the ends of the earth and kill them if his identity was ever divulged, explained it clearly enough.

'My brother was a very dangerous man, as you saw for yourself,' he told her when she taxed him with it. 'I wasn't going to risk giving him any excuse to come after us, and you saw what happened to the man on the moor,' he reminded her sadly. Nevertheless Edward arranged for a small funeral ceremony for Grenville in Southampton. assuring Eleanor that she need not attend unless she wished, but she gritted her teeth and joined him for the service. After some hesitation Marianne accompanied them, saying matter-of-factly that the scoundrel was no longer in a position to do any more harm to them or to anyone else.

A farmer from Moretonhampstead had contacted Edward to express interest in purchasing Little Tor Farm, assuring them that the notoriety of recent events did not bother him in the slightest. He could see that the premises were in good order, and made a provisional offer which he hoped to be able to confirm in the new year.

As Roger Strong looked at the skies each morning and rubbed his hands to keep warm, he was happy to let the winter snows do their worst. Everyone for miles around was prepared for the regular white-out, blizzards and snowdrifts, or freezing water troughs, icy paths. It had happened before, and it would do so again. What did it matter? Christmas was coming, and the goose was getting fat. After the fun of Christmas Day they had the Boxing Day meet to look forward to. He and Mary always made a point of watching the start of the hunt, and often following the foxhounds a little way on foot.

At last life had returned to normal. They had listened open-mouthed at Maud Watts' account of the scene at the hotel. Mary reacted with instinctive sympathy when she mentioned Grenville Bridgman's cancer, though Roger couldn't stop himself from remarking that he was glad there was now one less rogue at large in the world.

'An' thank 'eaven George weren't a German spy after all,' was Mary's final comment. 'Always knew it in me bones that the young man were innocent, like.'

At the Red Lion, Isobel and Alf Cuthbert were equally interested in Maud's recollections. Alf was speechless at first, while Isobel remarked succinctly that she had had her suspicions for some time and that the final act of the drama came as little surprise.

Back at their house at Stafford Terrace, Alfred and Louise Hillman had Ralph to stay for a few days before Christmas. One evening they invited Canon Richardson to dinner. Over their meal they spoke of the sad events of the last few weeks – Ethel's death, followed so quickly by Dick Priestley's murder, and then Grenville's dramatic admission and suicide. Alfred was mildly piqued when Ralph teasingly mentioned that the 'cheap tawdry adventure stories' circulating around Holne and district had turned out to have more than a grain of truth after all.

'Well, at least it's all behind us now, and needn't take up any more of our time,' he grunted. Seeing the stormy look on his face, the Canon swiftly changed the subject of conversation to recollections of some of his Christmases in Africa and Louise joined in, discussing plans for a children's party which she was looking forward to organising. By the time they had finished, the other happenings had been forgotten.

After that evening at the hotel, Charlotte had shed a few emotional tears in private over the knowledge that the German Emperor must have carried such a torch in his heart for her mother. Had Ethel Stephens ever known how much she meant to the young Wilhelm Hohenzollern? How long was it since he had given that photograph to the man whom they now knew to be Grenville Bridgman? How had George managed to go through his life carrying the burden of such an extraordinary secret? It was probably just as well that he had laid that burden down with his life at so young an age. But, terrible though it was, at least that great shadow over her life had now been put to rest.

As for Grenville Bridgman – was it possible to feel pity for a man like that? At first she had thought him the devil incarnate, but maybe he had his more human side after all. What could have happened to him to make him such a monster? Still, his family must have suffered even more than she had. Perhaps it was only right to shut him out of her mind as best she could. Surely the memory of him would fade with time.

At first Paul and Charles had been incredulous to learn how events had unfolded. The more they thought about it, however, the less astonishing it seemed.

'It all fits together, doesn't it?' Paul remarked in the office one day. 'George always seemed such a secretive chap, but with all that funny business in the background, who can blame him?'

Charles nodded. 'If I'd had a mother like that, I think I'd have been a bit odd myself. Poor man.'

'To say nothing of a father like that as well!'

Oliver was relieved beyond measure that the mystery had been cleared up. While sorry that one of his most dedicated employees had been implicated, albeit in a manner beyond his control, it suited him to put the whole distasteful affair behind them. A friendly but firm word to George's colleagues that 'we need not dwell on these things any more' made his attitude clear.

One week later, James and Charlotte invited Paul and Charles with their wives to dinner at their house in Pimlico. It was their last night in the capital before they moved to Lower Brook Manor for Christmas, and the invitation had been accepted with some trepidation, but all of them had got along splendidly. Charlotte's shy little whisper to them while he was out of the room before they went to sit at table that 'he's not such a bad old devil, really' had only gone part of the way to reassure them. However, he readily put them at their ease and over dinner he allowed his wife to tell one or two gently self-deprecating stories about him.

'That wasn't the James Waters I thought I knew,' Paul remarked as they took a cab home that night. 'Either that man at dinner was an actor, or else Charlotte has tamed him in no uncertain manner. The first time I met her, she gave me the impression she was almost terrified of him.'

'I can see how the course of events must have changed him,' Charles remarked. 'Or rather, not exactly changed him, but at least made him think again. It would take a pretty hard man not to be moved in some way by all those things happening to his wife.'

> *'O come, all ye faithful,*
> *Joyful and triumphant,*
> *Oh come ye, oh come ye, to Bethlehem!'*

James and Charlotte Waters and the boys were at Lower Brook Manor, Charlotte singing to herself as she supervised Thomas and David in helping to decorate their tree in the hall with glittering baubles and silver tinsel. They joined in singing with her, la-la-ing in tune when they were not sure of the words. It was less than a week to go until Christmas Day, and it was a long time since they had seemed their mother so carefree. On their last day in London she and James had taken them to the Natural History Museum in Kensington and they had come out open-mouthed at some of the exhibits, particularly the prehistoric animals about which they had hardly stopped talking since. James had promised them all a visit to the pantomime on Boxing Day, and they were looking forward to *Aladdin* at the Theatre Royal in Aylesbury.

After supper that evening, when the boys had gone to bed, James poured them both a glass of port.

'I still think I owe you an apology,' he said as he took a chair opposite her and lit himself a large cigar. 'I misjudged your brother.'

'No, you didn't,' she smiled sadly. It was evident that the last few days had softened James. She had perforce accepted the ambitious young rising politician who put his career first and his family a rather poor second, but now she was seeing much more of the kindly, gentle man whom she had idolised during their betrothal and in the first idyllic weeks of marriage. 'You never really had much of a chance to get to know each other properly. I'm sure he would have liked you. But what's done is done, and it's all in the past. And now we know what happened.'

'That was the worst part of everything for you, wasn't it? Not knowing what was going on in Devon.'

'Partly that, yes. And that business about – well, about my mother's affair with the Kaiser. Throughout the years, I really thought she was making it up. I'd never thought there was a word of truth in it.'

'I thought exactly the same.' He shook his head sadly. 'Your brother went through life carrying the sort of cross you wouldn't wish on anyone. Only now do I realise what he must have had to go through all that time. Look at our boys, they know who their father is. And I hope they can be proud of him.' He laughed softly.

'Talking of the boys, look at this.' She got up and fetched a piece of paper from the other side of the room to show him. On it was a child's drawing in brightly-coloured crayons, with the words 'Uncle George' underneath. 'Thomas brought it back from school. He said it was a picture of his uncle going up to Heaven. You see, that's him on a cloud, with two angels and their trumpets flying behind him, showing him the way. Don't you think that's sweet?'

She blinked, and for a moment James thought she was going to cry. He held the drawing and looked at it, smiling fondly.

'That's very touching of Thomas. We'll keep that, won't we? It strikes me, your brother didn't know exactly who his father was. Or if he did, he had to keep quiet about it. I can't help thinking what absolute hell it must have been for him, every time somebody mentioned the blessed Wilhelm's name at work.'

He inhaled deeply and blew the smoke out. 'I have been giving the matter a good deal of thought. Sometime in the new year, maybe we ought to go and visit this church at Poundsgate. Or was it Holne? Wherever it was, the place where they had his funeral. We could go and meet some of his friends there.'

Charlotte nodded. 'He seems to have been well liked in the community there. We've met a number of them already, on the night when – well, when it all happened. But I think I'd like to make a special effort to see Mr and Mrs Strong. They obviously

181

looked after him well every time when he went there, and it would give me a chance to thank them.'

'It would indeed. And perhaps we could provide some sort of memorial to him as well. What about a stone cross or whatever they have on Dartmoor, or a stained glass window in the church to his memory? I'll pay for it, naturally. It's the very least I can do.'

'Oh James!' Impulsively she got up and hugged him before planting a kiss on his cheek. 'That is the best Christmas present you could give me.'

'But I wasn't thinking of it as a Christmas present.' He smiled as they embraced more tightly. 'No, it would be a little extra gift to you. To him if you like, and in fact to the whole family. Why don't we arrange to go there sometime in the new year? We would take the boys, and they could see where their uncle used to love to spend his holidays.'

'It was a pity they never knew their uncle either.' Her face fell, but only momentarily, and she looked at the Christmas tree. 'Is Sophie Clark better yet?'

'Not completely, but I hear she is well on the way to recovery. She's going to be taking it very gently over Christmas, of course. They had planned to go to France for a few days, but they've changed their minds on that. Physically I think she's fine. Oswald told me she confessed to him about what she'd been up to with Andrewitz, or should I say Bridgman.' He grimaced. 'Confound the man, I hardly know which name I should be using for him! Anyway, the two of them may have slept together. In fact, knowing her, I feel there's little doubt she did, but as far as the spying side went, no real harm was done. Apparently she went to meet him at a hotel to try and hand some facts and figures over, and he had pushed off back to Germany. Then he came round to her house a few days later, which resulted in that nasty little scene that Giannetta told us about. It's not surprising that the combined shock of that and her remorse afterwards resulted in that suicide bid.'

'Poor woman! Well, it was extremely foolish, but I still feel sorry for her. She was her own worst enemy, really.'

'She was. But Oswald has forgiven her, bless him. He told me that he will definitely be standing down from the Commons at the next dissolution. I think it's the right decision, whichever way you look at it. He never struck me as having the right sort of temperament for a member of Parliament. Knows his stuff all right, but he hasn't got the right cut and thrust when it comes to debates. Reasonable under-secretary material, but I can't see him as senior minister material somehow.'

'He seems such a gentle fellow. Do you think he blames himself in any way for what Sophie did?'

James looked at her carefully. He wondered if there was any sense of reproach in her question, but felt on balance that it was a perfectly innocent enquiry.

'It's possible, I suppose. He has been away from her a good deal since he was elected to Parliament, and maybe she found it difficult to cope with that. Especially with no children. I think she wanted some kind of excitement in her life, and she found the charity work wasn't really as fulfilling as she thought it was going to be, so she started playing with fire. One or two things he has let slip to me in the past – well, I know I shouldn't read too much into them, but she has been a little, let's say, excitable. Not quite – well, mad, but –'

'But it might not take much to push her towards it, you mean?'

'In a manner of speaking. Anyway, Oswald thinks he'll apply for the Chiltern Hundreds early in the new year, so they can think about retiring and go to live in France just that bit sooner. It's going to mean a by-election, of course, and his successor may have a fight on his hands to keep the seat. But there are more important things in life.'

'We ought to give them a farewell dinner here before they leave.'

'I was going to suggest that myself, Charlotte. Oswald's constituency association will presumably lay on something pretty grand for him themselves, and I'm sure they will want me there as one of his closest parliamentary colleagues. But we could always have a small dinner party for them at the house.' He laughed gently. 'You know, Oswald's quite a character. Most people think he's a bit slow and rather a nonentity, and I'm the first to admit he does tend to hit the bottle a bit too much for his own good. But once you get to see beyond that, he's a good chap. And he's got an endless fund of funny stories to tell. Never minds a good joke at his own expense, and there aren't many of our colleagues at Westminster of whom that can be said.'

183

James turned to look at his wife again, and smiled. 'What would you say if I told you I was thinking of standing down myself?'

Her eyes opened wide in incredulity. 'You're not!'

'Not seriously, I admit. But what if I thought I hadn't been spending enough time with you and the boys, and that I ought to give some consideration to a career in the city. Finance, banking, that kind of thing. It would be a comfortable living, and we'd never want for anything. And it would give me a routine enabling me to see much more of you.'

Charlotte thought hard for a moment, then shook her head.

'No, James. Everything is fine as it is. People are all saying what a splendid member of the Commons you are, and that you will go a long way. Give it a few more years, and if you think a financial career would be right after that – well, you've got your whole life ahead of you.'

He nodded, a little relieved to find that her ideas concurred with his.

Having had ample opportunity to reflect on their immediate future, she felt the moment was right to turn once more to plans for her brother's memorial.

'I've been thinking about George. He didn't go to church very often, as far as I know,' she mused. 'So I think a large stone outside on the moors would be the most suitable thing. Perhaps we could put his name on it, and his dates of birth and death. Best really to keep it as simple as possible. I wonder if we could get permission to put it up near the spot where he fell. It may be private land, but it should be easy enough to find out. Maybe people will leave flowers beside it, like we do on gravestones. And they'll do it long after we have gone as well. Something of the sort would look rather good, don't you think?'

As James turned towards her again, his features slowly broke into the genuine warm smile of which she had seen so little in her husband's eyes and face for so long.

'A stone monument on the moors. Of course!' he exclaimed, in a note verging on triumph. 'George would have appreciated that, wouldn't he?'

She glanced up towards the ceiling. 'Perhaps he's looking down on us and giving us his blessing as we speak.'

Smiling at him, she sighed with contentment as he took her gently in his arms.

Epilogue – 1979

Full of the joys of anticipation of a good Sunday lunch, Eileen and Jack York and their son Chris marched into The Old Coaching Inn, South Brent. It was a glorious sunny day in July, with just the faint hint of midsummer breeze to keep the midday temperature within reasonable limits, and they had booked for a bar meal to celebrate Eileen's birthday that week. The pub had only been open for ten minutes or so and half a dozen regulars were propping up the bar already, pints in front of them as they helped themselves to crisps and nuts, discussing the chairmanship of the village carnival committee for the next season, or exchanging views on the pros and cons of the newly-elected Conservative administration under Margaret Thatcher. Otherwise all was quiet except for a small mains radio behind the bar, playing *We Don't Talk Anymore*.

Chris ordered and paid for two pints of bitter and a tomato juice, placed them on a tray and took them over to a circular table near the unlit fireplace where his parents were making themselves comfortable. His mother was bending down to make a fuss of a small grey cat with white paws which had wandered over, tail in the air, to say hello.

'Cheers.' They all raised their glasses.

'I thought of something I was going to tell you about, Chris,' Eileen remarked. Her brow furrowed, then she clicked her fingers. 'I've got it. You know I was going for a walk on the moor around Holne on Thursday morning? Well, I saw something near the old road to Buckfastleigh I'd never noticed before. It's been there all the time, I mean, but I never thought of looking at it properly until last week. A large granite boulder, standing about four foot high, with a little posy of flowers beside it. I had to make a note of it, because I knew it would interest you with your passion for dates and history.' She rummaged around in her handbag. 'Where did I put it...or did I leave it at home on the kitchen table...no, as you were, I've got it here.'

She took out a small red pocket diary, thumbing through the pages of addresses and notes at the back. '"In memory of George Edward Stephens, born 20 January 1879, died 23 July 1913."'

Chris nodded. 'Just before the Great War, wasn't it.' He took another swallow from his pint. 'That's all there was?'

'Just that. I had a look in one or two of my Dartmoor books when I got home, and they said something about a chap from London who used to come to Devon quite often in the early years of this century. They think he was an office clerk who was found dead in rather mysterious circumstances.'

'And they didn't say what?'

His mother shook her head.

'I could have a ferret around in the back files of the papers at the local history library in Plymouth Central,' he suggested. 'It's going to mean winding through loads and loads of microfilm, I know. Hard work, but all the same it would be fun to find out. Or there might be some reference to it on the card indexes.'

They continued to drink in silence for a while, watching the cat stroll over to another table in search of tidbits. A group of five was seated there and the waitress was bringing their first course across on a tray. If the diners felt unequal to that plaice on the bone or their gammon, the winsome little four-legged dustbin wouldn't need to be asked twice to help out.

'But don't you think it would be more fun to make up your own story?' Jack suggested, and Eileen nodded.

Chris was temporarily lost in thought. 'That's an idea. Let me see – now, in 1913, things were a bit iffy between us and Germany, and the Great War was just round the corner. For sake of argument, let's suppose he was a secret by-blow of the Kaiser, or something of the sort, and the German military secretariat wanted to get him out of the way. Or he might have been a spy and the British army took it upon themselves to kill him, but they didn't want any scandal and it was important for them to make it look as though he had died of natural causes.'

'You ought to write a whodunnit about it,' Jack declared.

Chris grinned gently and picked up his pint. 'Would be fun, yes, one of these days. If only there wasn't so much to do in the garden at this time of year.'